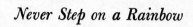

Never Step on a Rainbow

Never
Step
on a Rainbow

Winifred Wolfe

HARPER & ROW,
PUBLISHERS
New York

For three special men in my life,
for three separate and special reasons:
my husband, JACK
my brother, RICHARD
and my friend, OSCAR

Never Step on a Rainbow

There was all that blood over Broadway, so thick she could almost taste it. Jenny wondered why she had ever called sunset beautiful.

Six floors below on Forty-third Street nobody seemed to notice what was happening over their heads. If they did, they'd think it made a pretty picture. She knew better. Lately she had learned

1

there's more to a painting than what you see on top. Sometimes you have to keep looking until what's underneath shows through. That's when you understand what it really says.

She didn't have to look at Lou to understand what he was saying.

"I don't like talking to the back of your neck, Jenny. Maybe I'd like to break it, but I don't want to carry on a conversation with it. Turn around."

The sky was turning the color of the hallways in the brownstone. Mrs. Keefer once said dark red hid the dirt. It did something else— pulled walls together. Those stairs were bad enough, but to have walls squeeze in at the same time—all the way to the top—

At the top of his voice, Lou was shouting: "To blow a show before a weekend! You wanna mark yourself lousy in this business?"

The sky was getting bloodier; the day dying in agony. Before long it would burn itself out and go screaming into the night.—Lou was screaming now.

"For a smart girl, you're pretty stupid. There are hundreds of new girls pouring into this city every week—hungry for club dates. And they're young, Jenny; most of 'em look like the day after jailbait. Do you follow me? Am I getting through to you?"

"I wish," she said, turning from the window, "you'd stop yelling. You're giving me an awful headache."

"I got a flash for you. Right this minute I got one in fourteen different languages. One of 'em's in fluent Arabic."

She cupped her hands over her ears.

"You trying to dial me out?"

"No." To prove it, she let her hands slide the length of her cheeks and fan under her chin, lifting it gently. "Did you ever have the feeling," she asked him, "that if you didn't hold your head, it would come off and roll across the floor and maybe somebody will think it's only a doll's head and kick it halfway across the room?"

"This is a way to repay me for four months steady booking in New York? This is how to say thank you?—Aw," Lou said, "now I get it."

"Do you?"

He stood up, but not, she couldn't help noticing, all the way. Instead, he slanted his short body across the desk, arms stiff, hands spread for balance. That was to make her think that if he felt like it he could stand the distance and be taller than she was.

Quickly she sat in the big chair facing him, so he could straighten up if he wanted to and look down on her, and she thought how sad it was to be ashamed of what you can't do anything about, like being short, or getting old, or having skin a different color.

The trouble with me, she decided, is that I'm always feeling sorry for people. That's what starts it. Every time.

Just the same she was glad to be sitting. There was a dragging in her legs from that long climb to the office. Six flights. He had been right about one thing. She wasn't getting any younger. Thirty-three next month. Even Lou would be surprised at that. He probably figured twenty-eight the most. And she wasn't afraid of growing old. What she was afraid of most was—not growing old.

"It's so simple," Lou was saying, "I don't know why I didn't get it before."

"What?"

"You're trying out a new routine." He was eye level with her now. "It's the old gag. The Broadway agent who books this act in from the Coast—six acrobats, goddam giants every one—the runt of the bunch is six-ten. Contracts are signed. Publicity's out. He goes down to the airport to meet them."

"I heard it before," Jenny told him dully.

"—And six goddam midgets walk off the plane," Lou went on, as if he hadn't heard her. "He rushes over and says, 'Wha' happened?' And one of the midgets explains, 'On the way over we met this guy and he talked us into changing the act.' "

"I didn't laugh the first time," Jenny said.

"I'm not laughing now. Just tell me that's what happened to you. On the way over you met this guy and he talked you into changing the act. Right? Right?"

"Please," she said, "don't yell."

"From now on, you don't want to be an exotic dancer. From now on, you're going to be a comic. Well, you're about as funny as a crutch."

"I'm not trying to be funny." Most of the blood had drained out above the Paramount Building. Night was moving in fast. Between them, the two women had finally convinced her—that if she didn't get away before it came, she wouldn't be around to see another morning.

"Get me a booking," she begged. "Boston, Miami, Montreal— any schlock joint—four shows a night. Just so it's out of New York."

"What am I supposed to tell them at the place you're at now?"

"Tell them I'm sick."

"You don't look sick to me."

She turned back to him for only a moment. "I'm dying." When she looked out again, it was raining. Just like that, she thought, surprised. "Such a funny kind of rain," she said. "You can't even hear it."

"It isn't raining, Jen." His voice sounded worried and close. She knew he had left the desk and was standing beside her.

It sent a queer kind of shiver through her. If Lou was worried enough about her to stand right next to her and not even care she could eat beans off his head, maybe he'd be worried enough to help her. God, she needed someone to help her and God sure wouldn't—not now—not after she had been practically living with the devil. That meant even praying wouldn't do any good. The only prayer she ever memorized was the one with "If I should die before I wake" in it. Fine thing to teach little kids. Scare hell out of them. If the only legit prayer she knew was that creepy bit, maybe she was better off with the one old Alice had taught her. How did it go? *Harken to my prayer; free me from my sin*— No. That wasn't it. *Free me from my*— What was it? Why couldn't she remember?

She heard Lou ask, "What makes you think it's raining?"

"Everything's so blurry. The window's all wet." She crooked her elbow and rubbed her coat sleeve against the glass. "Isn't it?"

"No, Jen."

She shrugged. "Then I must be crying. I bet I look a mess. I always look a mess after I've been crying."

"Be a doll. Finish out the week. Then I promise I'll see what I can do for you."

"You need a hearing gimmick?" It was her turn to yell. "Then read my lips. I've got to get away from here. That's spelled—now."

"Not in any trouble with the cops, are you?"

"I'd welcome it."

"Man trouble?"

"Did you know your elevator broke down again? You ought to complain."

"What does he want?"

"Who?"

"That man—whoever he is—" He held the name back for a moment before he let it go— "Charlie?"

She shook her head. "I wouldn't even know where to start looking for him. It's a pretty big state."

"Don't you mean country? He could be anywhere in it."

"I meant state. Texas. Pretty big, you got to admit."

"When last heard from over a year ago that fire-eater you married started a ruckus at the club he was working. And when last seen he was coming out of Gilhouley's lit up like a Catholic church and headed for parts unknown.—What makes you think he's in Texas? He wrote you?"

"Charlie's not much for writing."

"How do you know then?"

"Three months ago—" She stopped. "I just realized that in a way everything began that day Charlie turned up again. But he's got nothing to do with this—trouble I'm in. Not indirectly or otherwise."

"He was here? In New York?"

"He's changed, Lou." Some old habits, she guessed, were too tough to break. Giving up sex or cigarettes was like nothing compared to giving up defending Charlie. "He's going to be a personality. Wait and see—a regular prominent person."

"Don't tell me he's still in business. He couldn't get himself arrested—not after the last time."

"He should care. My Charlie has his own club—in Texas."

"Nice." Lou smiled. "I'm glad."

"You don't believe me."

"Where in Texas?"

"He didn't say. All he promised was he'd come back for me. I expect him any day." She bit her lip. "He'll be disappointed when he won't find me, but I'll be sure to leave word with Mrs. Keefer. That's the landlady."

"Do that," Lou suggested.

He doesn't believe a word of it, Jenny thought. Well, why should he? He knows Charlie from way back. Not the way I do, though. Lou never got out of bed at five in the morning to see him stagger in practically paralytic. Lou never sat up with him and tried to get him to stop crying. There's something so particularly awful watching a man cry!—She had sat there and watched him and kept telling him, sure, it was the other guy's fault—always the other guy who started the new trouble that got him fired again—always the piano player or the waiter or an audience that deserved to be insulted—or a club owner who didn't have brains enough, only money enough, to run a club in the first place. Sure, not your fault, honey. Drink the coffee. Don't cry, honey. No—I won't walk out. What a thing to say. Jenny's here. Drink the coffee. I'm tired. I want to go to bed. I'm so tired—

"You look beat," she heard Lou say. "All flaxed out."

"I am."

"It isn't Charlie then?"

She was having trouble concentrating. What was it they had been talking about before?

"That guy," Lou reminded her, "whoever he is, what does he want?"

"He wants to kill me."

"You serious?"

"Yes."

"Maybe you ought to go to the police."

"What for?"

"Tell them."

"I don't have anything to tell them yet. When I do, it'll be too late. Will you help me?"

"Listen, doll," he said. "You know I've always liked you, but I can't get mixed up in anything. I can't afford to. And look at it this way: you're a taxpayer, entitled to police protection. You know what I mean?"

She knew what he meant. "I only wanted to know what you can do for me out of town."

"Oh, that—sure—anything I can do to help. I've always liked you—" He flipped open a large notebook on his desk and eagerly started thumbing through pages.

Jenny thought: He's not so hot on talking me into finishing out the week now. All of a sudden Mr. Big Heart wants to help.

"Of course," he was saying, "it's short notice and I don't know what I'm going to say to them where you're at now—but I'll think of something. Like I said—anything I can do—"

"I got off the subway," Jenny said, "a couple of stops before I had to. I wanted to walk. Did you ever notice how Broadway smells of salted peanuts and caramel popcorn? It was like I was smelling everything and seeing everything for the first time. Or maybe the last. An old woman was selling orchids right out on the sidewalk. I bought one." She tore a flower from her coat. "I think the old witch stuck a long pin through the stem to keep it looking alive. Poor thing. It'll be dead before night." With a shudder, she tossed it into the wastebasket.

"Mike's," Lou said, "South Boston."

"And there was a man selling toy bears. You wind them up and they walk." She reached into a large handbag and took out a toy.

He watched her twist the winder. "Do you want to hear what I've got for you or don't you?"

Before he could stop her, she put the toy on his desk. It began to waddle toward him. With one sweeping motion, he knocked it to the floor.

"Don't!" he heard her cry. "Don't hurt it." She fell to her knees and kept turning the small bear over and over—watching tiny paws walking and getting nowhere. When she was satisfied it hadn't been broken, she stood up again.

"I'm sorry," Lou said uncomfortably, "I didn't mean to—" It wasn't that he had been afraid of the damn thing. It was Jenny putting it there. Something about Jenny—

"You know a kid? Give it to her."

"I got a granddaughter. You wouldn't believe it to look at me, would you? That's one of the reasons I can't afford to get mixed up in—"

"I kept walking," she said, "and thinking—this city, it's so crazy and so beautiful, and if I let him kill me, I'll never see it any more."

Lou ripped a paper from a memo pad and scrawled: Mike's—South Boston. "I can book you there for two weeks."

"I'll leave tonight."

"You don't open until a week from Monday."

"But I told you—"

"Best I can do."

She ran her tongue over patches of lipstick that hadn't already been eaten off. "I'll check into a hotel in Boston. It'll be O.K."

"They wanted a singer."

"They'll thank you," she promised, stuffing the memo slip into the pocket of her trench coat. "They'll say I've got an act that starts the way everyone else's finishes—big." She glanced nervously at the door. "I hope your elevator's fixed."

"Want me to walk you down if it isn't?"

"You'd do that for me? And walk all the way up again—alone?"

"I'm not a bad sort, Jen. I do what I can. You know what I mean?"

"I would appreciate it—if it's not too much trouble."

"Let's go." He was anxious to get rid of her now.

"I just noticed—" she said, nodding in the direction of the over-sized desk. "You put my picture up." Covering every square inch of two sides and the broad front were publicity glossies: ventriloquists with dummies, dancers wearing little more than big smiles, glamorous head shots of singers, instrumental trios, the backwash of show business that overflowed into cheap clubs in and around Manhattan and masqueraded outside of New York as "Class Acts— Direct From Broadway."

She couldn't say why, but it made her feel warm for the first time since she had come into the office.

She remembered the Spanish routine she'd worked up once: the red rose—the shawl with the black fringe. Why had she thought of that all of a sudden? Oh, yes, she had been cold—her teeth clacking like castanets. Now, seeing her picture with all the others, she didn't feel cold any more. Maybe it was because she knew every one of those faces personally. Any one of them who walked in that minute would say, "Hi, Jen"—because they knew her. It was like being with friends all around. That must be why she felt warm. And safe.

"I'm in the middle," she said, pleased. "Thanks."

"I meant to put it up months ago. There wasn't room for a post-card, and I can't hang anything on these walls. Tried banging in a nail once. Plaster came down on me. That's when I thought of using the desk. You can bang nails into wood all you like."

Like coffins, Jenny thought.

"—So I've been waiting for a space for you." He was annoyed with himself for sounding so apologetic. "First one that comes up. That's what I promised myself. I said to myself, 'Jenny probably feels lousy about it, but she's too nice a kid to mention it.' "

"It did take me a long time to think up what to write on it," she admitted.

"I bet it did. I'm sorry."

"I wanted to write something clever—like Charlie did on his. Remember? He wrote, 'To Lou—with ten percent of my love.' I thought that was clever. I told him so."

"Yuh, sure was," Lou said, sorry now he had put up her damn picture. If he hadn't, it wouldn't have been there for her to notice. She'd have been on her way—out.

"I racked my brain," she told him, "trying to be clever like Charlie. In the end all I came up with was 'To Lou, my agent and my friend.' Pretty corny."

"I liked it," Lou said. "Simple and sincere. I liked it—and the first opportunity I had—"

"Who died?"

"What?"

"Somebody's missing. You must have had to take somebody else off to make room."

"That hoofer—the mick. You knew the kid—Kelly. Just like that. Heart."

"Sorry to hear it. I really am."

"There could have been other reasons. What made you so sure someone had—"

"Maybe," Jenny said, "I'm beginning to see around dark corners that aren't there—like Alice. Maybe I'm getting to be smart—like Alice."

And if I'm smart, Lou thought, I won't ask who Alice is.

"Anyway," Jenny said, "I'm sorry about the kid. I was on a bill with him once, but I am glad you've got room for me now. Is that an awful thing to say?"

"No," soothingly, "perfectly natural."

"Even if it may be just for a little while—because I imagine if I'm not around—you've got another one to fill in the hole."

"Jenny—"

She began to giggle. "Lower me in the hole, and cover me up so I'll be warm, but, oh, Lou, what'll I do for an encore?" Abruptly she stopped giggling and began to whimper. "If I'm dead, what'll I do for an encore?"

When the telephone rang, he bounded almost jovially across the room. That ringing was the most beautiful sound he had heard all day. He tore the receiver from the hook.

He shouted, "Yeah," into the mouthpiece, then cupped his hand over it. "Sorry, doll. I've been expecting this call. You understand."

She stood where he had left her.

"Well, where the hell were you last night? I got better things to do than sit around Lindy's on my butt waiting—" He cupped his hand over the mouthpiece again. "I'd ask you to wait, but this may take time." Why wasn't she moving? "You want to get out of New York," he reminded her. "That's what you said. Don't you have things to do? Like packing?"

Only her eyelids moved. They fluttered several times, making her look like a big doll somebody had thrown away.

"If this call wasn't so important, but it happens to be of the utmost—"

When the doll finally spoke, the words could have come from inside—from a playback. "I understand," she said mechanically. "Go right ahead."

"Anything I can do—just let me know."

"Sure."

"Wire me—phone me—reverse the charges." Hastily he added, "Only I can't afford to get mixed up in anything."

"Thanks, Lou. Thanks for everything."

He waited until she had gone before he began barking into the

mouthpiece. "No, I'm not busy. I can talk. And I've got plenty to
say to you.—All right. I'm listening."

But he was thinking: Going downstairs isn't such a big deal.
It's going up that's rough—and I would have been perfectly willing. Didn't I offer?

Was it his fault the phone rang as they were on their way out?

Jenny knew he had wanted to go with her. Hadn't she even said,
"You'd do that? For me?"

It was his sincerity she had appreciated. If she hadn't known
he was sincere, would she have autographed her picture the way she
had: "To Lou, my agent and my friend"?

"I'm still listening," he said.

But he only half-heard. He kept thinking about Jenny and
wondering who the man was who wanted to kill her—and why.

He could have asked. Then where would he have been? Involved.

She hadn't asked for that. If she had come right out and asked,
he would have been more than happy to get involved. That was
the kind of good-natured jerk he was.

Hadn't he done the one thing she had asked? Got her another
booking? She appreciated it. Wasn't the very last thing she said,
"Thanks—for everything?"

Her exact words.

Just the same he couldn't forget how scared she had looked and
how she had giggled, "Lower me in the hole, and cover me up,
so I'll be warm—but, oh, Lou, what'll I do for an encore?"

She didn't blame him. Nobody wants to get involved in other people's nightmares. If she was trying so hard to get out of it, and it belonged to her, why should anybody, who didn't have to, try to get in? Lou had his own problems. Jenny wasn't one of them.

That's why people buy tabloids, she decided, so they can read

2

about other people's problems, shake their heads and say, "Isn't it too bad? Isn't it awful?"—but what they're really thinking is: it could have been worse, it could have happened to me. Then they drop the paper somewhere—in the bathroom usually.

Tomorrow, she thought, if it's me they read about—I hope they at least drop me somewhere nicer. The living room. Or the kitchen. Then she thought: But if they leave the paper in the kitchen, somebody may use it to wrap up the garbage.

She could see her picture on the front page. The glossy Lou had tacked on his desk would make a nice clear reproduction. He'd be only too glad to donate it. Jenny could see that picture being wrapped up with leftover fish or unwanted fat or parts of a chicken nobody wanted to eat.

She felt sick and grabbed the railing. Those damn stairs. All the flesh had worn off and she was going to have to walk on the bones.

If she told herself a story maybe she wouldn't notice how they came up to meet her at the same time she was going down. So she held on tighter and began: Once upon another flight of stairs, I met a man.

No, that wasn't exactly true. She hadn't actually met him that way. In the beginning they had just passed each other on the stairs. Usually she'd move a little closer to the banister and turn her head the other way; but she could feel him looking her over, like somebody giving her the evil eye. She never used to believe in kooky things like the evil eye. A step rose up to slap the sole of her shoe.

"Mother," she whispered, "I'm scared he's going to kill me."

Then she decided it was stupid, really, that every time she was scared she called on a mother she didn't even remember.

"I've got to get to the bottom," she said aloud, scraping her teeth together to cover the sound of her own footfalls, and remembered back to those other stairs where she used to pass him.

You can't always explain why you're afraid of something. You just feel it so strong you understand it without having a real reason. But to feel sorry for him! That was something she didn't understand. That was crazy, wasn't it, Mother?

All of a sudden one day it occurred to her, she hadn't seen him for over a week. She missed him—the way you miss a tap that drips or a radiator that gurgles. After they're fixed, you realize you got used to having them around. Getting used to being afraid is like that. When there's nothing to be afraid of any more, a person feels free. And a little empty.

She asked Mrs. Keefer about him. "What's happened to the Beard?"

It was sort of a game—making up names for people. Alice Molland was "the Glob"—never to her face, of course, or in front of Mrs. Keefer. Those two she had lumped together as "the Dolly Sisters." They were almost always together.

There was a Beckstein living in the brownstone in the West Eighties, and an Adams and a Grosset. Others, too. She knew from mail left on the big table in the vestibule. They were *Day People*. Jenny was a *Night People*. She got to bed when they were getting up and hardly ever saw them.

Sometimes it seemed that the house belonged to just the four of them. Mrs. Keefer, with an apartment on the first—Alice Molland, a flight higher—then on three, only a thin wall between them, Jenny and a man whose name she didn't even know.

"Did he move out?" she asked. "I haven't seen him lately."

Mrs. Keefer was sorting mail. She handed Jenny something, a bill from the costumers. It sure was highway robbery what they charged for a handful of sequins and a quarter of a yard of black net.

"I knocked on his door Friday," Mrs. Keefer told her, "to give him fresh linens. I didn't stay long enough to take a good look, but I could see he was in bed. He looked terrible. Not that he could ever look good to me."

"He's sick?"

"That face," she said, "all sunk in at the cheeks. Made his eyes bulge."

"He's that sick, Mrs. Keefer?"

"All I hope," she went on, "is that he doesn't take it into his head to die in there. I'd have all the proper arrangements to make and it wouldn't be very pleasant for me."

Jenny could remember, even now, how that rubbed her the wrong way. Maybe it was because Mrs. Keefer rubbed her the wrong way.

"I don't suppose it would be very pleasant for him, either," Jenny had snapped, and had gone back up to the third floor.

The coughing started a couple of days later—raw and sore sounding and could have been coming from right inside her own room instead of from the one next door. One morning it woke her up. Half in, half out of sleep, she could have sworn he was lying beside her.

That woke her all the way, so she got dressed quickly and brewed coffee in the big percolator. She always made a lot and kept reheating until the pot was empty. The last stale cup made a new first cup something to look forward to. That was another game she played—finding things to look forward to. There weren't many. She put a low flame under the pot and left the studio apartment.

She didn't meet anyone on her way out. The Day People had gone. Neither Mrs. Keefer nor Miss Molland was around, and the house was very quiet. Maybe after she got something to eat she could try getting back to sleep.

It was going to be in the 90's again. Kids on the block had opened a fire hydrant and were drenching half-naked bodies that didn't look as if they could stand the force of the water. A Puerto Rican woman leaned from an open window, cooling herself with a Japanese paper fan. She was almost as far out of the window, Jenny noticed, as in it. Jenny couldn't help noticing, too, that the woman was about to produce another body to fight its way into the hydrant spray.

There was a newsstand on the corner, pushing the more sensational tabloids: "Raped and a Mother at Thirteen"—"Kills Husband to Spite In-Laws"—and "Buried Alive for Thirteen Hours." Jenny felt nauseated. Maybe it was the heat.

The supermarket might have been in space—a pleasant air-conditioned world. A medley of Noel Coward settled over everything from frozen foods to green stamps. Jenny picked up a dozen eggs, a couple of containers of milk, and some boxed doughnuts to "I'll Follow My Secret Heart." She took a can of roach powder from the shelf to "I'll See You Again," paid for everything at the checkout counter, and went out into the street.

It probably wasn't any hotter—only seemed to be after the market. A few minutes later she had returned to the brownstone, and the door closed solidly behind her—a door with stained-glass panels that had once looked down on people living in another time when the street had a cleaner face. Ahead of her were still the stairs.

"If I've got half the brains I was born with," she told herself, "I'll find another place to live. Nobody's forcing me to stay."

Her determination to move made the climb easier until she got closer to her own floor—their floor. Why couldn't she hear him coughing? Maybe he was better. Maybe he was even on his way down. Any minute now the shadow of him would come first and he would step on the heels of it. Choking down a cry of fear, Jenny gathered strength and pitched herself headlong to the top landing. She was glad she hadn't bothered to lock her door. That meant she wouldn't have to waste time rummaging for the key, and—more precious time fitting the key into the lock. Another second now— she'd be in the room.

She was alone, finally, leaning gratefully against the other side of the door. In the darkness she had made to happen simply by closing her eyes, she heard a voice:

"What kind of dreams do you have, Jenny? Tell me about them and I'll tell you what they mean."

The cry of fear she had managed to stifle on the stairs broke. She opened her eyes and realized she wasn't alone after all.

"Dream of beetles crawling on you," said the Glob on her bed, "and you'll have bad luck in money matters. Dream of rats, watch out for your health. Dream of travel—"

"I never dream, Miss Molland." Jenny wasn't sure whether she was more relieved than angry. "You know you scared me? You just scared hell out of me."

Alice Molland looked as if she had been poured onto the bed from some giant taffy-making machine, and left to harden. In 90-degree heat she never would, and Jenny wondered if she'd have to scrape her off—great big spoonfuls of the lady. It wasn't anything to look forward to—especially on such a day. She carried the shopping bag into the utility kitchen and began putting things away while she worked on getting her breathing back to normal. After that, she'd figure out how to get rid of her uninvited guest.

"Little dear," Alice Molland said, rearranging the mass and shifting it in Jenny's direction, "are you sure you're telling old Alice the truth? Was it really me that scared you? Was it me who chased you up those stairs?"

Jenny put the eggs and the milk into the tiny refrigerator, left the doughnuts out for coffee, and didn't answer. When there was no further comment from the bed, she was sorry she hadn't. Not answering was practically an admission, and admitting it to someone like the Glob made it even worse somehow.

The mattress springs groaned. "My, such a lot of lovely lumps."

"Doesn't bother me," Jenny told her pointedly. "And I won't force you to lie on my bed if you're not comfortable."

"Now that's sweet of you worrying over my comfort."

Jenny turned to watch her miraculously gather the mass together and pull herself to a sitting position.

"Didn't I always say you were a generous girl? Didn't you prove it when you let me borrow this for the party?" She removed one of the sparkling bits of costume jewelry from a dress already over-ornamented with amber and jet beads, a gold pendant, a twisted silver chain, a cameo, and a glittering sunburst. She gazed hungrily at the pin she had just taken off and, moving slowly and reluctantly to the dresser, put it down. "The truth is, Jenny, I prefer a mattress with a few good lumps here and there. That Mrs. Keefer! Thought she was doing me a favor buying me a new mattress. Do you know I haven't had a bad dream since I got it?"

The complaint made Jenny smile for the first time that morning. It was on the tip of her tongue to say, If you don't have nightmares, old girl, it's because you already are one. But she controlled herself. "Tell you what," she offered, "I'll change with you."

"You mean that? Don't forget a dream tonight warns you what tomorrow will bring."

"Since I don't ever dream, it's kind of a pity to waste perfectly good lumps."

"I'll make the switch myself." She said it as hungrily as she had taken leave of the borrowed jewelry. "We won't tell Mrs. Keefer, will we?"

Jenny shook her head soberly. Moving might be a mistake. Most people have to pay for sideshows. This was on the house—already in it would be more accurate.

"You are a generous little soul," Alice Molland said. "I knew it from the day you moved in. There were vibrations all around you—impulses. I knew we had moved into each other's orbit."

"You bet," she agreed, and opened the wall cupboard.

"You don't understand, do you?"

"The only vibrations I understand," Jenny told her dryly, "are the ones I do at the club—for the paying customers." As she reached for a cup and saucer she did a quick and dirty grind and bump to illustrate her point.

"Never mind. As time goes on, you'll discover I'm right. I was destined to influence your little world. —You really mean it about the mattress?"

"It'll be a pleasure." She frowned. "Damn, I was sure I turned that coffee on before I left. It would have been ready by now."

"It is, dear. Just heat it up again. I turned it off and poured a cup for myself."

"Oh?" Jenny said annoyed. "Did you?"

"I was sure you wouldn't mind. You and me being neighbors."

For the first time Jenny noticed that a cup and saucer had already been taken from the cupboard. Alice Molland picked it up and sipped noisily.

If Glob is a good name for her, Jenny decided, more annoyed with herself, then Slob is a better one for me—a good-natured Slob, and I'm sick of having my good nature taken advantage of. "Listen," she said, "I don't mind you helping yourself to the coffee—"

"Of course, you don't—and how many times have I asked you to call me Alice?"

Jenny ignored that. "What I do mind is having you walk in when I'm not here."

"Did you know that the last woman to be hanged by the neck in England for being a witch was named Alice Molland? That was in 1685, little dear."

"Did you hear me? I don't like anybody walking in when I'm not here."

"I knocked first. The door practically swung open by itself."

"I'll bet!"

Oh, what was the use? She was already there and it was too muggy and too much trouble to fight over a cup of coffee. She poured one for herself. "Tell me, Alice," she asked, taking the chair opposite her at the table, "that other Alice—was she a relative?"

"Now, that would be interesting to know, wouldn't it? It's possible, of course, since I have the gift, too."

"What gift?"

"The black art of prophecy. It's both," she winked knowingly, "an art and a gift. And don't let anyone tell you different."

"Oh, I won't," Jenny promised, and opened the box of doughnuts.

"An art and a gift," Alice Molland repeated, "and my, I do like doughnuts."

She was looking even hungrier than she had when she returned the pin and accepted the mattress. Jenny offered the box. Her guest took one, and dropped a second into the pocket of her dress.

"For later," she explained.

"Why not?"

"I'm lucky," Alice said, biting away half of the one she had selected *for now,* "to have been born in my own time. In other days, they would have hanged me or burned me or worse."

"Tell me," Jenny humored her, "are you a witch?"

Alice Molland did a peculiar thing then. She widened and closed her eyes quickly and, when she did, somehow caught Jenny in them. No matter how hard she tried, Jenny couldn't look away.

It's because I'm tired, she thought, frightened. That's why.

"Tell me," Alice dared, "if you know."

She managed to wrench her eyes from hers. "I only know I don't believe in such stuff."

"Then you don't believe in the Bible?"

"Did I say that?"

"To deny the existence of witchcraft is to deny the Bible itself. 'Thou shalt not suffer a witch to live.' Exodus, Chapter 22, Verse 18. 'A man also or woman that hath a familiar spirit, or that is a wizard, shall surely be put to death: they shall stone them with stones: their blood shall be upon them.' Leviticus, Chapter 20, Verse 27."

"That in the Bible? No kidding?"

Alice Molland finished her coffee, pulled herself up heavily once more, and lumbered back to look down on the bed. "That's placed wrong."

"What's wrong with it?"

"It should face either north or south. The north side position is best. It gets beneficial magnetism from the earth that way."

"That in the Bible, too?"

"It's just fact."

"Sure." Jenny nodded. "Absolute one hundred percent positive fact."

"Why do I have the feeling," Alice asked, "that you're laughing at me?"

Jenny had the feeling that if she didn't watch out she'd be caught in those eyes again. "Sorry," she apologized, looking away quickly before it happened. "It's just that I don't believe in—stuff like that. I already told you."

"That's a pity. Then you won't be interested."

"In what?"

For answer, she reached into the bulging pocket of the dress that had once been purple—before age had streaked it many colors. "I was going to read the tarot cards for you."

"What are those? Some kind of fortunetelling cards?"

"The most marvelous science of the occult—a consultation with the spirits."

"Thanks a lot," Jenny declined, "but, no, thanks."

"I usually get paid well for doing it, but I was going to give you a reading for nothing, because you were so nice to let me borrow the brooch.—It was greatly admired, by the way. Not in so many words, of course. Society people are like that. They consider it vulgar to pay compliments. But I noticed the way they all looked at it."

"It is kind of pretty," Jenny said, pinning it on.

"You were wearing it the day you came to rent this room," Alice said.

"Was I? I don't remember."

"I said to myself: Nobody could tell that from the real thing. Nobody could even guess it's only colored glass and rhinestones."

"Then how come you guessed?"

"You didn't look like you could afford the real thing."

"And that," Jenny said, "is more one hundred percent positive fact. If this costume junk were legit, I wouldn't be caught dead living here."

"That party I was at last night, the china was edged with real gold and the glasses were genuine crystal. You only had to tap them lightly with a silver spoon to know that. And the centerpiece! —purple grapes and fat pink roses. Oh, very effective, I can tell you. And over the table, Jenny, a chandelier hung with amethyst drops—big as your fist—"

"This," Jenny said, looking around the room, "must be quite a comedown."

"I prefer informality. It's less of a strain. —Would you like to know what they served?"

"Some other time," Jenny said, and hoped she wouldn't take her up on it. "If I don't get a couple of hours' sleep I'll fall flat on my face tonight, and I've got three shows to do."

"I was surprised to hear you leave so early. Not even ten o'clock. Don't you usually sleep till noon?"

Jenny stiffened. "Then you knew I wasn't here when you knocked, didn't you?"

"Now you're angry." When she looked unhappy, dozens of fat creases in her face turned upside down.

"And the door didn't practically swing open by itself, did it?"

"You *are* angry."

"Next time I'll lock the door."

Alice Molland drew herself up with a dignity Jenny couldn't help admiring. There she stands, Jenny thought, all three hundred pounds of her—in an egg-stained dress, my doughnut in her pocket, and in another minute she'll have me apologizing to her.

"You think," Alice said, as if she were Queen of the goddam latrine, "that I came to steal something?"

"Miss Molland, I don't have anything to steal and I kid you not."

"Then why all the fuss? I wanted to return the brooch. Did I tell you it was greatly admired?"

"You told me."

"And I wanted to lie on your bed."

Suddenly Jenny was on her guard. There were all kinds—male, female, and the various assorted others in between. She had been propositioned more times than she cared to remember by the various assorted. Show girls with 38–22–36 were the ones that had surprised her most and most often in the past. Lately she was harder to surprise, but there was something so particularly repulsive about the suggestion coming from Alice Molland.

"Now, wait a minute," she began, "if you've got any cockeyed ideas about me, Lady—" And if the Lady had, and tried to carry them out, just what was Jenny supposed to do? Yell for help to the man next door?

"Is that what you think?" She narrowed her eyes to slits and smiled through them.

"Why did you want to lie on my bed?" Jenny demanded.

"The vibrations," Alice told her. "I thought I could find out something about your future that might prove useful to you."

"You are kidding. You have to be."

"On my soul." Without warning, she reached out and swallowed up one of Jenny's hands in both of her own. Still holding it, she pressed it against the broad soft cushion of her breast. Amber and jet beads bounced. "You have to believe me," she said, "if I swear on my soul."

"O.K.," Jenny said uncomfortably. "Let me go and I'll listen. What did you find out?"

Alice released her and Jenny stood where she was, rubbing her hand.

"There were disturbing elements," Alice Molland said. "It could have been the way the bed was facing. On the other hand—"

"It could have been the lumps. Look, I really have to get some sleep. I didn't get much this morning with that coughing—" She checked herself. "Thanks for returning the crown jewels. Next fancy party you go to, you're more than welcome to—"

"His coughing keep you up?"

"Whose?"

"That one. Next door. I heard it myself when I was lying on your bed waiting for you. That's what really disturbed my psychic contemplation. Poor little dear, no wonder you couldn't sleep."

"Why don't you take another doughnut? I mean—in case you get hungry on the way down to your room."

"I'll be honest with you, little dear. I don't know if I really am a witch—"

Jenny thought: You've got my vote if you want it.

"—or what they used to hang for being one," she continued. "I just know that sometimes I can see around dark corners that aren't there. I can look back to tomorrow as if it happened yesterday, but always for other people. Never for myself."

"Why not for yourself? That against union rules for witches?" This creep was making her nervous, but something told her that if she let it show, Alice Molland could do more than take her eyes.

"Stay away from that man next door," Jenny heard her say. "Listen to me. I'm your friend."

"I don't even know him. I just pass him on the stairs."

"And I've watched. He frightens you, doesn't he? That why you were running up the stairs before? Afraid you'd meet him coming the other way?"

"Why should I be afraid?"

"Why are you?" She nodded toward the bed. "The walls are thin. It was as if he was lying in the bed beside me—coughing. That the way it seemed to you?—as if he was lying in the bed beside you? That black devil! No wonder you couldn't sleep. Do as I suggest and move the bed."

"You get out of here!" Jenny shouted. "Get out of here with all your crazy talk! Look what you're doing to me. I'm shaking like a leaf." She held out her hands and tried to steady them. The next thing she knew, Alice had slid the cards out of her pocket once more.

"Shuffle first, then cut. But to the left. Always to the left."

Jenny went to the door and opened it wide enough so that no part of Alice would have any trouble getting through. "I don't need my fortune told. I just need sleep."

"One day you'll ask me to read them for you. I won't have to ask you."

"Let's leave it at that," Jenny said. "Don't call me, I'll call you."

Alice Molland spread the cards and fondled them. "See the colors —so brilliant—and transparent. Here, the Empress—and here, the Hanged Man—and here, the Wheel of Fortune." She looked up and ordered, "Take one."

"Will you go if I do?"

"I never," Alice Molland informed her coldly, "stay where I'm not wanted."

Jenny sighed, anxious to do almost anything to get rid of her. If taking a card from the pack would make her happy and make her go— "What's this one?" she asked, not caring much one way or the other.

"You're holding it in reverse."

"What'd I tell you? This isn't the game for me. I do it all wrong."

"Reverse just has another meaning. Five of cups—arrival and return. It must signify something for you, if you chose it from all the others."

"An accident," Jenny said, pleased to see her on her way at last.

"In tarot there is no accident."

Jenny didn't bother to answer. She didn't have time. Because just then Charlie returned.

Arrival and return.

Five of cups.

Reverse.

He smiled. "Hello, little girl. Is your mother in?"

Jenny stared dumbly at him. All those months, not knowing where he was—or *if* he was.

He wouldn't dare walk in like this, Jenny thought, so casually, and make with the flip opener. Not even Charlie.

3

On second thought, who else had that kind of polished brass?

"There was a sign over the bell," he said. "Out of order."

And that, she wondered bitterly, explains everything?

"Don't tell me about the sign," Mrs. Keefer mumbled. "I hung it there."

For the first time Jenny noticed her. She had been standing behind him. If she couldn't be seen before, it was because Charlie was so tall. Whatever he had been up to agreed with him. He was thinner, even better looking.

"He told me he wanted Mrs. Frye," Mrs. Keefer said. "I told him it was Miss, not Mrs."

"Don't tell me about the missus," Charlie quipped. "Just like the sign on the bell, I hung it there." He appealed to Jenny. "She doesn't believe I'm your husband."

"You better prove it," Mrs. Keefer said. "I'm not letting anyone move in just by saying—"

"He's not moving in," Jenny assured her. She said the words slowly and clearly. They were meant as much for Charlie as for the landlady.

"You have a husband?" Alice Molland asked.

Alice didn't seem particularly happy about that. Afraid she's slipping, Jenny decided; all those vibrations, and not one of them shaped like a wedding band.

"He's been away," Jenny told her, a little pleased at putting one over on a gypsy fortuneteller.

"Did you expect him today?"

Jenny looked at Charlie. "No," she said quietly, "I didn't."

"You should have. Five of cups—arrival, return." Satisfied to leave her with that, Alice moved down the hall toward the stairs.

For a moment Mrs. Keefer looked startled, then she ran after her. "Miss Molland!"

"Not today, Mrs. Keefer."

"I wanted to ask about the party. Did you have a good time?"

"It tired me. You know how it always tires me."

"And no wonder," they heard Mrs. Keefer say. "It takes so much out of you. —Would you like to come down to my place? I have some Danish—"

"Cheese?"

"Prune, too."

Charlie closed the door. "Prune," he said, pursing his lips.

She tightened hers.

"All the way over in the cab," he said, not quite so sure of himself any more, "I rehearsed what I was going to say when I got here. Funny, I can't remember any of it."

She didn't try to help him.

"I can remember the way it opened, though. Like this: I missed you."

She wondered how many mailboxes he had missed in his travels. A letter would have satisfied her, or a postcard. It didn't even have to have a picture on it.

"Maybe," he prompted, "the rest would come back to me if you threw me a line. Something like: 'I missed you, too.' "

"You came in a cab?"

"Why?"

Her handbag was on the bed Alice had told her wasn't getting beneficial magnetism from the earth. She opened it and took out her purse. "How much?"

"Jenny." He sounded hurt.

She knew him well enough to know how hard he was trying to sound that way. "Let's not keep the meter running too long. It has a sneaky way of climbing."

"That isn't nice, Jenny."

"Sorry." She dropped the purse back into the handbag and snapped the lock shut. "Bad habit I developed when we were married—paying your bills. You had pretty expensive tastes. Just ask me and the Diners' Club."

"We're still married."

"I hadn't noticed. Not lately." She waited for him to answer that one. It might even be interesting. —Come on, she dared silently, it's showtime at Jenny's Place. You're 'on.' Try to remember what it was you were rehearsing on the way over. Or just ad-lib it, Charlie. Say something clever. You've had cold audiences before. This one would freeze the tail off a comet.

He shook a cigarette from a pack, lit it, and offered it to her. The only move she made was to fold her arms. —Bad piece of business, her eyes told him. Doesn't work. Try again, Charlie.

"I hoped," he said, laying the cigarette in an ashtray in case she changed her mind, "that maybe you'd be a little glad to see me. I figured maybe you'd think I had been killed or something."

"I would have been notified if you had."

"Did I ever tell you," he asked, "that I've GI insurance? Maybe I should have gone under that cab, instead of in it. At least you would have got something out of being married to me. It's not much, but it's something."

That was the line that did it. That was the one that worked. "Don't talk like that," she said. "Don't ever talk like that." He opened his arms and the next thing she knew they were around her and he was holding her almost close enough to make up for all the lost time.

"I promised myself," she began, "that if I ever laid eyes on you again—"

"You are glad to see me," he said. "I can tell." He was the one finally who pushed them apart. "Let me have a good look. Smile. Maybe I'll even take your picture."

"Don't." She turned her face to the wall. "I look awful. I hardly got any sleep this morning."

"Poor baby. It hasn't been easy, has it?"

"I survived," she told him dully. "It's not much, but it's something. Do you want to tell me where you've been? I could be curious."

The cigarette he had put aside for her was still burning. She picked it up while he shook another from the pack and lit it for himself. "How far back do you want me to go?"

"Never mind going all the way back to the last place you worked in New York. That day, almost a year ago, when you didn't come home, I went down there. What was the name of that club?"

"What's the difference?"

"I found out what had happened. Oh, Charlie, it was bad enough telling them off—but did you have to hit him?"

"He got me sore. He said—"

"I don't care what he said."

He took one of the cups from the table and held it out. "Any more coffee?"

It was while she was rinsing the cup that it came back to her. Speak of coincidences—this one was wild! "That card—it said an arrival. I didn't believe it."

"What card?"

"That woman who was here when you came. She tells fortunes."

She dried the cup, filled it, and brought it over to him.

"How much does she charge to haunt a house?" He drank some of the coffee. "You're not having any?"

She shook her head. Something was bothering her. She wasn't sure what, but it was more than that silly card. "She asked me,"

Jenny said slowly, "what I dream about. I told her I never do." She stared at him. "It's not true, Charlie."

"Did you ever dream about me? Lie and say you did. I don't deserve it, but make me happy."

She took the chair opposite him, the same one she had been sitting on a little while ago when Alice Molland was there. "That's what I'm trying to tell you. I did dream about you. Last night. How do you like that? I just remembered it now. That crazy old coot could probably even tell me what it was exactly—but all I can remember is that you were here—"

"I am."

She held her hand to her face. "And that you slapped me."

"Hey!" He put the cup down so hard that some of the coffee splashed into the saucer.

"It was just a dream, Charlie." But for all of that, it had been so real. She could feel the stinging on her cheek.

"You don't need any headshrinker," Charlie said tightly, "to figure out that one. Just ask me."

"What do you think it meant?"

He got up and started moving about the room. She couldn't help noticing that he didn't forget to take the coffee with him. "Don't make me put it into words, Jen. You know as well as I do. Maybe I never hit you, not actually. Not where it would show. But inside—in the gut. Don't deny it."

She hadn't intended to.

"You can't say I didn't warn you. That day at City Hall I gave you a last chance to back out."

"It was too late. I already paid for the license." She got the box with the doughnuts. "Want one?"

"No, thanks." He sounded hurt again.

"That wasn't nice either, was it?" She shrugged. "Maybe you're right."

"I made you so many big promises."

"Well," lightly, "you never promised to keep them."

"I'm a good M.C., Jenny, and not a bad comic. I know that. I've worked dozens of crummy clubs from here to L.A., but never played one of them a second time. I couldn't figure out what was wrong."

"I told you often enough. You and your lousy temper, always telling off the owners."

"Because they were stupid."

"Maybe they didn't like being told that by the hired help. You still haven't told me where you've been. I'm still curious."

"Curious—or do you care? Because the two aren't one and the same. We'd better have an understanding first. I've got to know if you care."

Wasn't that just like him—trying to twist it so it would end up her fault if he didn't tell her? Maybe she should have kept that promise she had made to herself and not let him back in. But there he was drinking her coffee. And he hadn't been invited either. Well, he was more her type than Alice Molland and, in spite of everything, more welcome.

"How did you find me, by the way?"

"Lou told me. I talked him into it."

"You were always good at fast-talking yourself into everything but holding a job. You were always too good for whatever you were doing."

"I was made for better."

"If I thought that way I'd starve to death. Lucky I don't. I just do the best I can with my—natural assets."

"You think I liked that?" He wasn't acting now. She could tell. "You think it made me feel good knowing you were putting yourself on exhibition for the cheap drunks and the slobs with fat cigars— making yourself into a dirty joke three times a night?"

Jenny put her hand to her face. "You might just as well have slapped me. Same thing."

He was sorry he had said it. She could tell that, too, but it didn't make her feel any better.

"I only meant—"

"I never enjoyed the act. I can't say that, but I'll tell you one thing: it's going to be a lot tougher to do from now on, knowing that's what you think of it."

"I wanted you to quit. I wanted to take care of you."

She turned her back to him. "Dirty joke, three times a night. That's what you said."

"Listen," Charlie said, "please."

She swung around furiously. "Why'd you come back? I got used to being alone. I didn't even mind it any more." She was on her way to talking herself into believing she had even enjoyed it, when a loud rasping cough cut the room in half and she knew she couldn't ever make herself believe that—no matter how hard she tried.

Charlie looked startled. "What was that?"

"Just somebody who lives next door. You haven't answered me."

He walked over to the wall and stood next to it. "He could have been right here in the room with us. Doesn't it bother you?"

The only thing that bothers me right now is why you came back."

"Listen," he said again, "forget this last year."

"I couldn't if I wanted to."

"Want to change hells with me, Jenny? If you could, would you do it? No questions asked? I warn you—you'd ask for your own back."

This wasn't acting either. She let him talk. "Don't be curious, Jenny," he said, "and don't even care—if you can't. Just listen."

What did he think she was doing? "Go on," she told him softly.

"Who was it said that drowning isn't going down? That what it really is—is not coming up?"

"I don't know," she said, but hearing him talk that way, like a man for once—not a half-baked cocky kid—made her feel that maybe the last of the bubbles hadn't all risen over her head either.

"I decided I didn't want to drown," he told her. "It was as simple as that. And once I decided, things began to happen. I won't go into details, how I met this Texan, but he uses a ten-buck ante in the poker games he plays, and throws in his wife just to make the game more interesting."

"What's he got to do with you?"

"He's going to let me put some of his well-oiled money where my big mouth is. Now I'll show those bright boys around Broadway how a good club should be run."

"This on the level, Charlie?"

"Give me three months to prove it and I'll come back for you."

She looked toward the wall where the coughing had come through. "You're not taking me with you?"

"I can't. Don't you understand?"

"No. No, I don't."

"I have to prove it to myself first. If I mess this up, I don't want you around to see me doing it."

She wanted to tell him it wouldn't matter, that nothing would matter if only he wouldn't leave her behind. She didn't get a chance to get the words out. He kissed her quickly, as if he had a plane to catch. Maybe he did.

"If I do come back, will you be here?"

"Yes," she said, forgetting that earlier she had decided to move. She had forgotten about that, even forgotten about the man next door. "I'll be here."

"That's what I came to find out. Thanks for the coffee."

She rushed after him to the door. "Will you write this time?"

"If I'm not back in three months, you'll get that GI insurance in the mail. Don't spend it all in one place."

When he opened the door, Jenny saw Mrs. Keefer who had just dropped something white outside the room halfway down the hall. It couldn't be sheets and towels. What would be the sense of dropping anything clean on that floor? Mrs. Keefer looked sharply at Charlie, who winked at her. "I'm leaving, sweetheart. Eat your heart out—but take care of my girl."

"Charlie," Jenny asked again, "will you write?" She had asked it for the last time, because a moment later he wasn't there to answer and there was nothing in the room to let her know he had been there except a cup with a little coffee left in the bottom. Alice had left hers like that. Maybe it was the same cup. Maybe Charlie hadn't been there at all.

"I want to talk to you," the landlady said.

"What do you want to talk to me about?"

"Mind if I come in?"

Jenny forced a smile. "It'll be a novelty. You'll be the first this morning who's waited to be invited."

When they were alone, Mrs. Keefer said, "Did she give you a reading?"

"Did who give me a what?"

"Miss Molland."

Jenny laughed. "The ta-ra-ra-boom-tee-ay cards—or whatever you call them?"

"Tarot, Mrs. Frye," Mrs. Keefer said shortly, "and don't make fun of it."

"You mean if I don't like it, don't knock it. Hey," she said, "you know what you just did?"

"I asked you if she gave you a reading."

"Do you realize you just called me Mrs. Frye?"

"Well? Is it or isn't it?"

"You bet," Jenny said, and went quickly to the window—in time to see him hail a cab.

"It isn't fair," she heard Mrs. Keefer say.

"A lot of things aren't fair," Jenny agreed. "What can you do? Survive."

"After all, I do let her have her room for nothing."

That was enough to make Jenny turn from the window. Besides, she couldn't see the cab any more, but she was sure now that she hadn't imagined it. He had been there. What's more, he was coming back. How many promises can a man make without eventually keeping one? It was practically the law of averages.

"I'm giving you notice, Mrs. Keefer," she said impulsively, "three whole months. That should satisfy you."

It didn't even seem to interest her. "Did she give you a reading?"

"No," patiently, "she didn't. Say, you were kidding about letting her have her room for nothing, weren't you?"

"I heard her mention the five of cups."

"Oh, that. Well, I picked one out of the deck at random. She said, 'Arrival and return.' " She smiled to herself. "Then Charlie came. How do you like that for a coincidence?" She picked up the cup he had been drinking from and finished the last of his cold coffee—holding the rim up to her mouth where his had been, and moving her lips back and forth against it.

"That's all you did? Just picked a card? She didn't lay them out for divination?"

Jenny took the cup to the sink and washed it. Oh, brother! First that other kook; now this one. Old Alice sure had a few marbles scrambled, and Jenny wasn't about to swear for Mrs. Keefer.

"Well, did she?" Mrs. Keefer demanded in a shrill little voice.

"Did she what, for God's sake?"

"Lay them out for divination?"

"No—Alice didn't—whatever you just said."

"Better not let her hear you call her Alice. She won't like it."

"She asked me to."

"Oh?" Mrs. Keefer said, tight-lipped. "She's very formal with me. She must like you."

"She says we travel in the same orbit." All of a sudden it struck her as being funny. She widened and narrowed her eyes in imitation of Alice Molland and moved slowly toward Mrs. Keefer. "You know how she knows?" she said mysteriously. She shot out both hands, fingers outstretched. "Vibrations!"

"That so?"

Jenny let her arms drop. "You don't think it's funny?"

"You do?"

"I think it's a hoot if you want to know the living truth. Look, if you want to let her go rent-free, that's your business—but if you want to know what I think, I think she's a nut. That stuff she filled me with! I wondered what she had been smoking."

"She smokes," Mrs. Keefer said soberly, "cigars."

"Figures. You know what else she told me? All about a high society party she went to—with gold plates and fancy crystal and—I wonder what's in that cigar."

"It's true. Anything she told you is true."

"You can prove it?"

"Alice Molland mingles with the best, the rich ones and the ones with power—big names in politics. And movie stars—oh, lots and lots of movie stars."

Jenny looked slantwise at her. "She doesn't give you a puff on that cigar now and then?"

"I saw an invitation she got once from one of the richest men in the world to spend a weekend on his yacht. And I saw a letter from a prince—"

"Oh, come on now," Jenny said. This was beginning to be a bit much.

"It's true," the landlady insisted. "They know she's got the gift."

"So she told me."

"And people with money or power or both have more to lose than the rest of us. It helps to know what's ahead—what to watch out for."

Mrs. Keefer had said more to her in the past few minutes than in all the time Jenny had lived in the house. It hadn't, she decided, been worth waiting for—to hear such garbage.

"So our Alice," she said, "tells everybody what to watch out for. I'm glad, Mrs. Keefer. You may not believe it, but I'm very happy to hear it."

"She's never been wrong with me, but nobody's forcing you to believe."

If I have to get down on my knees, Jenny thought, and beat my bazoom and wail: I believe, oh, lordy, I believe—so help me I'll do it. I'll do anything if only you'll get out and let me get some sleep.

As she was thinking it, a sound split the room in half again and Jenny knew she wasn't going to be able to sleep—not with that going on. If it kept up steady, it wouldn't be so bad. It was not knowing when to expect it—like not knowing when she was going to pass him on the dark stairs—

"I don't like to complain," she said, "but I wish there was something you could do about that coughing. I really wish there was. It's driving me nuts."

More violent coughing almost smothered the last of the sentence. She had to shout over it. "You try to sleep with that going on."

"I'm sorry if it bothers you," Mrs. Keefer said. Jenny didn't believe for a minute that she meant it. "I'm sure I don't know what I can do about it."

That, at least, Jenny couldn't argue with. What did she expect Mrs. Keefer to do about it? The spasm stopped as suddenly as it had begun and no sound at all came from the other side of the wall. It was almost too quiet.

There's no satisfying me, Jenny decided grimly, and surprised herself by saying, "What does he do about food?" What business was it of hers anyway?

"I was thinking of bringing him something to eat," Mrs. Keefer said, "but I'd make good and sure I'd poison it first."

Jenny frowned. What did those words remind her of? She couldn't remember. It had happened to her before—something was spoken—just words and she would try to put them together with other words. "I'd make sure I'd poison it first." Probably the punch line to a funny story, not a pleasant funny story if it ended that way, but when you come right down to it, how many really pleasant funny stories are there? Every one of them has something to do with something unpleasant for somebody. "Make sure I'd poison it first." —It would bug her for days until she remembered. It was silly and stupid, but that was the way she was.

Suddenly it hit her. She wasn't going to have to wait for days. It wasn't a punch line after all. It *was* a story, but one that had happened in real life a long time ago—almost twenty years, but she remembered it like a week ago Wednesday.

It had happened in the little town upstate where she was from.

There was a dog, a mean-looking cur who didn't belong to anybody. Everybody was afraid of that dog and hated him and one day Jenny heard the butcher say to another man, "I was thinking of giving that mutt something to eat, but I'd make sure I'd poison it first." And later that same day he threw him a slab of meat. The dog looked surprised, but he came over and ate it anyway. When he was lying in the middle of the road good and dead, Jenny got closer to him than she had ever dared when he was alive. He didn't look mean then—just dead, and sort of sad. She remembered how she had gone home and cried.

"That was a rotten thing you said just now, Mrs. Keefer," she told her. "It really was."

"Why don't you bring him something to eat if you feel that way about it?"

"Maybe I will," Jenny shot back, without stopping to think if she meant it.

"I wouldn't set foot in that room, but you can do as you please. Do you know what I did?" she went on, looking proud of herself, "dropped his linens outside his door. He knows it's Friday. Maybe he'll think to look."

So those had been the sheets and towels after all. "Don't take this too personally, Mrs. Keefer," Jenny said, "but I've walked on cleaner floors in my life. Just dropped them? I think that stinks. I really do."

"Then pick them up yourself," the landlady said, obviously taking it very personally.

I should care, Jenny thought; she stinks, too.

"Go on," Mrs. Keefer said, "pick them up and give them to him, Mrs. Frye."

"And maybe I'll do that, too! How do you know I won't?"

When she was alone for the first time since she had returned from the supermarket, Jenny reheated the coffee. There was a whole carton of eggs and a fresh loaf of bread for toast.

The coughing started again.

There should be plenty of doughnuts left, unless Alice had

sneaked a few more into her pocket when nobody was looking.

He was really coughing up his insides this time. Why didn't he have sense enough to get up and get a glass of water?

There was cheese. That was always good with doughnuts. Or she might be better off filling a bowl with cornflakes. Nice and cool on a hot day.

Maybe the reason he didn't get any water was because he wasn't able to get up and get it. That could be the reason.

There was even a banana. She could slice that into the cornflakes—and add milk. Cold milk. Why didn't he stop?

When he finally did, Jenny took the eggs from the refrigerator and set them on the table. She put the cheese next to that, and the fresh loaf of bread and the rest of the doughnuts. She added a package of unopened oleomargarine and a half-filled box of cornflakes.

"What am I kidding myself for?" she said out loud to no one in particular. "I'm not going to eat all this stuff and I know it."

She put everything in the supermarket bag. Quickly. Don't think, she ordered herself. Don't think of anything except that if you were dying she'd wait around to make the proper arrangements for you.

The coffee was hot. She turned off the light under it—picked up the percolator—looped her arm under the handle of the grocery bag and left her room.

Outside in the hall there was a moment when she came close to changing her mind, but she saw the clean sheets looking as dead as that dog had looked twenty years before and as lonely somehow. Anything that's thrown away, she thought, always looks so lonely.

She knocked at his door.

When he finished coughing, Jenny heard him say, "Who is it?"
Right there was when she should have run, turned and run down
the stairs.

Three months later, on a landing halfway down other stairs, she
knew it. She thought she'd known it even then, but she had had that

4

awful feeling you get in a dream sometimes, of not being able to
move. Worse, you've forgotten how to wake up.

"I said who is it?"

It had been a deep voice that went with the cough. Three months
to remember. Three flights to walk unless Lou's elevator had been
fixed.

She pushed open the exit door. There were a couple of offices:
an accountant—a music publisher. Clack-clacking of a typewriter
came from one of them. At the far end of the hall, inside a sound
studio, a girl rehearsed. She sang a few bars, stopped and tried
again.

Jenny offered her some silent free advice: Go home, if you've
got a home to go to. This city's no place for a girl unless she's got
somebody to take care of her.

The girl wouldn't pay any attention even if she could hear. Who
takes advice from a stranger? Had she taken Alice's?

She pressed the elevator button. Still out of order. Even buttons
get tired of being pushed. Jenny knew exactly how they must feel.

Push me once more, damn you, and you can whistle—or walk. She went back to the stairs.

"It's Jenny Frye," she had answered, when he had asked.

"Who?"

She took a first step down. "Jenny Frye." Then because she had known the name wouldn't mean anything to him, she had added, "I live next door."

He said, "Come in."

Before she did, she managed to pick up the linens with her free hand. Light filtered in from the hall and the room was full of shadows.

"I just wanted to ask you—"

She felt not only frightened but foolish, because she couldn't remember what it was she wanted to ask him. One of the large shadows belonged to him. Jenny couldn't make him out any more than that.

Once, on a dark night, she had driven in a car with Charlie, and someone, like the shadow in the room, ran across the street. Charlie jammed on his brakes and swore. "Wouldn't you think they'd have brains enough to wear something white—even a handkerchief? How the hell do they expect you to see them on a dark night?"

This shadow was like that one had been—all black. To be perfectly fair, she thought, everything looks that way and it can't all be. Something must be a little gray in the room.

Another seizure gripped him. It was louder right there in the same room with it, yet, in a peculiar way, it didn't bother her as much as it had those other times when it jumped through the wall from his room to hers. His room was where it belonged, and she remembered why she had come into it.

"Anything I can get for you?"

He didn't answer.

Shadows began to turn into things. A large one near the door was a table. She set down the linens, the groceries, and the percolator. "That's a bad cough you've got. Seen a doctor?"

The shadow began to rise from the bed at the same time her heart shot up to her throat.

"Get out!"

She stumbled back, into something, and jumped to get out of its way. She didn't realize she had bumped into the door, until it swung shut behind her, turning her into one of the shadows.

"The door." It was a hollow whisper. "I can't find it."

No answer came from the other side of the room. Jenny couldn't see clearly, but she knew he could and that he was propped up on one elbow, watching her. She hadn't moved very far. The door had to be somewhere. All she had to do was find it and feel for the knob. Too flat—must be the wall.

"I can't find the door," she said, a little louder. "I can't find the damn old door."

Suddenly she was angry, because he was just watching her, not even trying to help her—and she had come to help him. She was close to crying now. Once she got out, if she ever got out, she didn't care what happened to him.

Her foot kicked something—like a hard ball. It clattered as it rolled across the room. She probably screamed then, because he said, "It won't bite."

"What was that?"

"Just a head. A very little head."

Oh, Mother, Mother, she prayed.

"A doll's head."

"A doll's head?" she repeated weakly.

"Now I know who you are. I never heard your voice before, but I recognize you now."

Jenny raised her hand. "I'm not even sure how many fingers I've got up. You're more used to being in this dark than I am."

"I had a grandmother," he told her, "who always said people see better when they're in their graves."

That did it! "Well, so long," she said, and turned back once more to where the door should be. Frantically, palms open, she searched for it. She knew where it should be. Only it wasn't. Could it have melted into the wall?

"Are you that afraid of being in the dark with me?" He sounded amused, as if it was some kind of joke.

Only I'm not laughing, Jenny thought. "Please," she begged, "where's the door?"

"What did you want anyway?"

"Mrs. Keefer said you were sick. I thought maybe you could use something to eat."

Even in the dark she could tell he was looking suspicious. Then his shadow fell back heavily.

"You're very kind."

When he said that, something popped behind her eyes—or seemed to—and she could make out a lot of things, like the door. She opened it.

"I was beginning to wonder what to do about food," he said.

Jenny took a deep breath. "I'm glad you can use it. I brought in the linens, too. Mrs. Keefer dropped them outside the door."

"Thank you. Thank you very much."

What was wrong with her anyway? She could go now if she wanted to. "I didn't think that was very nice. I told her so. They didn't get too dirty."

He started to cough again. She had the distinct feeling that he kept it from going on too long on her account.

"There are some eggs," she told him, "and some bread. And—"

"I'll be glad to pay you whatever it is as soon as I'm better."

"I didn't mean that," quickly. "I only wanted to tell you what's there. Say, how sick are you? Are you even able to get up and get any of this stuff?"

"I'll be all right."

She heard herself ask, "Where are the windows?" Don't think, she had told herself before she left her room for this. Just do it. —She was doing it again and not giving herself time to think.

"What did you say?"

"I asked where the windows are." She pointed to the wall. "In my room they're over there. Don't you have any?"

He was looking suspicious again.

"I'm not much of a cook to begin with," she explained. "So why give myself a handicap and work in the dark?"

"You're going to cook for me?"

"Just a couple of eggs. Coffee's already heated." If he wanted it he better hurry. "Tell me where the windows are," she warned, "before I have a chance to change my mind."

"If you thought it over, would you run?"

Damn right I would, she thought.

"Are you still afraid of me?"

Damn right again, but all she told him was: "I meant I was planning on getting some sleep. I didn't get much this morning. You cough pretty loud."

"There's a skylight," he said. "Can you see the cord? On your right."

She rolled it back and let in the sun. It was a large attic room, full of dust and rags and glass jars with paint brushes stuck in them. Everywhere she looked there were dolls' heads, all pink and painted with blue eyes and smiling red mouths. Finally, she found the courage to turn and look at him.

He was a big shaggy animal of a man with tight crinkly hair and dark skin that glistened in the heat. The whites of his eyes were blue-white. She had always noticed that about him. And he had a beard—crinkly and black to match his hair. He hid behind it and watched her.

For the sake of saying something, she said, "Mrs. Keefer was right, you do look terrible." It seemed to her she could have thought of something better than that.

"You didn't have to stay," he reminded her. "I didn't force you."

"Who says you did?"

She carried the groceries to the stove, took out the oleo and dropped a hunk into a frying pan already there. The oil melted and spat up at her.

"Isn't that the worst possible sound," she said, "on a hot day?"

She broke in a couple of eggs, then grabbed for a spatula hanging on a hook. "I hope you like these scrambled. I started to fry them; but they decided they'd rather scramble." He sure wasn't much of a talker. "You know," she said, "there's nothing to making a couple of eggs—providing you're a chicken."

She heard him laugh.

"Oh, boy," she said sympathetically, "you must be sicker than I thought if you so much as smile at that. It's like you; it has whiskers. —Where are your cups?"

He nodded toward the cupboard.

Cups, saucers—dishes were stacked and put away with care. She took out what she needed. "Where's the sterling?"

He pointed to the drawers flanking the cupboard.

Knives, forks, spoons were divided into separate compartments. It was more than she could say for her own system.

"Something wrong?" she heard him say.

"Everything's so neat."

"You sound surprised." His voice had a cutting edge.

"Listen," she told him, "I'm too tired to start hacking away at any chip on your shoulder. I made a plain statement of fact. If it offended you, I apologize." Had she said that to him? Where had she got the nerve? She held her breath.

"I'm the one who should apologize," he said quietly.

"I suppose I was just surprised," she explained," considering the condition of the rest of this room."

"It doesn't usually look this bad, but the night I took sick, that table got in the way when I fell. The place is a mess."

"Forget it," Jenny said.

She poured the coffee. She started to ask him if he wanted it black, but the word made her self-conscious—which was stupid, but there it was. "You want cream and sugar?"

He said, "Black."

"Sure."

She brought it over and placed it on the small table beside the bed. "Toast?"

"Don't bother."

"It's no bother."

"Will you have coffee with me?"

"No, thanks." She made the mistake of refusing too quickly.

"It's your coffee."

She went to the cupboard and took down another cup and saucer. "I never did get to finish the first cup I made for myself this morning. The morning's been full of surprises. First, Alice Molland walked in on me. Then—"

"That old witch!"

"She'd probably be the first to agree with you. She's proud of it."

"I hate that hag of hell." He threw up the words from somewhere dark deep inside of him, from a place she couldn't see and wouldn't ever know—and she wondered all over again what she was doing there.

"The eggs!" she cried, glad of the excuse to go to the stove and busy herself.

"Did she tell you I almost killed her once?"

She wished he would stop talking about Alice Molland. Wasn't being alone with him enough? He had eyes that made her nervous, too. A person could fall in and drown in them. He didn't have to open them wide and snap them half-shut the way old Alice did. All he had to do was look at her.

"Did she?" he asked.

"What?"

"Tell you I almost killed her."

She dumped the eggs onto the plate and buttered a couple of slices of bread to go with it. "Did you?"

"I pushed her," he answered. "I wanted her to get out of here."

Jenny smiled. Now he was talking her language. Wanting to get rid of Alice was something she understood.

"If you ask her," he said, taking the plate from her, "she'll tell you I broke her arm. It's not true."

"I won't ask her then."

"Don't you want to know why I pushed her?"

"Not particularly." It was true. It wasn't any of her affair. "Frankly," she said, "I felt like giving her a good shove myself, but for me it would have been like shoving the side of a mountain."

Without warning, without giving her a chance to think of a good answer, he said, "If just passing me on the stairs frightened you so—and don't deny it—why aren't you afraid now?"

"Maybe," Jenny said, "because I know you're in no condition to break my arm."

He smiled and started on the eggs.

"What's wrong with you anyhow?" she asked. "Fine time for me to ask if it's contagious."

"No," he said, "and it's my own fault. I have a weak lung. I should have known better than to walk in the rain."

For what seemed to be a long time neither of them said anything. She sipped her coffee and watched him eat. She always enjoyed seeing people eat something she had made herself, and always wished she knew how to make it turn out better. "I'm a little ashamed," she said.

"Of what?"

It had been on her mind to tell him she was ashamed she was such a rotten cook. Instead she heard herself say, "Of being afraid of you—when I didn't know you."

She must have looked surprised and even embarrassed. She sipped the coffee and hoped, somehow, he hadn't heard.

"You don't really know me now."

"Don't ask me to explain. I can't." Suddenly she was glad she had said it. She went further. "And I'm sorry you're sick, and sorry Mrs. Keefer dropped your clean linens on the dirty floor, and I'm sorry the butcher poisoned the meat. That dog really never hurt anybody. He just looked vicious."

"I don't understand."

She had said enough. "Never mind." She put down her cup, went over to the corner, and picked up what she saw lying there. "This *is* a doll's head. That's something else for me to be ashamed of—being afraid of this." She looked around the room at all the others. "They're bald—but cute."

He laughed again. "They'll get hair at the factory—and bodies. And then somebody will put pretty dresses on them, and soon a little girl will go to sleep holding a doll that has a head that frightened you so."

"What do you have to do with them?"

"I paint the faces."

She turned the little head over and over in her hands. She didn't know what made her tell him, "I never had a doll." Gently, she put it on the shelf with the others. "You're the first artist I ever met." She picked up several big tubes of paint from the floor and laid those on the shelf, too.

"I'm not an artist," he said. "I paint faces on dolls."

"Well?"

"Well, that's not art."

"I think it's great. I really do. I admire people with talent. You don't need talent for what I do. Just a gimmick."

It was obvious he didn't understand.

"I'm an exotic dancer." As soon as she said it she regretted it. Was it because of what Charlie had said before? She tried to dismiss it by explaining. "I'm not the headliner. I just help warm up the audience for the star attraction." Why didn't she shut up? He wasn't interested. If he was, he shouldn't be. "What I mean is, I know what I've got, so I don't have to show it." She was making it worse, not better. She thought she knew how to make it better.

"Say, this ought to interest you—since you're an artist."

"I told you before," he said, "I'm not—"

"My gimmick is this: I call myself the Mona Lisa." She waited for him to react. "You've heard of the 'Mona Lisa,' haven't you? It's a famous masterpiece."

"I've heard of it."

"Well," she went on, "this is my gimmick. I do the whole bit wearing nothing much but some chiffon, and a smile that looks like it's been painted on. It's the smile that gets 'em. The customers try to figure out from that just how far I'm going to go. —The hell with them. Let them suffer. —I went to the Metropolitan Museum a while back, when they had the 'Mona Lisa,' and I tried to copy her smile. That's where I got the idea for the routine. It came to me while I was standing there. As an artist, what would you call that—inspiration?"

She had hoped to "dress up" what she did, in a manner of speaking, by dragging in a reference to the Metropolitan Museum. Somehow it wasn't coming out as high-toned as she had hoped.

"What did you think of da Vinci's painting?"

She brightened and hoisted herself up on the table. The other girls should see her now discussing art that really was for art's sake and with a real artist.

"In my opinion," she said elegantly, "I think she looked kind of green around the gills."

"The bulletproof glass they put over it affected the color."

"No kidding?"

"Time hasn't been kind to it either."

"That so?"

"The green pigments have come through more strongly as the colors have faded."

"Pigments," Jenny parroted.

"But the painting," he went on, "is more than the paint. Do you know what Leonardo said about taking lifeless material and forming it into the human face?"

"Who?"

"Leonardo da Vinci."

"Oh," she said, "sure. Leonardo." Referring to the artist by first name was like being with it—all the way. "What did he say?"

He drained the cup.

She jumped lightly from the table. "Refill?"

"Is there more?"

"Plenty." She carried the percolator from the stove. "You were saying?"

"He called it the mirror of the soul."

"What do you know?"

"Do you understand?"

"Not completely," Jenny admitted.

"He meant the soul of the artist. That's what makes it a work of art. The soul of the artist is in the face of the model."

"I still don't get it. Which one of them was doing the smiling? Leonardo—?" What the hell! Why be so formal? "I mean Leo," she corrected herself, "or Mona?"

From what she could see of him behind the beard and the cup, she had the distinct impression he was looking amused again. But it wasn't the same as it had been earlier when he seemed to think it was a large joke that she had lost the door.

"The lady was doing the smiling," he said. Even his voice was different, not the same as it had been when he had said, "Are you that afraid of being in the dark with me?"

"Why was she smiling?" Jenny persisted.

"Legend has it the artist hired an orchestra to make her feel less sad—to help make her smile."

"What'd she have to be sad about? —Oh, I know, someone had died. I could tell from the way she was dressed."

"The real story," he told her, "isn't as pretty as the legend. It's said her husband forced her to wear mourning clothes so no one would suspect he had pawned her jewelry."

Jenny nodded knowingly. "Anything to put up a big front. Don't tell me. I'm married to a guy like that." Hastily she added, "The front's legit now. He has his own club. In Texas. I'm going there in three months. —Hey!"

"What's the matter?"

"I just realized. Here we've been talking—" she cleared her throat, "discussing art and masterpieces and all things like that— and I don't even know your name."

"I'm just a man who used to frighten you on the stairs."

"What's the point of dragging that up?" she asked, annoyed.

"Forget I mentioned it."

"Boy," she said, "you sure are sensitive. Do you want to tell me your name or don't you?"

"Conner," he told her. "James Conner. It doesn't really belong to me. One day a long time ago I picked it out of a New York telephone directory."

"Mona Lisa doesn't belong to me either," she said, "but I got mine from a classier place—the Metropolitan Museum. —Anything I can get you before I leave?"

"No," he said. "You've already put yourself out—" He jerked the bedclothes to his mouth and managed to stifle a fresh cough. When it passed, he continued, breathing heavily, "—more—much more than you had to."

"I didn't *have* to do anything."

"That's what I mean."

She grinned. "Maybe Alice Molland's the one you ought to thank for the banquet."

He looked confused.

"She told me to stay away from you."

"Oh? Did she?"

"Maybe I was nice to you just to spite her."

"I think," James Conner said, "you were nice—because you are."

"She makes me nervous."

"I don't?"

"Not any more. I told you that. Didn't I?"

He didn't answer.

"Well," she said, "I'm telling you now."

Three months, she decided, wasn't long. She might just as well wait there for Charlie and not bother moving, after all.

"Now, if I can only figure out a way to get old Alice off my back," she said, thinking aloud. He was looking confused again. "You see," she explained, "it all started with this." She patted the rhinestones and colored glass Alice Molland had said no one could tell from the real thing. "She liked it, so I let her borrow it. No skin off my nose. Only now, she wants to be my pal."

"Give it to her," he said.

Her hand went to her dress and she put a protective hand over the glittering pin.

"If it'll help you get rid of her," James Conner advised, "give it to her."

"You're pretty generous with my property," she said indignantly.

"It suits her," he said. "Not you."

"You don't like this?"

"Will you be insulted if I tell you something?"

"It all depends."

"It's cheap," he said. "You're not."

For a moment she didn't answer. When she did she said, "I wouldn't mind being insulted like that every day of the week."

Charlie could be blamed for a lot of things that had happened to her, but could she honestly blame him for what she said next to James Conner?

"Tell you what. Since I shop for myself anyway, why don't I get a few things for you until you're up and around?"

Was that Charlie's fault—just because he had told her she was a dirty joke three times a night, and a man who had picked his name from the New York telephone book told her to give away some junk jewelry because it was cheap—and that she wasn't?

"I wouldn't want to trouble you," he said.

"No trouble," she had answered promptly.

That did it. That started the whole business. During the next week she knocked at his door to make out a list of things he needed and itemized afterwards, on another list, what she had spent—to the penny. He was extremely particular about that and always left money under the sugar bowl on the table.

She never saw him out of bed, but the studio couldn't have cleaned itself. Every day it looked a little better. So did he.

The longest she spent with him was that first day. That first day was when they found the most to talk about, too. If she became more involved afterwards, was that Charlie's fault?

Or were the two women, Mrs. Keefer and Alice Molland, to blame—making her just mad enough to tell them to mind their own business when they interfered? The crazy part of it was, up until the moment they did there hadn't been anything really to interfere with.

"You did a lot of shopping, I see," Mrs. Keefer said one morning, stopping her on the second-floor landing.

"The way I figure it is this," Jenny told her sarcastically, "why quit when I'm ahead? The more I buy, the more stamps they give me."

She tried to get by, but the landlady barred the way. "Miss Molland wants to see you."

"Some other time."

"Now."

What was this? A royal command? "Sorry, I've got things to do."

Once again she tried to move up the stairs to three. Again, Mrs. Keefer blocked her.

Jenny was beginning to get annoyed. "Now, just a minute—" She cut herself off short when she noticed Mrs. Keefer shaking all over. Every bit of blood had drained from her face. She was either scared or angry. The next moment Jenny realized it was a little of both.

"You were in my reading," Mrs. Keefer accused. "Those were—my cards. What were you doing in them?"

"Oh, come on," Jenny said impatiently.

"It's not fair. It was my reading." With a great effort she clenched her fists into tight balls and controlled her trembling. "That's what Miss Molland wants to see you about."

"You must be kidding," Jenny said.

Mrs. Keefer bit her lip. "I'm afraid that's true."

"O.K. Then let me get by."

"What I meant was—she doesn't want to see you."

"Good. That makes us even."

"She says you should come to her. She's right, of course. Alice Molland doesn't go around with her palm out—waiting to have it crossed with silver."

"I've got news for you," Jenny told her. "I won't even cross it with green stamps."

"She has the true gift," Mrs. Keefer said indignantly. "Do you think she has to beg people to take it from her?"

The bag of groceries was getting heavier. "Tell you what," Jenny suggested, "maybe later—like next month, I'll be glad to—"

"She's doing it for me," Mrs. Keefer shrilled, "as a favor. She doesn't always show it, but Miss Molland is very fond of me."

Jenny smiled sweetly. "I may not always show it either, but I'm very fond of you, too. I'll like you even better if you let me get upstairs."

"To him?"

Jenny tightened. "Who?"

"I'd be more careful how I pick my friends, Mrs. Frye."

"It's not up to you to pick them for me, Mrs. Keefer."

Unexpectedly, Mrs. Keefer stood aside. "All right, go on. If you're that afraid."

"I'm just in a hurry." Jenny shifted the weight of the groceries.

"I said—go on, then."

Instead of going, she asked, "Why should I be afraid?"

"Why are you?"

Strange the way the same words kept coming back. In the past it had always amazed her that so many thousands of songs, millions maybe, had been written using the same eight notes—give or take a few sharps and flats. Yet, the songs were all different. And she used to think, too, how interesting it was that two eyes, a nose, and a mouth could be scrambled to make so many different faces.

But words! There were enough of those to play around with, which made it strange how often the same ones kept coming back.

For instance, on that morning not too long ago she talked to Alice Molland about a man who lived next door. She didn't know his name.

"Why should I be afraid?" she had asked then—the exact words she had just used again.

And using Alice's exact words, Mrs. Keefer had just answered, "Why are you?"

It was stupid to have been afraid of Mr. Conner—stupid now to be afraid of Alice Molland. "O.K.," she agreed, "but I won't let her read my cards. I don't have the time, and if I did, I think it's a good way of wasting it."

"It's my cards I want you to see," the landlady told her. She hesitated.

"Well," Jenny prompted, "do you want me to go, or don't you? It was your idea."

"You won't say anything to make her angry?"

"I'll be a doll," Jenny promised. "Let's get it over with."

Alice Molland, wearing the same streaked purple dress, didn't bother to look up when they entered. She was sitting at a small table looking down on picture cards that had been carefully laid out. Dozens of other pictures, covering the walls, interested Jenny more.

Mrs. Keefer had told her once that Alice Molland mingled with the best—important people in politics and movie stars—oh, lots and lots of movie stars. It was possible, of course, that all those photographs had been bought in Woolworth's. They're thrown in free when you buy frames. Alice could have autographed them to herself. Jenny wouldn't put that past her. Still, though she hated to admit it, they didn't have a Woolworth look about them. And you don't get snapshots of celebrities in the five-and-dime. She was startled to see Alice in a few of those snapshots, standing next to some pretty well-known actors and actresses.

Now that she thought of it, she remembered reading how some really big stars sign new contracts or get married again only on days their horoscopes give them the go-ahead. There were a lot of crackpots in the world! Maybe some of them even consulted Alice Molland. Jenny was willing to give her the benefit of that. But no more.

The sun beat down on the other side of the drawn shades. Only slivers of it found their way into the room. Once inside, Mrs. Keefer fell silent, but she was being silent with all her might, imploring Jenny with her eyes not to antagonize Alice—who studied the cards intently as if they were giving forth all the light that was needed in the room.

She suddenly turned to Jenny. "Beautiful, aren't they? See the colors—so brilliant—so transparent. Here the Empress, and here the Hanged Man—and here the Wheel of Fortune."

Deliberately, Jenny yawned in her face. Mrs. Keefer emitted a soft little moan of dismay.

Alice Molland only smiled. "You should cover your mouth when you yawn."

"Forgive me for my bad manners," Jenny apologized dryly.

"It isn't a matter of bad manners. It's an ancient belief. Cover your mouth when you yawn or the devil will jump in."

That time Jenny laughed in her face. It wasn't deliberate. She simply couldn't help it. "You really believe that jazz?"

The smile spread. Jenny had never seen one quite like it. It didn't make her face look any happier—just wider. "Is it any more stupid," Alice asked, "than knocking on wood, or marking a floor in a modern building 12-A and not 13?"

Jenny couldn't argue with her there.

"The ancients had their fools, too, but only a twentieth-century fool would turn her back on the secrets they left us."

Jenny couldn't help noticing that Alice made a point of saying "her" back. She couldn't help taking it personally—undoubtedly the way it was meant to be taken.

"Thousands of years ago," Alice said, tapping the cards with a fat finger, "priests fled when the temples were destroyed and desecrated by infidels, and carried with them—these—hidden in their robes."

"All I can say," Jenny commented, "is that those cards are in pretty good condition considering the fact they're thousands of years old."

"A deck like them," Mrs. Keefer murmured.

"She knows what I mean," Alice Molland snapped. "And stop whimpering like a four-legged bitch in heat. You make me nervous."

Oh, boy, Jenny thought, she doesn't always show it, Mrs. Keefer, but she really is very fond of you. Just like you said. You bet.

"Priests of old," Alice droned on, "would still recognize these as their own children."

"Nice way to talk about priests," Jenny said.

Alice Molland ignored that and tapped the cards again. "They gave birth to them, and nursed them. In these you will find the wisdom of the lost Egyptians, who took it from the great secret of the Hebrew Cabala."

"They just lifted the act, huh?" Jenny said irreverently. "Well, that's show business." Beside her, she heard Mrs. Keefer murmur reproachfully, "You promised. You promised."

What had she promised? Oh, yes, not to make Alice Molland angry. It wasn't easy. She'd have to try harder. "I haven't got all day. What did you want to see me about?"

For the first time the Oracle at the table did seem angry. "Who said I wanted to see you?" She glared at Mrs. Keefer. "You?"

"I said—" the other woman stammered, "I only said you would see her."

Annoyed, Jenny asked, "What is this? Are you saying I asked to—"

"You wanted to see my cards," Mrs. Keefer told her. "Remember?"

"No," Jenny told her firmly, "I didn't. You wanted me to. O.K., as long as I'm here, I'm looking. What am I supposed to see?" The sooner I cooperate, she reasoned, the sooner I can get out of this booby hatch.

Mrs. Keefer moved forward eagerly. "Show her, Miss Molland."

"Ten of pentacles," Miss Molland said, "—this one—signifies a house or a dwelling."

"That would be my house, of course," Mrs. Keefer interrupted. "This house. And that—" She pointed down.

"It's kind of pretty," Jenny admitted.

Alice looked steadily at her and smiled again. "You are—very pretty— A Fair Girl. That's you, Jenny."

"Has it got my name on it?"

"You're the only fair girl living in this house," Mrs. Keefer said.

"And this," Alice continued, "is a Dark Man. Does it have to have his name on it? Are you going to tell me you don't know who the dark man is?"

"I never should have rented that room to him in the first place," Mrs. Keefer wailed, wringing her hands.

"Oh, so that's it! Me and Mr. Conner."

Alice had stopped smiling. "I understand you're in there every day."

"He even has her doing his shopping for him." As proof Mrs. Keefer nodded toward the bag of groceries.

"I wonder," Alice said, "what your husband would say about it. He was your husband, wasn't he?"

"Damn right, he is," Jenny replied, picking up the groceries and going to the door. "—And he'd tell you what I'm telling you now— to mind your own business."

"Would he?" Alice asked. "Are you so sure?"

With obvious disgust, Mrs. Keefer added, "Show people! Never mind the color as long as he's a man."

Jenny figured she had taken as much as she was going to take. She slammed the door behind her.

All the way up the stairs to the third floor she heard the landlady calling after her, "Mrs. Frye! Mrs. Frye, come back. Miss Molland hasn't told you what the tarot cards predict about the Fair Girl and the Dark Man."

After that she started having her main meal of the day with him. Two o'clock every afternoon, they would spend an hour together. He'd sit up in bed, a tray across his knees, and she'd push the kitchen table closer so they could talk.

Although she never let him know, it was her way of showing

5

Mrs. Keefer that she didn't need anyone to pick her friends for her. That went double for old Alice.

Then an odd thing began to happen. She realized it when she awoke around noon as usual one day and tried to remember what it was she had to be glad about. There had been very few times in her entire life that she had awakened like that. She lay perfectly still, enjoyed the feeling, and tried to figure out why it was here. When she did, it came as a big surprise. She was looking forward to that hour with Mr. Conner!

After a while a whole week went by and she hadn't once thought of the two women who, between them, had been responsible for pushing her into that room in the first place. She didn't think about them because an hour isn't really very long and there was so much to talk about. He had a way of getting words out of her that she hadn't guessed were in her. And he seemed so interested in listening to everything she had to say. Nobody else, not even Charlie, had ever been interested in quite the same way.

"If my grandmother could see me now," she said one day. They had finished eating and she was washing up the dishes. She turned the water on full and laughed softly to herself over the sound of it.

"Your grandmother?"

"She brought me up," Jenny told him. "She was the only relative I had in the world and vice versa. We lived in this little town upstate—" She switched off the tap, turned to him, and leaned against the sink. Was he darker than usual, or did he only seem to be because of what she had been thinking? "I could tell you something about myself, but I'm not sure how you'll take it."

"Don't tell me anything about yourself you'll regret later," he advised. "It's never a good idea, Mrs. Frye."

Jenny shook her head. "You don't understand, Mr. Conner. This isn't about me—completely. A lot has to do with you."

It was obvious he didn't understand.

"I never saw a colored man," she said, "until I was ten."

He sat across the room, black and watchful—waiting for her to continue. Even as she wondered why she had started, she knew the answer. It was simply that she wanted to tell him. "I still don't know," she said, "what he was doing in that town—or why he stayed. Nobody made him feel very welcome. My grandmother—" She closed her eyes. Her lids seemed to lock, and behind them she could see it happening all over again. "—She used to yank me by the arm and pull me to the other side of the street whenever she saw him coming." Her eyes opened and she stood there awkwardly, holding the dish towel, not sure what to say next. The only thing she could think of was: "I shouldn't have told you."

"Is that why you were so afraid of me on the stairs?"

She shrugged. "Maybe. That chin armor didn't help."

"What?"

"Whiskers, Mr. Conner. That's night-club talk. It was funny about you. What I mean is: working clubs the way I have, I've run into a lot of colored people—in the band or on the same bill. I never bothered with them and they never bothered me. Why was it just you who bothered me, Mr. Conner?"

"Mrs. Frye," he said, "I can't answer that. You'll have to."

She thought about it for a moment. "I guess there was some-

thing about that other man, the one I told you about, that reminded me of you. You think that's possible?"

"It's possible."

"He was a loner, too, which was how you always struck me. He
never talked to anyone either. And just like the way you kept turning up on the stairs when I least expected to see you—was the way
he kept turning up in places I never expected to see him—coming
across the empty lot I used as a short cut to get home, for instance,
and once in a doorway I ducked into to get out of the rain. There he
was, tall as you are now, only I was much shorter then. I ran out of
the doorway into the pouring rain, and kept on running. And another time—" she stopped to take a breath,—"another time, I met
him along the river. There wasn't even anyone within yelling distance."

"What did he do to you, Mrs. Frye?"

"Looked," Jenny answered without hesitation, "the way you did.
That's all." She hung the dish towel over the rack. "Well," she
said, "do you understand?"

"I understand," he answered, "why you wanted to tell me."

Which is, Jenny thought, more than I do.

"Thank you, Mrs. Frye," he said.

"Don't mention it." But she wasn't sure what it was he was thanking her for. Never mind. It was done. The sooner forgotten the
better. A lot of things were better that way.

"I felt awful when she died," she heard herself say next. "My
grandmother, that is"—and proved to herself by saying it that some
things aren't that easy to forget after all. "She was really very good
to me, even if she did think having any kind of fun was a mortal
sin. But she loved me. That's the reason I felt so awful when she
died." She took another deep breath and finished with, "You see,
I never even liked her." Why, she had never told that to anyone—
not even Charlie.

What was it about this man that got her to unwind like a broken
clock that goes wild and starts to race backwards? How had he
made her tell him that she hadn't liked her grandmother? That was

something she had only told herself, and only once, during the funeral service.

Afterwards she had felt so absolutely rotten to have thought it that she spent longer than was necessary at the casket looking down at the body with the wax face which, a long time before, had hit her across the mouth when she learned that her granddaughter had stood up in Sunday school and refused to renounce the Devil and all his works. Jenny had said she wouldn't unless somebody could prove to her first that there was a Devil. She had said she just didn't believe it.

Had she told that to Mr. Conner, too? She couldn't swear she hadn't. How did he do it—pull all those things out of her? Just by being there to listen? Maybe. She couldn't remember the last time anybody else had been so available.

Charlie was typical of most of the big-time listeners. He was all for it, on the condition that the talk was about him. "We've talked about me long enough, baby. Now let's talk about you. What do you think of my talent, my personality, this new venture I'm working on? What do you think of its possibilities? Tell me. Tell me. I'm all ears."

It was possible that Mr. Conner wasn't really interested in anything she had to say about herself. Perhaps he was being polite because she was helping him out when he needed it. It didn't matter. Soon he'd be better. She wouldn't have any more to do with him and she would have two things to show for it: she wouldn't be afraid the next time she passed him on the stairs and she'd have talked herself out—enough to last a lifetime. It would probably have to last that long.

"See you tomorrow," she said.

He had turned his face to the wall and wasn't answering. That, Jenny thought wryly, really is the limit! I talked him to sleep. No wonder nobody ever wants to listen to me. I'm not interesting.

"So long." She said it softly. There was no point in waking him.

He surprised her by saying, "My grandmother raised me, too." His head was still turned toward the wall. He could have been talking to it instead of to her, but at least she had the satisfaction of knowing he *had* been listening before.

"We've got something in common then," Jenny said. She doubted, however, if her grandmother would have found anything in common with his. Why bother to mention that? It was another one of those pure statements of fact, but he might take it personally, and she had probably hurt his feelings enough for one day—spilling over with all that stuff about the other colored man, the one who had given her nightmares when she was a kid just by looking at her.

Mr. Conner said he understood about that. He had even thanked her. That was the part she still had to puzzle out. Good, she thought, it'll give me something to work on later, when I go into the act.

Thinking about other things was something she had learned to do, once she gave up trying to convince herself that, with a differ- ent audience, what she was doing could pass for art—that a high- class crowd might even call it "Interpretive Dancing." Who was she kidding?

"She brought me with her when she left the Islands," he was saying.

"Who? Oh, your grandmother. Well, that's interesting. I'll bet they're very pretty—the Islands. I've seen travel folders."

"My mother," he said, "just—left me." The way he said it made it clear what he meant by that.

It's getting late, Jenny thought. I ought to be going, but since he let me tell him all those things about myself, I suppose it's my turn to listen—except that there's a big difference. What I had to say dealt directly with him—with the reason I felt the way I did about him. Nothing he could tell me about himself can have any relation to me—not possibly.

She would be polite and listen anyway. Fair was fair, and there was no one and nothing to tell her how much it would have to do with her later on when it was too late for him to take back the words, and too late for her not to have heard them.

"When I was twelve," he began, "I painted some display posters for a store in our neighborhood. They let me pick out a shirt and a pair of shoes for doing it. I was proud. So proud."

"I'll bet you were." Jenny tried hard to picture him at twelve. She couldn't.

"My grandmother—she burned the shoes in the furnace and tore the shirt to shreds."

Startled, Jenny asked, "What'd she do that for?"

"Because," he told her quietly, "I had put the shoes on a shelf higher than my head, and that could have brought death down on me, of course."

Jenny stared openly at him. Had he said "of course"?

"And the buttons on the shirt—those could have closed me in so I couldn't breathe. That's what she believed."

"Did you?" If he said yes, it would end right then and there. She would never again be able to discuss anything serious with him.

"That first day you came in here," he said, "you talked about being ashamed. Do you remember?"

"No," she said.

"You told me you were ashamed of being afraid of me when you didn't even know me."

"Yeah—I guess so. What about it?"

"Mrs. Frye, you don't know what it is to feel shame. I did— every time someone came to get a love potion from her, or a little bag stuffed with the feet of a chicken and the foot of a rabbit, some ashes and a broken piece of razor, so they could make hoodoo against an enemy."

Fair was fair, but this was more than she had bargained for. He didn't look like he had any intention of quitting either.

"And I felt shame," he said, "when they asked for dust from a fresh grave to keep the hoodoo away."

Nice talk for after dinner, Jenny thought distastefully. Personally, I prefer mints.

"As soon as I could," he said, "I ran away—changed my name. Hers was the only one I ever had. And she loved me the way your grandmother loved you. But I was ashamed of her. That's worse— much worse than just not liking—"

He started to cough, worse than any time she had ever heard him.

"Hey," she said, "want me to get you some water?" She didn't wait for an answer but went directly to the sink and filled a glass. "Here," she said, "drink it slowly. Try breathing into it at the same time. It's got something to do with oxygen, though I'm not sure what. Anyway, it helps sometimes."

When he was better he said, "Thank you."

"You all right now?"

"I'm all right."

"Sounds like your grandmother could have even given old Alice a few pointers. That's saying something, since she sees around dark corners that aren't there. Her words, not mine."

Chicken feet and fortunetelling cards! What a slapstick world it was and the only ticket a person needed was to get born into it. If nothing else, the show was good for laughs.

Mr. Conner wasn't laughing. From the expression on his face she realized that he didn't much care for the comparison linking up his grandmother with Alice Molland.

"Anyway," she said lamely, "I'm sure she did love you. Well, I've really got to go now."

He managed a smile. "Thank you again for your trouble, Mrs. Frye."

"See you tomorrow?"

"It's up to you. I'll be here."

"O.K.," she said, "tomorrow," but she made up her mind it would be different then. There were a lot of things to talk about besides things that hurt—better ways to spend an hour besides scraping scabs off old sores. Maybe the scabs would never disappear, but a person could learn to live with them as long as they were covered up so outsiders couldn't see. What was the point of exposing them? Did he really care how she felt about her grandmother? Did she honestly care what his had been like? —All it had succeeded in doing was making them both feel bad and that was too bad because up to that day it had all been pleasant. Well, the next day would be again.

Still, she couldn't help being glad he didn't believe all those things his grandmother believed. She would have been disappointed in him if he had, and in herself for wasting so much time in his company.

It was a summer to remember—in the 90's fifteen days in a row and still no sign of relief. The next afternoon she made up a plate of cold cuts and brewed the coffee twice as strong, so it could take being watered down with ice.

"I bought something today," she told him proudly, and waited. "Aren't you going to ask me what?"

"If you want to tell me."

Exasperated, she said, "Sometimes I have to buy words from you, Mr. Conner."

"I'm sorry, Mrs. Frye."

"Never mind. Ask me what I bought." She didn't wait for him that time, but continued with a flourish. "Prints—reproductions, they told me, of famous paintings."

"That's very nice. For your room?"

The question seemed to take her by surprise. "What'd you say?"

"I asked if you were going to hang them up in your room."

"It never occurred to me," she told him honestly. "I didn't buy them for that reason." She started to unwrap the brown paper from a large flat package. "Do you know the Columbus Avenue Art Gallery? That's where I got these."

"I know where it is."

"I've walked by it lots of times, but never went in. If you want to know what I think, I think they call a lot of pure junk art. How do they get away with it, Mr. Conner?"

"Art," he said, "is often a matter of taste, Mrs. Frye."

"You mean one man's junk is another man's art?"

"Sometimes."

"They had these little figures carved in wood," she remembered. "One in particular really threw me—a skinny woman with no hips and pointing in the front all the way to Staten Island. And there were weird masks I wouldn't give house room—so help me." The fingers struggling with knots in the string paused for a moment. "There were other things, too—candlesticks and ashtrays and bowls. There was one bowl shaped like a boat. All the colors ran together—like a rainbow in a gutter. Have you ever seen a rainbow in a gutter, Mr. Conner?"

He nodded.

"Did you step on it or over it? I'm curious."

"Over it," he told her soberly.

"Same here." She laughed, then looked thoughtful. "Do you think I should have bought that bowl?"

"If it would have made you happy living with it—yes, I do."

"They were asking an awful lot—nine-ninety-five. Well, maybe next week." She was impatient finally, trying to undo the knots and snapped the string. The brown paper fell open and Jenny lifted out three large prints. "I spent enough extra for one week on these. They weren't giving them away, I can tell you. I paid quite a lot for each one and they came without frames."

"I'm still not sure why you bought them."

"Didn't I tell you?"

"You said you didn't want to hang them up."

"Why should I? I don't like them—two especially. The third one is kind of cute. It's different. I bought them so you could explain them to me—the way you did the 'Mona Lisa.' I found that conversation we had extremely interesting. —Something wrong?"

"You may be giving me more credit than I deserve."

"Meaning what?"

"I may not know anything at all about those."

"Sure you will," confidently.

"You should have bought prints you liked," he insisted.

"Do you think," she asked, "they'll let me take these back? Apply the difference toward the bowl?"

"They might."

"Good! I'll really get my money's worth then. First you tell me about them, then I'll return them. Be careful and don't get any finger marks on them." She handed him the first. "What I want from you," she said matter-of-factly, "is your honest opinion. You like that?"

"Yes, I do. It's beautiful."

"Oh, come on now." She had a mental picture of these fat women some artist called Rubens had called "The Three Graces" walking out on the floor of the club wearing luminescent pasties. *It's showtime, Ladies and Gentlemen.* "What's graceful about them?" she demanded.

"You mean they don't belong on a calendar, is that it?"

"Calendar!" Jenny exploded. "They're cows, for crying out loud."

"They're strong healthy animals."

"Didn't I say it? Cows."

"Never mind the figures," he suggested. "Study the faces."

Jenny did. "They don't look embarrassed," she said, with some surprise.

"Perhaps," he said, "because they don't have anything to be embarrassed about."

Jenny studied it with new eyes.

"And they're not looking for trouble either, are they? Or whistles."

Could she honestly say as much for the girls who would walk around the floor later, balancing themselves on heels that made their legs seem even longer? If those girls—Miss Mona Lisa included —didn't get whistles, they'd be worse than dead. They'd be out of a job.

She looked down at the drawing of bare feet planted firmly on earth, and strong hands grasping sturdy arms. All three of the Graces were bathed in brilliant sunlight. "I'll bet," Jenny said, "women like that had no trouble having a dozen kids."

He seemed pleased with that observation. "I wouldn't be surprised."

"Or bringing them up either. One step out of line and—pow!"

At that he threw back his head and laughed.

"What's so funny?"

"Let me see the next one."

"This," she said, "is a self-portrait of the artist. How do you pronounce him?"

"Cézanne," he told her slowly.

"See," victoriously, "you do know all about them! Now tell me this: What makes him so conceited?"

"What makes you think he was?"

"Couldn't he afford any models?"

"I'm sure he could have found a model if he had wanted one."

"My point exactly. Why paint himself?"

"It takes courage."

"And also saves a model's fee," she commented dryly.

"No one knows the artist better than he does himself. Think how much of himself he's giving away to strangers just by letting them know what he's thinking."

She cocked her head and examined the picture. "You know what he's thinking, Mr. Conner?"

"Live with it," he said. "I think you will, too, after a while."

"Nuts," Jenny said, slipping it back into the brown paper. "He's dead now, so he's not thinking anything. I'd rather have the bowl." —She started to take out the last print, then stopped. "Did you ever do one?"

"One what?" he asked, but she was certain he knew exactly what she meant.

"Self portrait," she said pointedly.

"Mrs. Frye, how many times have I told you that I—only—"

"Paint faces on dolls."

"That's right."

"You bet," Jenny agreed and didn't believe him for a second. He could be telling the truth, but wasn't. Of that she was sure. She couldn't even draw a straight line, but this man was lying if he said he couldn't do that and a lot more besides.

Funny how she could always tell when people were lying. That was a special knack she had developed. How often had she caught Charlie off base by listening very patiently until he had finished talking and then saying, "O.K., that's a good story. Now let's have the real one." Poor Charlie—always so sure he was getting away with it. In a way it was too bad she had to spoil it for him. He worked so hard trying to make it convincing.

Once, his jaw dropping, he'd asked, "How'd you know?" And she had answered, "Think they could use me on the police force?"

"I wouldn't want to be in any lineup," he said, "with you looking me over."

"Why, Charlie," she had told him sweetly, "you just were." But it was an amusing thought just the same—so amusing she forgot to be mad at him that time. She could imagine herself down at headquarters.

"All right, Jenny," the inspector would say, "they're all yours. "You've heard their stories. One of them is lying through his teeth. Which one are you going to finger?"

And without further hesitation, she would make the accusation. "Third man on the left."

"Positive, Jenny?"

"Positive, sir."

"How did you know?"

And Jenny could imagine herself answering, "You have to look behind the eyes, inspector. There's something behind the eyes that lights up and says 'tilt'—only you've got to learn to recognize it when it happens."

It had been an amusing thought, but in real life maybe she had Charlie to thank for all the practice she had had—learning to recognize the tilt sign whenever it came on. She had seen it just now light up behind James Conner's eyes as he told her, again, that all he knew how to do was paint faces on little wooden heads. Strictly his affair, of course. She wasn't going to pry.

"Is there another?" he asked her.

"Another? Oh—print. Yes. One more. This I may keep."

"I'd be interested," he said, "to see what it is you like enough to keep."

"It's kooky."

"What?"

"Off beat. Way out."

"I see," he said. "Modern art. What is it you like about it? The colors?"

"Oh, no," Jenny said quickly. "It's not what you think it is. I mean it's not one of those things nobody can understand—blobs of paint that don't look like anything except blobs of paint. As a matter of fact, this hasn't any color. It's plain black and white."

He held out his hand.

"It's a woman," Jenny said, reaching into the paper parcel for the third time, "sitting in front of a mirror. My grandmother had a photograph taken once, a long time before I was born, wearing a dress that looked a lot like this. So I don't suppose you could call it 'modern art,' could you? —Here," she said, and gave it to him.

She had expected that his reaction might be interesting. Certainly she hadn't expected it to be violent. She wasn't prepared for it.

Without leaving the bed he lunged forward, reminding her of a black panther that had been shot in the throat. His voice was hoarse and terrible.

Jenny drew back from the sound of it and from him. The shade to the skylight was rolled back and she could see the room clearly enough, but there was a thundercloud passing over the sun and she wanted to get out fast before she was left in the dark with this panther who might hurl himself at her and sink his teeth in her throat because of what she had done to him. What had she done?

"Who put you up to this?"

"I don't know what you're talking about, Mr. Conner."

"Alice Molland?"

She was too stunned to answer.

"Was it that old witch?"

"No!" she cried.

"Why did you buy it?"

"I don't know," but she wished she hadn't, and wished even more that she had never shown it to him.

"You must have had a reason."

"I told you. I thought it was different."

Suddenly he was different. He seemed to have worn himself out, torn himself to pieces. Exhausted, he fell back against the pillows, hardly breathing, and not saying a word.

Alice Molland hadn't put her up to it, but she *had* warned her against this man. If anyone else had warned me, Jenny wondered, would I have listened? Should I have listened to her?

"Mrs. Frye," he said, with that other voice, the deep gentle one she had grown used to from him, "did I upset you?"

She couldn't help it. She started to laugh. "Are you kidding? Look at my hands." She showed them. "That's a peculiar thing that happens to me whenever I get mad or nervous. They get all puffed up and red." She could feel the heat coursing through them and knew that the only way she could get her ring off, if she wanted to, was to soak her hands in epsom salts and wait for the swelling to go down. "Upset me, Mr. Conner? You just scared me to death."

He appeared to have returned so completely to the man he had been only a minute before that she found the courage to say, "I want to know why."

He looked directly at her and answered, "It bothered me that you wanted to return those others and intended to keep that—trash."

Tilt! Jenny thought, looking behind his eyes, you're lying, Mr. Conner.

"The others," he continued, "are examples of good art. I was pleased you wanted to know more about them. I was flattered you thought I could tell you about them."

I'll buy that, she thought. Go on.

"But this—" The print wasn't any heavier than the others, but he seemed to be having great difficulty picking it up. "This and others like it were quite popular around the turn of the century. But tastes change, Mrs. Frye. It won't live."

"It lived this long," Jenny reminded him.

"It didn't deserve to."

"Because you say so, Mr. Conner?"

"Keep the others," he advised, "or, if you return them, return this too. Get your money back."

Jenny was still curious enough to ask, "How did Alice Molland come into this? You were so sure she had something to do with it."

"She's a coarse and stupid woman," he answered. "And a cruel one. She takes advantage of other people's ignorance. I thought perhaps she had been responsible for talking you into wasting your good money on this."

Tilt! Tilt! Tilt! Oh, Mr. Conner, Jenny thought, I don't believe one single word you're saying. Whatever it was set you off isn't what you're claiming now.

The same streak of perversity that made her want to help him in the beginning made her say now, "You think it's nice to call me ignorant, just because I don't know much about cultural things?"

"I didn't mean that the way it sounded," he apologized.

"Didn't you say before that art is a matter of taste?"

"Yes," he admitted.

"Well, maybe I've got low tastes. Maybe I like this better than the fat ladies or the conceited man. I like novelties—things that are different. This happens to be. That's why I'm going to keep it."

"Do as you please," he said stiffly.

"I think it's clever."

He didn't answer. She reached out, took it from him and looked almost defiantly at the print titled "Vanity."

A tightly corseted woman, hair piled high in the fashion of the day and wearing a bustled gown, sat before a mirror, apparently pleased with what she saw. What she obviously didn't see was a second face overlying her own reflection in the mirror—the face of the Devil. The shape of his head, horns and all, was composed from other shapes belonging to the woman. It took its shape from the folds of her dress, the curve of her arm, the rise of her hair.

"It's damned clever," Jenny said, "in spite of what you say. There she is, so busy admiring herself that she doesn't see the Devil staring back at her—and she's the one who put him there by being so vain."

"That's another reason you shouldn't have brought it to me." His voice brought in the only cold air in the room. "You understand it quite well."

She turned to him. "Explain this then. Tell me why it's bad."

"I already have."

"I wish I could draw this good. Don't you, Mr. Conner?"

He didn't answer.

I'm getting him mad again, she told herself. Why don't I stop? What's the matter with me?

But she knew what it was that was making her do it. She had to find out what it was about the drawing that had turned him into a panther. She wanted to know that so badly that she risked having him turn into one again.

"You see, Mr. Conner," Jenny said, "I don't accept your explanation of why this is trash. It tells a story, which is more than I can say for that self-portrait. You told me I'd have to live with that to find out what the artist was thinking. This one tells a story right off. I don't have to think about it. Vanity is another name for the Devil, right?" She shoved the print closer to him—and noticed how he retreated from it. "This artist," she said, "must have had to work very hard to get it to come out like this—to draw one face and have you see two. Don't you think he had to plan it very carefully— know just exactly what he was doing?"

Then it happened. He seized the print from her hand and, with those large ones of his, ripped it savagely in half. But this time, because she had expected something to happen, because she knew she had been deliberately asking for trouble by needling him, Jenny was on her feet in an instant and halfway across the room when she said, "That was mine, Mr. Conner, bought and paid for."

He seemed confused, almost surprised to look down and see the torn print. It was as if he wasn't quite sure who had been responsible for destroying it.

I am, Jenny thought. It's really my fault. And she was terribly sorry, not about the picture—that didn't matter—but for trying to trick him into telling her what it was about it that he hated so.

Whatever it was was still a mystery and would stay that way, if
that was how he wanted it.

"I'll replace it," he said, "give you the money to buy a new one."

"Don't bother," Jenny said and meant it. He had taken all the
fun out of it. Another would only remind her of what had happened
to the first.

"I'd like to explain." As he had once before, he turned his head
and talked to the wall rather than to her.

"Don't bother," she said again.

"I get on my own nerves, day after day, never leaving this room.
Lately, though, I've been a little less useless. I've set up my paints
on this table and been able to get some work done."

"I've noticed," she said. "There's a whole new shelf of heads
done now."

"But I haven't been able to deliver them. I just stay here in this
room."

"You'll be better soon," Jenny told him, and at the same time
told herself: And once you are, Mr. Conner—that will be that.
It will have been nice knowing you. And maybe I'll think of you
sometimes, not often, only once in a while, and I'll wonder if I ever
really knew you at all—even a little.

"I get short-tempered," he was saying, "for stupid reasons like
before. For no reason." He was having great difficulty finding the
right words. "And the heat, Mrs. Frye. It's very hot again, isn't it?"

"There's more iced coffee," Jenny said, "in the refrigerator—
if you want it."

She said nothing about seeing him again the next day. That
was something she would have to think very seriously about—and
then decide.

The decision was easy—because the next morning he made it for
her.

She saw herself knocking at his door.

"Who is it?"

"Jenny Frye!"

And she had that awful feeling you get in a dream sometimes of not being able to move—

6

"Who is it?"

"Jenny Frye. I live next door."

Worse—she had forgotten how to wake up.

"Get out!"

"What was that I kicked?"

"Just a head. A very little head."

"I can't find the door. Where is it?"

"Who is it?"

"Jenny Frye. I live next door."

"Who put you up to it? Alice Molland? It won't live. It doesn't deserve to."

"Please. Where's the door? What was that I kicked?"

"Just a panther. A very black panther."

Then she was outside his door knocking again, and she had that awful feeling you get in a dream sometimes. She wanted to move, and had forgotten how.

Terrible—just terrible, to know you're dreaming—and not be able to cross the road back. Maybe if she tried—harder—

"Who is it?"

That time Jenny knew she was the one who was saying it. Somehow she had managed to wake herself up. Knocking was still coming from outside the door, but from outside her own door—not his. She stared up at the ceiling.

It's interesting, she thought, how I can always tell what is a dream and what isn't.

How could she be so sure she was awake now and hadn't been before? That room she had been in only a minute before, in her mind had looked exactly like the studio next door. She had seen the shelves with doll heads, the table, the chairs—the stove where she had made those first eggs, the ones that decided they'd rather scramble than fry. She had seen the same skylight with the roll shade. And the bed—she reached out and touched the wall—was exactly like that real one on the other side of this. How did she know it had been a dream? How could she tell the difference? It was a screwy idea. And a scary one.

Maybe one day she would be wide awake, but not know that she was. What could she wake up from then? There would be no place to go—except crazy!

The knocking stopped. Interesting, too—the way sounds you hear in real life are the ones you wrap dreams around. She could hear heavy footsteps moving away—going down the stairs. Mrs. Keefer probably. Typical of her not to have answered. Too much trouble in too much heat. She must have left a package.

I'll get it in a minute, Jenny decided. First she had to decide something else. It seemed very important; perhaps, because she had never thought of it before. But now she had, she had to know. One day she might need to and wouldn't have the time to figure it out.

She picked up the little clock on the night table. Not quite noon. No rush. Think about it. How can a person really tell when she's awake and when she isn't?

Jenny closed her eyes. There was nothing to see now, but next time she had a dream she'd be in it again. She was sure of that. Whenever she dreamed she was always in it. It wasn't like watching a movie or TV. It was more personal, and whether she liked it or not, she always had the leading role.

She sat up and smiled. So simple, really. Why hadn't she figured it out right away?

I can always tell I'm dreaming, Jenny told herself logically, because I can always see myself. It's like standing two feet in back of myself, watching things happen to me. And when that happens, I know I'm asleep and it's not real. If I can only remember next time, I won't be afraid.

She jumped out of bed, went to the dresser, and grinned at her reflection. "You look like something the cat dragged in, girl." Still it was reassuring to know that the only way she could see herself was in the mirror—even if what she saw wouldn't win any beauty contests.

I would have been better off, she thought, if I had forced myself to stay up. I could have sewed in that zipper or done some ironing. What's the good of sleeping, if it doesn't do any good?

She had been tired when she fell into bed. She was exhausted now. In the bathroom she opened the medicine cabinet. Pills for everything; some to keep people awake, others to put them to sleep. If somebody could only invent a pill to keep people from dreaming. It might solve the whole world's problems. Most of the time when you read the papers, Jenny thought, it's like reading about a bad dream somebody had. To get rid of it, he woke up and passed it on to three other guys. Then they kept passing it on and on to more and more people and that, she decided, brushing her teeth vigorously, is how wars begin.

She wondered what package Mrs. Keefer had left outside her door. There wasn't anything she was expecting and ordinary mail was never personally delivered. Except telegrams! Charlie! She slipped her robe over a baby-doll gown and ran to the door. Three months weren't up yet and she probably was out of her mind to count on his turning up again when they were. Still, he had been so different that day. For the first time seeming to know where he was going. Wherever it was, couldn't he have changed his mind about wanting her there with him—just in case it didn't work out—just in case he needed her around to tell him it had been somebody else's fault?

She flung open the door and looked down for the yellow envelope. What she saw instead was a long box—neatly gift wrapped.

Even before she opened it she knew what it was. The shape told her that, and, at the same time, told her who it was who had knocked to let her know it was there, before he went down the stairs. Those footsteps had been much too heavy to have belonged to the landlady. She should have realized it, but she had been groggy, just over a nightmare.

There wasn't a note in the box. There didn't have to be. Jenny put the long bowl on the table. It was even prettier than she had remembered. He had given it to her for two reasons and she knew them both. The first was to apologize again—for tearing up that print; the second—to thank her for giving up some of her time these past couple of weeks.

Suddenly she remembered she had been planning to think very seriously about giving up any more of that time after what had happened the day before. It was all settled now. Since Mr. Conner was well enough to go out and buy that bowl, he was well enough to take care of himself.

It was getting to be a drag anyway. Throwing a meal together for herself was one thing; when it comes to two, it becomes a production. It involves deciding what to make and what to shop for; then going to all the trouble of preparing it and making conversation with a person she honestly didn't have a thing in common with.

"I'm glad it's over," Jenny said out loud. Then she looked down at the bowl filled with colors that ran one into the other, and felt mean thinking what she had. Still truth was truth. It was going to be a lot easier thinking only about herself, especially if the hot spell didn't end soon. That afternoon it rained.

Jenny pulled the table next to the window and looked out. The sky had opened and let down sheets of water. Later, if the sun came out again, the gutters would be full of rainbows—and she remembered how Mr. Conner had told her he never walked on them either, always over them, the way she did. Well, maybe that was the one thing they did have in common. That—and both of them being brought up by grandmothers.

The stale heat that hung over the city was washed away, and after a while much of the memory of those hours spent next door washed away with it. Like everyone else in New York that summer, Jenny had been sure it was never going to rain. Once it did, she was sure, like everyone else, it was never going to end.

If she thought about him at all, it was with mild disappointment that she never once passed him on the stairs. Actually, she had looked forward to that—to the satisfaction of seeing him and standing still. She had it planned.

"Good morning, Mr. Conner."

"Good morning, Mrs. Frye."

"This is the first chance I've had to thank you for the bowl."

"Do you like it?"

"Very much."

"I'm glad."

"Well—good-by, Mr. Conner."

"Good-by, Mrs. Frye."

He would nod, she would smile, and they would go in opposite directions. She might even run the rest of the stairs, not because she was afraid, but because she wasn't.

Only she didn't see him, except once from her window—head bent, walking toward the corner.

What a jerk, Jenny thought, annoyed. He got sick last time from walking in the rain. If he gets sick again, he's asking for it.

The next few days she waited for the coughing to start all over. It didn't. Every once in a while she heard him moving about. Alice Molland had been right about one thing: those walls were thin, almost like paper. She was wrong about something else though, Jenny thought. She warned me to keep away from him. If I ever get the chance, I'll tell her she was wrong. I gave him a helping hand when he needed it and got two nice presents for my trouble:

that bowl and, much more important, those stairs don't bother me any more.

Tell all that to the Glob? Risk having her think she was trying to be cozy with her? That would be the absolute height of insanity. Come to think of it, she hadn't seen old Alice around lately either. One day Mrs. Keefer offered some information about that when Jenny went down to get the mail.

"I wouldn't mind changing places with her." Mrs. Keefer sighed.

"With who?"

"Miss Molland. Now that the weather's so perfect—not too hot, and it's finally stopped raining."

"Speaking of rain," Jenny told her, "I've got a leak in my ceiling."

The skin around Mrs. Keefer's mouth shrank, making it seem even more pinched.

"Well, I didn't put the leak there. I'm just telling you about it. Are you going to have it fixed or not?"

"It'll be attended to," the landlady said. "There's no need to keep at me about it."

"Keep at you?" Jenny said exasperated. "I only just mentioned it."

"Exactly what I mean. You've only just mentioned it. Now give me a chance to have it fixed, will you?"

"Oh, brother," Jenny muttered, and continued to thumb through the stack.

"I was telling you about Miss Molland. She's certainly having a nice little vacation for herself."

"Glad to hear it," Jenny said. "Where'd she go?"

"She's on the water."

Jenny couldn't help it. She laughed. "What's she doing? Being launched? The S.S. *Alice*. You can't tell her S from her front."

When Mrs. Keefer looked disapproving, it was as if she was being squeezed between bookends. Everything about her became thinner—more pointed. "You can be very crude, Mrs. Frye."

"Yeah," she admitted, "that was. Sorry."

"Miss Molland is being entertained."

"On a yacht?"

"Naturally."

"Naturally. Not much mail, is there?" She tried to sound casual about it. "You—uh—couldn't have put anything for me in somebody else's stack, could you?"

"Couldn't and didn't. That's all you got. Your husband's not much for writing, is he? I haven't noticed any letters postmarked Texas."

Annoyed, Jenny told her, "Nobody asks you to look at the postmarks. All you're supposed to do is sort the mail." With difficulty, she restrained herself, and continued rather grandly—not that it was easy to pretend to be grand on the heels of making that corny and—crude—pun about Alice, but she did her best: "The truth is, Mrs. Keefer, I told Mr. Frye not to bother writing. He's much too busy getting everything ready for when I get there."

"And you manage to keep yourself busy while you wait for him, don't you?"

And there's no mistaking what she means by that crack, Jenny thought. "I always manage to keep myself busy," she snapped.

"Mr. Conner is better, I see."

Jenny couldn't resist, "Then you must see him more than I do." What an old gossip she was and just the right nose for it.

Mrs. Keefer did something that surprised her then—reached out and patted her on the shoulder. It was an odd little pat, timid and almost friendly. Jenny couldn't have been more surprised if the other woman had kicked her instead. She would have known how to react then—kicked her back. This way she didn't know what to do, so she did nothing—just waited for Mrs. Keefer to explain.

"You believed them after all, didn't you?" She sounded pleased with Jenny.

"Believed who, Mrs. Keefer?"

"The cards."

Jenny was disgusted. Were they back to that again? "Mrs. Keefer," she said patiently, "I don't know anything about those cards."

"You're not supposed to, dear."

Dear? Jenny repeated silently. Since when am I dear?

"As long as Miss Molland is here to explain them to us."

"In case it slipped your mind, I didn't stay long enough to have anything explained."

"But they were pointed out to you. Don't you remember? A fair girl—a dark man and—"

"And I left." She started to do so again. She was halfway up the first flight when she heard Mrs. Keefer call after her.

"You're sure?"

Jenny spun around, holding onto the banister for support. "Positive."

Mrs. Keefer frowned. "We discussed it for such a long time that afternoon—Miss Molland and me. —I remember now. She really studied the cards. Oh, she's very conscientious. She wanted to be sure she had read them right, that there was no mistake." She shook her head meaningfully. "There wasn't, Mrs. Frye."

"You're dying to have me ask what she saw, aren't you?"

"Aren't you even a little curious?"

"Not even a little," Jenny said.

"It doesn't matter now anyway," Mrs. Keefer said.

"It never did."

"What I mean is: we are all masters of our own destinies up to a point. That's what Miss Molland says. And if we can be warned in time— It'll be all right," she finished, "as long as you don't have anything to do with him any more."

"Mrs. Keefer," Jenny said, "you know something? You're wasting your time. You don't need cards. You are one."

After that she went out of her way to look down the spiral of stairs that wound from the third floor to the vestibule—she could see it clearly—and if no one was there, except perhaps one of the Day People who happened to be at home, she would run down to get her mail. It was seldom worth the effort.

Usually there were just bills and ads, and once a letter from Candy who had been known as "Cotton Candy" when they worked the same club. She had hair dyed pink to match the puffy cotton balls pasted on in suitable places. Little by little every night she would pick them off and toss them into the audience. She had lent Jenny money once when she really needed it, and acted surprised and even grateful to get it back, as if it didn't always happen that way. She had been a good friend really, even if she did have the face of an angel and a mouth like a garbage disposal. After every show, Jenny remembered, Candy circulated with the out-of-towners encouraging them to buy more drinks—something Jenny always refused to do, insisting that wasn't in her contract. Candy didn't object. There wasn't much of anything she did object to—including marrying one of the out-of-towners, moving to Cleveland, letting her roots grow out, and registering Republican.

In the letter she said all the members of the PTA thought she was simply wonderful to have given up a brilliant Broadway career to become a Den Mother. It was funny in a way and went to prove something. Jenny wasn't quite sure what.

Another letter, forwarded from her last address, really was funny. It came from Charlie's sister in Detroit. Did Jenny know where Charlie was, because family ties were very important—especially when people start to get older and it wasn't right to see each other just at funerals. So if Jenny would write and tell her where he was, she would appreciate it and would write and apologize for the things she said to him last time she saw him over a year ago.

Jenny hadn't even known he had been there. It was probably one of the stops he made after leaving New York that other time, and he probably hadn't been sober enough to know he was being insulted anyway. She decided not to answer. What could she say? Dear Helen: If you know where Charlie is, I'd appreciate it if you'd let me know. Then I'll be very happy to write back and let you know.

Of course, she could be more helpful if she wanted to, and tell her he was somewhere in Texas. More specific than that she couldn't be. Just somewhere. As the days went on, she counted less and less on his ever coming back—from wherever that somewhere was.

Four o'clock one morning he telephoned.

She had been home for about half an hour and was sitting at the kitchen table eating cornflakes and trying to decide if that was the morning she would finally wash out the perk and put in fresh coffee, so all she'd have to do when she got up later was turn on the flame under it. Too much trouble. Too tired. Still a good idea— for tomorrow. If she wasn't too tired. If it wasn't too much trouble.

There's a thick stillness about four o'clock in the morning. The ringing made a knife cut through it.

"Hello," Jenny said.

"I figured you'd be getting in about now. Was I right? It's two hours earlier here."

Pick up a phone and dial the New York code number. No long-distance operator to prepare the party on the other end first. Progress! Who needs it? "That you, Charlie?"

It wasn't a brilliant opening, but she hadn't been given time to think of one.

"Who else calls you at this hour?"

"I'm kidding. I recognized you right away. Well," she said, "this is a surprise."

"A nice one?"

"Sure. I wasn't asked first if I'd accept the charges." Now that, she thought bitterly, was brilliant. No wonder he walked out the first time! There I am ready with the needles again. I wouldn't blame him if he hung up. "Charlie? You still there?"

He was still there, but his voice was withdrawn, taking him even farther away than he really was.

"I wanted to let you know how things are going—if you're interested."

"You know I am."

"That well-oiled Texan I told you about—remember?"

"The one who uses a ten-buck ante in poker games and throws in his wife just to make the game more interesting?"

He laughed. "Greatest guy in the world! When you meet him, you'll love him."

"When did you say that would be?"

"He's introducing me to all the right people down here—taking me everywhere—footing all the bills."

"He must like you."

"Flipped over me," Charlie said. "Thinks I'm the greatest thing since mother's milk."

"What about the club? That still on? Or has he been too busy laughing at your jokes to remember that's what he got you down there for?"

"You know, Jenny," Charlie said, "sometimes you have a very unfortunate way of putting things."

"What'd I say?"

"You make it sound like I'm freeloading by entertaining the local yokels."

"I heard a couple of new stories last night," she told him. "One of 'em's clean, but still funny. Maybe it'll be good for a couple of drinks."

"So long, Jen," he said reproachfully.

She yanked the telephone cord to her, as if that could bring him closer. It couldn't any more than she could split it open and pull out the words she had poured into it.

"I'm tired," she said hastily, and wondered why she always had to pick his bones whenever he got within hearing distance.

There were so many soft things she wanted to say to him. Why did she keep spitting burrs? It didn't make sense, not when she was so glad he had called. Relieved was a better word. She was like those mothers she was always seeing on Riverside Drive park. They'd rush over when their kids fell out of trees, pick them up, dust them off, and start whacking them, just because they were so relieved they hadn't been killed—just the way she was so relieved to hear from Charlie now. But he wasn't a kid, even though he was the only one she had ever had. Given half the chance maybe he could even be a husband.

"What about the club?" she persisted.

"I don't get the impression," he said with dignity, "that you take it seriously."

"I told you I'm tired. I mean—was. I'm fine now. I do want to hear about it."

"It's going to be small," he said, excited, "but intimate—more like a cabaret. The tables are going to be so close together, the customers will be playing kneesies with each other; but they won't mind, because they'll be playing it with the right people. You know how we're going to make sure only the right people come? They're the only ones who'll be able to afford to pay the tab. And what do you think of this, Jen? Instead of applauding the acts and jabbing each other in the eyeballs with their elbows, we're going to request them to snap their fingers. Cute gimmick?"

"Cute," Jenny said, smiling into the mouthpiece. He was full of lively enthusiasm again. Helen needn't have worried. Charlie never stayed insulted long. "Your sister wants to know how to get in touch with you."

"What dragged her up all of a sudden?"

"She wants to apologize."

"For what?"

"How should I know? I wasn't there. Something she said last time she saw you. Where can she write you?" —What she was really asking was: where can I?

"The hell with her. I haven't got time to be a pen pal."

"She's your sister."

"O.K., I'll write to her when I get the chance. Right now I'm busy getting ready to open a club. Remember I told you three months?"

She reminded him: "You told me that's when you'd be back to get me."

"I said if I didn't mess it up." She thought the line had gone dead until she heard him say, "Will I mess it up, Jenny?"

He wasn't asking for an answer. He was pleading for the one he had to have. At that instant she knew the real reason he called. It was two o'clock in the morning and he was alone. Awake and alone—maybe for the first time in weeks—not tired enough to sleep, no one around to listen to his jokes. And he was scared.

This, Jenny told herself, is my chance to soften the burrs. They'll be so soft that afterwards he'll plump them together into a fat pillow and go off to sleep like a big baby. When he wakes up he won't be scared any more.

"Of course you won't mess it up," she crooned. "Didn't I already tell you that? Not this time."

"What've you got?" he asked eagerly. "Something like a premonition? Something like that?"

"Yes," she lied, "I've got a premonition. A real strong one. This is the big one, Charlie." Another minute and she'd be rolling her eyes to heaven and spouting, "It's in the cards"—like Alice Molland.

"I'll need to hire a good M.C., someone who can really pull them in."

He was being the perfect straight man—feeding her all the right lines. "Why look for outside talent? You won't find anyone better than you, Charlie."

"Get the picture first, hon."

She could see him sitting on the edge of the bed while he talked, unbuttoning his shirt with one hand, kicking off his shoe. He was already feeling more relaxed, almost ready for sleep. Just a little more crooning.

"This will be a different kind of audience. More on the elite side. Sophisticated."

"You can handle them."

"You think so, Jen?"

"Would I lie to you?"

She heard him laugh. He was over a thousand miles away and she knew he had just kicked off the other shoe. Even his feet felt better.

"Well," he said, "I've got a big day not too far off. We're seeing contractors at ten. I just wanted to call and find out how things were going with you. So long, hon."

"Take care of yourself," Jenny said.

She hung up. What was that he had said? "I just wanted to call and find out how things are going with you?" She dumped the rest of the cornflakes into the sink strainer and decided that was the morning finally—to wash out the perk and put in fresh coffee so all she'd have to do when she got up later was turn on the flame under it. While she was doing it she laughed softly to herself. Well, they had talked about her, hadn't they? "We've talked about me long enough, baby. Now let's talk about you. What do you think of my talent, my personality, this new venture I'm working on. What do you think of its possibilities? Tell me. Tell me. I'm all ears."

What difference did it make? The only thing that mattered was that when he needed someone to talk to, none of those new "contacts" could do for him what she could.

She looked at the clock. By now he was already asleep. What kind of dreams do you have, Charlie?

It wasn't until she was in bed herself that she remembered that unpleasant one she had had the night before he came back—not too long ago. In it he had slapped her—hard—across the face. Stupid dream! No matter what his other faults, Charlie Frye had never lifted a finger to her. That was the one thing she wouldn't have put up with. Other girls did. Hadn't she seen the bruises? Sometimes they even showed them off—like medals.

Jenny flipped the pillow over to the cool side. She shouldn't have told him about that dream. It made him feel bad.

Isn't it nicer to make him feel good—like just now? It makes us both feel better and maybe I wasn't lying. Maybe this will be the big one. For us. It's been a long time coming. For us.

The pillow had been better on the other side after all. She flipped it back.

More of a cabaret than a club. Everybody snapping fingers instead of applauding. Cute gimmick. Very. She fell asleep—counting tiny café tables—pushed close together so that the right people could play kneesies with each other.

When she awoke it wasn't much past 8:30. Yet she felt rested and full of energy. Excitement can do that, and having something to look forward to. Unless he hadn't really called. She closed her eyes, remembered back, and was certain she had been able to see the room clearly—walls, sink, table, cornflakes sopping up the rest of the milk in the bowl—everything down to her own hand holding the telephone, but not once had she been able to see the *whole* of herself. Wasn't that what she had figured out? Didn't that prove it hadn't been a dream? She almost hopped out of bed.

Something else could help her prove it. She turned on the flame under the percolator. Just turned it on. Ten minutes later she was dressed and drinking fresh hot coffee.

Not long after that, barely nine o'clock, she left the house. Odd feeling, leaving with those others who took the bus crosstown or the subway downtown to offices or stores. She said good morning and wanted to tell them, "I'll be saying good-by soon. My husband called from Texas." There wasn't one of them she knew well enough for that.

For the first time she wanted to go out of her way to look for Mrs. Keefer. She would say, "Remember that leak I told you about? No, never mind any excuses. I just wanted to inform you not to put yourself out if it's too much trouble, which it obviously is. You see, it's quite definite now that I'll be leaving here."

I'll look for her later, she decided, when I get back. It's too beautiful a morning to stay indoors.

She crossed Riverside Drive into the park, where there were two ways of getting to the boat basin and the tangy smell of salt water. Either she could take the long way, down the path where there were always kids on bicycles, mothers pushing carriages and people walking dogs; or she could take the short cut down the broad flat steps that wound between leafy bushes and small overhanging trees.

She decided on the steps, but at the top she hesitated for a moment. "Go on," she ordered herself. "You're through being afraid of steps, remember?" Her shadow went first.

To the left, on the West Side Highway, she could see cars flashing by. Beyond that, the sun made the Hudson River sparkle. The next moment she could only hear the roar of the motors and couldn't see the water. All she could see were the stairs and the leaves. A caterpillar dangled on the underside of one of them. She stood very still for a moment and watched it inch its way up to safety.

Why didn't she feel safe? Broad daylight, the sun was shining— dozens of people above on the walk, hundreds of them in cars on the highway not a hundred feet away.

People in cars with loud racing motors, who wouldn't be able to hear her if she screamed. And others on the walk above, who wouldn't bother to find out what was the matter if she did. She should have gone the long way. If she found herself alone on the path, it wouldn't have bothered her. It was the stairs—

I'll hate myself later, Jenny thought, but I can't help it. I'm going back.

Before she could, two men came bounding into sight, moving up toward her. If she turned now, wouldn't it look as if she were running to get away from them? If they hadn't any ideas about her, wasn't that a pretty good way of giving them a few wrong ones? Nothing to do but continue moving down until she passed them.

Men? More like boys, eighteen—perhaps nineteen. Why was she so sure they weren't nice clean-cut American boys out looking for the same thing she was: fresh air and sunshine? Because she could always spot a couple of rotten evil-minded little bastards out look- ing for trouble.

When she met them finally, they stood one step below her, but close enough for her to feel breath from insulting mouths that laughed without uttering a single sound. She hated them for being able to stand so still while she cringed inside. The secret was in the way they stood—in their shoulders, the lift of their chins. Maybe she could copy it if she tried, and make them back away.

"Excuse me," she said.

Only their eyes moved. She could feel them crawling over her body, like the caterpillar. She shivered in the sun.

"I said excuse me."

She moved to the right. They moved to their left. Then their right—her left—in rhythm—the three of them dancing but not touching. Not yet.

Then one of them, the one with the tattoo on his arm, reached up and tapped her on the cheek with a rigid finger—a light tap, but her skin burned.

"Soft," he said. "You're soft."

"I'm in a hurry."

"We're not," the other boy said. It was in the middle of hot July, but he had frozen eyes—with no expression in them at all, not even pity.

The first one, the one who had called her soft, was humming in an almost inaudible voice. Her hands began to tingle. That meant she was getting nervous.

Once more she tried to move past them. Once again they blocked her. Her elbow jerked outwards, as she raised her arm and tried to find shelter behind it.

"What's the matter?" Frozen Eyes said. "You don't like us?"

"Get out of my way," Jenny said, trying hard to remember that they were just boys, little punks, "or I'll call the cops."

Her stomach turned over and she closed her eyes for a second, opening them again quickly when she felt the stairs gliding away under her feet. When she did she saw two long shadowy arms raised behind her own shadow. How could they be behind her and in front of her at the same time? She let out a cry of fright and helplessness and whirled around.

"Good morning, Mrs. Frye."

"Mr. Conner!"

"These two friends of yours?"

"No." She wanted to laugh and cry at the same time. She had been looking forward to meeting him on the stairs. She hadn't known they would be these particular stairs. She hadn't known just how glad she would be to see him.

The two punks don't look so big any more, she thought. Maybe that's because Mr. Conner is so much bigger. She watched them bolt the rest of the stairs without looking back.

"Were they bothering you?"

"They're not bothing me now," she answered. "I was on my way to the boat basin."

"So was I."

"Well," she said, "this is the first chance I've had to thank you for the bowl."

"You liked it?"

"Very much."

"I'm glad."

Just the way she had planned it, only they didn't go off in opposite directions. They walked along together through the arched underpass that was scrawled with black crayon: "Gonzales is a fink"— "Johnny Crime"—"T.K. and Lottie." And "The 84th Street Rockets." Not far ahead she could see the river.

It was pleasant along the water. People fished from the pier, sunbathed or just sat on the benches. Jenny and Mr. Conner took one of the empty ones.

"See that Chinese junk?" She pointed it out to him. "It's a real one, a couple of hundred years old. Some smart publicity guy rents it out for parties." For the first time she noticed he had been carrying a sketch pad. He opened it and began to sketch the junk with quick sure strokes. "I thought you just painted faces on dolls."

"Did I say that, Mrs. Frye?"

"Didn't you?"

"I don't draw people."

"Just—things?"

He nodded and kept on drawing.

"Will it bother you," she asked, "if I watch?"

He shook his head. It was pleasant, just sitting in the warm sun, not talking. After a while he said, "You don't have to tell me if you don't want to, but I heard your phone ring, about three or four o'clock this morning. I wondered if there was something wrong."

She laughed. "That was Charlie, my husband. He called all the way from Texas—just to find out how things are going with me. That's the way he is."

"Are you still leaving for Texas in three months?"

"I told you that a month ago. You can chop that down to two now."

"I'm glad for you."

"Thanks," she said. "Who knows? If things work out, maybe next summer Charlie and I will float back to New York on a yacht —big as that one out there. I'm kidding, of course." She squinted in the sun. "That must belong to somebody pretty important. Wouldn't you say?"

He nodded again and concentrated on his drawing.

"Draw that next," she suggested. "It's a beauty. Could you go to Europe in one like that?"

"I wouldn't be surprised."

Suddenly a little service boat left the pier and motored out toward the big yacht. Jenny squinted again. "Somebody's getting off. That must be why they sent the boat."

"Probably."

She leaned her head back and looked up at the sky. "It must be nice to live like that. —Do you suppose, Mr. Conner, that if we could live like that, just for a weekend, we'd be satisfied? Or would what we had to go back to afterwards seem even more grubby?"

"You're forgetting something."

"Forgetting what?"

"You won't be going back to Mrs. Keefer's much longer."

She smiled and sat up straight. "That's true." She shot up even straighter. "Mr. Conner—" She stopped abruptly, unable to find words to continue.

All she could do was fix her eyes on the boat that had taken its passenger from the yacht and was heading back. It hardly seemed strong enough to hold the weight of the almost crushing bulk seated in it—a bulk wearing a purple dress streaked with age and brilliant sunlight and overlaid with a glitter of jewelry that was almost blinding. Jenny's eyes teared from it, or perhaps she was staring too hard.

"Mr. Conner," she stammered again, "that's Alice Molland."

There was no mistaking the colossal figure being maneuvered from the boat onto the dock. Three men rushed over to assist in the operation.

Jenny watched and afterwards still wasn't exactly sure how they did it, but somehow there was the Glob standing upright on the dock holding onto a huge brimmed red straw hat with one hand and waving with the other in the direction of the yacht.

Jenny watched her lumber like a huge animal toward the shore. A few minutes later, followed by one of the men, she disappeared into the private underground garage.

"And if I had a big red straw hat," Jenny murmured, "I'd eat it."

Eyes glittering, Mrs. Keefer announced: "She came back—in a Cadillac limousine."

"Who?" Jenny asked, deliberately offhand, as if she didn't know exactly who *who* was.

"Miss Molland, of course."

7

"Back from where?"

The glitter of borrowed glory began to dim. "The yacht," Mrs. Keefer said between compressed lips. "I told you about the yacht."

Oh, it's mean, Jenny thought, to deny her this little victory if it gives her so much pleasure. "Sure," she said, "I remember now. I'll bet it was one of those big ones, too—that could go all the way to Europe." Why not go whole hog? —What did it cost? "You know what, Mrs. Keefer," she continued generously, "I'll bet they even sent a special boat to bring her back. I'll bet anything they did. You ask her."

Mrs. Keefer's face was flaming. "All right," she said in a strangled voice, "don't believe me, Mrs. Frye. Everything I told you is true, but you don't have to believe me."

"But I just told you," Jenny protested. "I believe every word."

"You say you do. But you don't. Not really."

Jenny started to answer, then changed her mind. Either way, she couldn't win. She went upstairs.

She had left Mr. Conner at the boat basin, still sketching *things*, not *people*. Because of Mrs. Keefer and now with old Alice back again, it was probably smarter not to be seen walking home with him. An accidental meeting could be misunderstood.

Chances were she wouldn't see him again for weeks. Hadn't it been almost two since the last time? That's the way it is in New York. A person could live right next door to someone and never even see him. If it should happen that she didn't see him again for eight weeks and Charlie returned for her, or sent for her, then she would knock at his door to say good-by. It would be a nice gesture, especially after what happened that morning. Better not think of what might have happened if he hadn't turned up when he did.

He had astonished her by appearing so suddenly, almost from nowhere, a familiar and welcome figure. He astonished her again, a few nights later, by reappearing—still a familiar figure, but one not so welcome. He turned up at the club.

She might not have known he was there until it was too late if it hadn't been for Lou. Seldom, if ever, did she bother to look out from behind the curtains that hid the dressing rooms. What was it to her how many "toads" came to the club—as long as there were enough to keep the place in business and her working; but Lou had said he'd drop by.

She arrived, as usual, about eight o'clock, put on her makeup and got into her Mona Lisa costume. While she did she tried to decide whether to tell Lou about Charlie. There was a lot to tell, up to and including the phone call the other night. Jenny could hardly wait to see the look on his face when she dropped such impressive words as "contractors," "Texas oil man," "intimate café," and "elite." "Elite"—that's spelled m–o–n–e–y. Every chance he got, Lou had always knocked Charlie. The particular words he used were never impressive or complimentary; words like "funnel"—or "gas hound"—or "hooch heister." That was all in the past. Charlie was a sober citizen now. Hadn't he sworn to her he was on the wagon? —Well, he had, hadn't he? —Jenny was sure he must have said *something* about it. He must have *meant* to mention it, if he hadn't. He couldn't very well be getting ready to open a club in a couple of months if he was—intoxicated.

"Fried to the hat," Lou would say.

The hell with Lou! She wouldn't tell him anything. Besides, it was her one superstition: Don't *whammy* things by talking about them before they've happened. It wasn't actually a superstition. Jenny prided herself that she was intelligent enough not to have any of those, but she had learned a long time ago that when a person flaps her tongue about something big that's going to break and it fizzles, then that person wishes she had cut out her tongue first. It would have hurt less.

She wouldn't say a word to Lou. She'd sit with him, have a drink with him, and if he mentioned Charlie, she'd answer honestly: "I don't know where he is."

Lou hadn't told her whether he was going to show up at the 9:30 show or one later. That was the reason she happened to lift the side of the curtain and look out. That was how she happened to see Mr. Conner.

He was seated at a table close to the dance floor, where, in a little while, she was expected to walk into a blue light that would discolor her white skin and bathe her in a mysterious glow. She would whirl about in the transparent black shroud as the music played her theme and finally, just before the spot went out on her altogether, she would do what *the smile* had been suggesting, teasing, promising, and withholding from the beginning: step out of the shroud.

He was alone, although she couldn't be sure he wasn't reserving the chair next to him. He had put a large box on it, the shape of a shoe box. Jenny didn't wait to see if he was being joined by a friend. She turned and ran back to the dressing room and, without stopping to take off her stage makeup or change back into street clothes, put a light trench coat over her costume, belted it, and went into the owner's office.

"What's the matter, Jenny?" She must have looked the way she felt.

Good. That would make it easier. "I don't know. All of a sudden I've got the most awful pain." She clutched her stomach. It was the truth. Her stomach felt as though it had turned over.

"Maybe if you lie down for a while."

"I'll lie down at home. I've got to go home."

"Who am I going to put on instead?" he began; and she doubled up and pretended to heave. "O.K.," he said anxiously. "Go home. Want me to get you a cab?"

Wordlessly, she nodded, and let him lead her out to the street from the side door. "I'll be all right," she told him, as he slammed the taxi door. "Probably something I ate."

"Call the doctor when you get in."

"Maybe I will."

But she knew she'd be fine as soon as she got away from the club and Mr. Conner, who was sitting at a table so close to the floor that if she had come out on it, he would have been able to lean forward, and stretch out one long arm—and touch her. If he wanted to—

In twenty minutes she was back at the brownstone—stretched out on the bed, still wearing the trench coat. When she felt better, she would get up and take it off. Funny—at the club she thought she was only putting on a different kind of act by playing sick. She must have done a better job than she realized—and talked herself into it. She really was feeling peculiar.

Served her right. What had she gained by running out—a rain check until the next night? If he came once, he'd come again.

"Damn you," she said aloud, and raised her eyes to the leak Mrs. Keefer would attend to, eventually, when part of the ceiling fell down on someone's head. Not on Jenny's head. It would take a lot more rain to weaken the ceiling that much. By then she'd be in Texas.

I wish I was there this minute, she said to herself. I wish it was eight weeks from now. Or four weeks ago. Mr. Conner wouldn't have starved. How often do you pick up a newspaper and read about somebody starving to death in the middle of New York City? He had had a couple of cans left—some instant coffee. When he used those up, he could have gone out just long enough to buy a few things. He would have managed somehow. The supermarket's only at the corner. Who asked me to be a Girl Scout? Damn that dog, the one the butcher poisoned.

She decided it was all the butcher's fault. As she was damning the butcher, someone knocked. "Who is it?"

"Mr. Conner. Are you all right, Mrs. Frye?"

Jenny sat up and pulled in the belt of her coat. "I'm O.K."

"I was at the club."

Was he telling her anything she didn't know? Wasn't that why she had run from it?

"They announced you were taken ill," she heard him say from the other side of the locked door.

"That's right. I'm sick. Please go away."

"I have something for you. Shall I leave it outside the door?"

Jenny thought about it for a minute. Settle it now—once and for all. Let him know how she felt, or risk having him show up tomorrow night. She opened the door.

He seemed surprised to see her still wearing her coat, and she pulled the belt in even more. Any tighter and she wouldn't be able to breathe at all. As it was, she was finding it hard. Was it because of the belt, or seeing him standing there in the dimly lit hallway and remembering him sitting at the club—a shoe box on the chair next to him. He was holding that box out to her now.

"What's that?" She sounded unfriendly and knew it.

"It's for you—it's why I went tonight—to give this to you." He was still holding it out. There was nothing to do but take it.

When Jenny opened the box, she saw a doll wearing a plum-colored velvet dress, fitted at the waist and falling in thick folds to the tips of little gold slippers. White fur edged the hem and circled the sleeves. Jenny stroked gold hair that was puffed high on a small perfect head and styled in an oddly familiar style. There was something familiar about the face of the doll, too.

"That first day," she heard him say, "you told me you never had a doll."

Jenny stared down at it.

"I had it made for you," he told her proudly. "There's not another like it. Money couldn't buy this."

Gently, because it was so beautiful, she lifted it from the box.

"It was to be a surprise," he continued. "That's why I didn't say anything about it that day on the Drive."

For a brief moment Jenny held it close and felt the tiniest heartbeat against her. Perhaps it was only her imagination, or the pulse in her own fingertip touching her throat, but she couldn't swear to it. She dropped the doll back into the box.

"Why did you go there?" she demanded furiously. "Who invited you?"

All her muscles tightened, not just in her fists, which she held stiffly to her sides, but every muscle in her body, still wrapped in the trench coat to hide what she was wearing underneath.

"I wanted to give you that."

"I saw you." As if telling him was a signal, tears began to roll down her cheeks. She didn't try to do anything about covering them up or wiping them away. "I saw you!" She hurled it at him like an accusation. "That's what made me sick. Seeing you. I told them I couldn't go on." She wanted to scream the words and had to fight to control her voice. "I didn't want you there," she said softly. The second time she was even more successful. She could whisper them—hoarse, but unmistakable. "I didn't want you there, Mr. Conner."

"You're right," he said, obviously fighting to control the strength of his own voice; but he couldn't control the resentment in it, or the hurt that comes from rejection.

Bewildered, Jenny realized that he was taking it wrong—all wrong. *I never meant it the way he thinks I did.* She thought, realizing it was too late, that of course it must have sounded that way. "You think I don't want to be seen in your company?" She put her hand to her face. It felt sticky. Maybe tears dried faster in the summer. "That's what you think, Mr. Conner?"

"It doesn't matter. I'm well again. You don't have to have anything to do with me any more."

She tried to answer but couldn't.

"Only now," he said, "maybe you won't be afraid of passing me on the stairs." He said it angrily, in the deep voice that had once ordered her to let him alone. He was ordering it again.

"You don't understand."

"Don't I, Mrs. Frye?"

"No—no, you don't. I was embarrassed."

"I told you. It doesn't matter."

This was awful. She had to explain. "Mr. Conner—"

He waved a big hand that made it clear he didn't want explanations. All he wanted was to go. Well, it was all right with her, but not this way, thinking what he did.

"All of a sudden," she told him, "I remembered what Charlie said—a dirty joke three times a night. That's what he said I was. I didn't want you to see me." Weren't artists supposed to be sensitive? Shouldn't he have understood without making me go through all that—mud? "It's what you said I wasn't," she cried. "Cheap!"

He still didn't understand. If he did, would he just stand there, filling the doorway, not moving or saying anything? Did *she* have to draw pictures for him? O.K., if she had to.

Before she knew what she was doing, had done, she wrenched the belt from the coat and let the coat fall to the floor.

He shut the door.

A little moan escaped her. I must be crazy, she thought. This is why I ran away earlier—only there were other people around then. Now there's only the two of us.

It could have been minutes, not seconds, until he said, "You couldn't be cheap. I told you that once."

Jenny felt herself close to a frenzied kind of giggling. How long could he stand like that, just concentrating on her face, not once going any farther down than her chin? Sooner or later he had to weaken, and there wasn't a thing she could do about stopping him, like putting on her coat, for instance. All she could do was stand there, like a block of ice, because that's what she had turned into. Even her blood ran cold.

What do you know, she thought hysterically—inside air conditioning! The middle of July and I'm freezing to death. I wish I were. Oh, God, I wish I were dead.

"You're shivering," he said. "Put on your coat." When she didn't, he picked it up for her. "Put it on," he said roughly.

While she did, he took the doll out of the box again. "Now," he said, "tell me if you really like this."

Jenny felt as tired as if she had actually done three shows that night, and wondered if she had the strength to hold the doll. It didn't weigh too much. She tilted it upright and looked into the eyes.

She couldn't remember seeing any quite that color before—not on a doll. Usually they were blue. These were more on the hazel, flecked with yellow. Where had she seen eyes like that before? A few hours earlier, perhaps at the makeup table when she had swept black mascara over her own lashes—?

"Is that real fur, Mr. Conner? Feels like it."

He nodded quickly, dismissing it, as if the fur were the least important thing about the doll. "Look closely at her face. Don't you recognize yourself?"

"Go on. I'm not half as pretty as that." She gave a self-conscious laugh. "You think so?"

She didn't wait for him to answer, but went directly to the bureau and held the little painted head up to the mirror, side by side with her own. He didn't have to answer. It was the same face, but with differences and improvements.

The pink glow in those cheeks wouldn't wipe off with cream and that hair was a memory—her own at ten, long before it had known what it was to be permanented or bleached.

But the eyes were the best part, because there was no memory in them at all—nothing of what had happened to her since she had been ten. Yet it wasn't the face of a child. It was Jenny now—only enchanted.

The mouth was shaped like the one she smoothed with lipstick every day, but a nicer mouth that had never told a "blue" story, put off a bill collector, answered an indignity with an insult, pitched hate words at a man who had earned them or wasted love words on one who couldn't appreciate them.

And all the little giveaway lines of worry and approaching age had been wiped clean.

Enchanted was a good word. If Charlie, she thought, could only see me looking like this, maybe he'd want to take care of me.

But Charlie might not recognize her face on a doll. A picture, though, a regular painting, would be different. "Mr. Conner," she said, turning to him, "I just got an idea. How'd you like to paint me?" She didn't wait for him to answer, but went on enthusiastically: "I mean it. I'd sit so still you wouldn't even know I was breathing."

"I've already painted you." He nodded toward the doll.

"I meant a real picture. I'd get a fancy frame for it and give it to my husband—as a surprise." She hastened to add: "I'd pay you for it, Mr. Conner."

"I wouldn't expect you to pay me, Mrs. Frye."

"You'll do it?"

"No," he said simply, "I won't."

That was when she remembered he didn't draw people, only things. There was no reason for her not to believe him if that was what he had said. No reason, either, for her to rub it in and make him feel bad if he couldn't. It did seem peculiar though.

"Never mind," she apologized. "I just figured if you could do this—" Her fingers traced the features on the small round head. "Maybe it's different if you have to paint a face flat. That it? I don't know why it should be, but I guess it is." She shrugged. "What do I know about things like that? If you don't know how, you don't. Forget it."

He surprised her by saying, "I know how!" What surprised her most was the way he said it—sullen and confused, as if he despised her for somehow making him betray an unclean thing about himself. Jenny was confused, too—the way she had been that afternoon in his studio when she had innocently showed him a print she had bought and unleashed a panther.

"Three years ago," he told her, "a gallery, one of the best, wanted to exhibit—"

Exactly as he had the other time, she seemed to watch him use up all his strength to yank it back on an invisible leash and bring it under control.

"What do you mean exhibit? You mean somebody thought your pictures good enough to hang up—sell to strangers?"

"They thought so."

"So what happened?"

"Something happened, and I burned all the portraits. All but one."

"The way your grandmother burned the shoes," Jenny asked, "just because you put them on a shelf higher than your head?"

He didn't take any more kindly to that comparison than he had to the one linking his grandmother to old Alice. Jenny didn't regret saying it. The truth was she was a little excited because she sensed that she was getting very close to another truth—one that was none of her business—but she had gone this far—

"I hope," she pushed on, "you had a better reason, Mr. Conner."

"I can't paint your portrait. Yours or anybody's. Not ever."

"But why?"

"Because I as much as murdered the last model who posed for me."

O.K., girl, she thought, you asked for it. You got it. Right in the face. Satisfied?

There was a chair behind her, so she sat down on it. Lucky for her it was there when her knees buckled. The window over the street was open. Nothing in the room was stirring, only the damp chill that had moved in and settled there. Jenny huddled inside the coat and listened.

There was a step behind her, so she sat down on it. Lucky for her it was there when her knees buckled. The door to Forty-third Street was open. Nothing in the back hall was stirring, only the damp chill that had moved in and settled there. Jenny huddled inside her coat and remembered how she had listened to him that night in her room two months ago.

Funny, she thought, it seems almost that long since I left Lou's office. Maybe it seems that way because I've relived so much on the way down, going over everything from the beginning, exactly the way it happened—because perhaps that way I'll find out I'm making a lot out of nothing.

But when she had reached the part where he had told her about that last model she got the bends all of a sudden and just had to sit down.

Mr. Conner never had been what she would have called a Talker. That was one of the first things she had noticed about him, but that particular night, once he started, he couldn't stop. It would have been like trying to stop a flood, or like trying to keep these same words from flooding back to her now. He had talked quickly and feverishly, as if he had a need to hear the sound of his own voice. Jenny had that same need now. Her own voice was like company, and there was no one around her to hear.

"I remember," she said softly, "how he told me that painting portraits was what he used to do. That didn't surprise me. It hadn't made sense to me that a person could only paint faces on dolls. He had studied all over—in Europe even—and people were beginning to talk about him; and then that night came when he did this last portrait and there were never any more after that. It was three years ago when it was finished; and his model left—"

She cut herself off in the middle of the sentence. If somebody walked in and saw her sitting there babbling to herself they'd put in a fast call to Bellevue. She pulled herself up. Only a short distance to the street, then out—and back uptown to pack.

She remembered, but silently this time, how he had said: "That night, after she left the studio, I stood in front of the easel and looked at the work I had just finished. An artist always knows when it's his best. It has something of himself in it."

Still holding the doll he had given her, she had asked, "And you liked what you had done?"

I'll bet, Jenny thought, if I could write it down on paper, it would be letter perfect. That's how clear it is in my mind.

"Yes," he told her, "at first I did—because it wasn't easy to see at first. Once I found it, it flew out of the canvas like acid burning my eyes."

"Mr. Conner," she said, "I don't even know what you're talking about."

"Where the girl's arm bent was the top of the—thing. And the curve in her hand made one of the big hollows for the eye sockets. I saw a death's-head."

The whole story sounded familiar, as if she had heard it before. Or seen it before. Seen it! Sure! That was it. "Hey," she interrupted, "wait a minute—" But he wouldn't wait.

"Like a crazy man I ran down those stairs after her—screaming inside all the way. I had to find her because I knew Death had been standing beside me, painting over my shoulder—"

"The way the Devil in that print I bought had been looking over the lady's shoulder? That it, Mr. Conner?"

"Except that I hadn't meant to put it there." He looked directly at her for a moment and murmured again, "I hadn't meant to put it there." Then he looked away. "Any more than I ever intended to tell you any of this."

"Well, you should have," she said, "that day you ripped up the print I spent good money on. I would have understood, if you had only explained."

"Didn't you understand what I told you before? Weren't you listening? I as much as murdered that girl. Don't you want to know what happened to her?"

"What happened to her?"

"She used to take a short cut through an alley. That's where I found her. On the ground was her handbag, the money gone. She must have tried to fight off her attacker, and he picked up something heavy—like a rock. Smashed her head in with it."

"Are you the one who picked up the rock, Mr. Conner?" She asked it coolly, and watched him take a step back as if she had just bounced one off him herself.

"No!"

"Then what's all this got to do with you not doing any more portraits?"

"Because I marked that girl."

"Oh, come on now." It was so ridiculous that she felt the corners of her mouth starting to twitch.

That was an unfortunate habit of hers, wanting to laugh at the wrong time and in all the wrong places. At her own wedding ceremony, for instance, when the justice of the peace made the mistake of saying, "Retreat after me"—and corrected it to "Repeat after me," she nearly died with silent convulsions. And that had been an extremely serious occasion.

Obviously, Mr. Conner took this just as seriously. It was interesting the way a dark skin can get even darker. Maybe it was the whites of his eyes getting whiter, and streaked with tiny red lines, like they were beginning to bleed. Seeing that, and the expression in them, made her change her mind in a hurry—about wanting to laugh.

"Something in me," he said, "put the death's-head in the painting. I know I marked that girl. Don't laugh at it, or at me, Mrs. Frye. The police laughed at hoodoo, even the black ones who should have known better, and they sent me back here. Maybe that's why I stayed; because I believe it, even if they didn't. As long as I'm in this house I'll remember it, and won't let it happen again—not to anyone."

She hugged the doll, rocked, holding it and told him lightly: "It wouldn't happen to me."

The whole thing struck her as being crazy. Here, Jenny thought, is an artist everybody used to say had a big future and what does he do? Tosses it over, because he gets it into his head he's a jinx. I could prove to him how screwy it is if I could just get him to let me pose.

"No," he said, "I wouldn't take the chance, Mrs. Frye."

"You realize what you're saying?" She was frankly shocked. "You know what I think? I think you're a jerk—a big, dumb, superstitious jerk. I'm sorry, Mr. Conner—I really am sorry, but I thought better of you."

"What's the matter with your hands?" he asked her.

"They're getting all puffed up and red." She said it as if he was the one who was to blame. Well, he was. "That's a peculiar thing that happens to me whenever I get mad or nervous. Right now, I'm so mad, I—" From dancing, she had learned a little about breath control to relax the body. She inhaled and exhaled once or twice—slowly. At least one of them had to sound like an intelligent person who knew how to think. What he had to do was so simple and he couldn't see it.

"Listen to me," she said. "Every once in a while a person gets born and God gives him an extra little pat for luck and He says, 'That's so you can grow up and do something special—like being able to sing or dance or paint pictures—' "

"Mrs. Frye," but she was wound up, really mad, and just kept on going.

"There's nothing special," she admitted honestly, "in the kind of bumps and grinds I do, but if God had picked me for that extra little pat, I'd be so proud—"

"Good night, Mrs. Frye." He went to the door and opened it. "I'm glad you like my present," he said, and left them alone—Jenny and the doll with a face that looked so much like hers.

He's running away, she thought furiously, and it's not the first time. She rushed to the door and flung it open again. He was already halfway down the hall to his own door. "Hoodoo!" she shouted. "Hoodoo—hoodoo!"

It hadn't been necessary to say it three times. Once would have been sufficient, she thought. He got the message the first time—got it and turned to face her.

Better to keep her voice down, she decided, or she'd have them both up there—the Dolly Sisters; and this was strictly between her and Mr. Conner.

"Isn't that what you ran away from? Well, how are you going to run away from yourself? I never should have brought you food to eat. You know what I should have brought you? —A little bag stuffed with the feet of a chicken and a razor blade and, oh, yeah—some dust from a fresh grave."

Deliberately she slammed the door and went back to stand in the middle of her room. He'd be back. She knew that would bring him back. She didn't have long to wait.

A moment later he returned and this time didn't bother to knock. "What do you want from me?" he asked quietly. "Tell me what you want from me, Mrs. Frye."

Jenny wasn't sure she liked him like this, so pleasant and obliging. Something about it made her vaguely uncomfortable. She had deliberately gone out of her way to get him mad and instead she had this quiet man with the low voice—an uninvited stranger in her room.

"Well, Mrs. Frye?"

Because there was nothing left for her to do but finish what she had started, she answered, "Paint my picture."

"Make sure," he said. "Make sure you want me to."

It was ridiculous to wonder if he had planned it like that from the beginning, worked it so that she would be the one to suggest it. Of course it was. Ridiculous.

"Won't Charlie be surprised," she said gaily, and reached for the doll. "Can you make me as pretty as you made her? She looks alive—almost." She let out a cry of pain and dropped the doll.

"What's the matter?"

"Something stuck me." She put a finger to her mouth and sucked her own blood back in again. Funny the way the tiniest pinprick can make a person's entire arm hurt—all the way to the shoulder, because she was sure it had been a pin.

"Here," he said, and pulled it out.

Jenny had watched him pick the doll up after she had dropped it and couldn't help but notice that he seemed to know exactly where to look for the pin—a little above the heart—if it had had a heart. A coincidence. Life was full of them, like Alice saying, "Arrival and return," and then Charlie coming. What made her think of Alice Molland now?

"When the doll was dressed," he was saying, "someone at the factory wasn't very careful."

"No, I guess not."

"She's fine now."

"Yes."

She stood very still as he held the doll high, next to her face. "And she does look so much like you, doesn't she, Mrs. Frye?"

She didn't answer.

A few days later they started the painting.

As Jenny pushed open the side door to the building on Forty-third Street, she saw a man leaving by the front entrance, and wondered which particular step she had been on when the elevator began working again; not that it made any difference now. She started toward Broadway.

8

Someone bumped into her and didn't bother to say "Excuse me." Then someone else did it. That was the trouble with New York: people too busy to be polite—in too much of a hurry to lift their heads and see all that blood. They don't give a damn, she thought, that a perfectly innocent day is being murdered, or that if I'm still in this city when dark comes— Dark will come after me, too.

She was astonished to hear a woman shout, "You deliberately walked into me! Deliberately! Are you drunk?"

Jenny blinked back sudden hot tears. It wasn't nice of the woman to embarrass her in front of strangers. Not nice, either, to accuse her of being drunk when it wasn't true. Most of all, it wasn't necessary to hurt her by calling everybody's attention to the fact that she was the one who had been doing the bumping. My fault, she told herself miserably; only I'm not drunk.

The woman looked as if she had had one too many herself. A feathered hat was tipsy over one eye. Jenny knew that must have been her fault, too, and began to snicker. The woman did look so ridiculous standing there with a crooked hat.

"Drunk!" the woman croaked, and flew away, straightening her head feathers as she went. Jenny blinked again. Impossible; yet the woman was gone.

"Wait," Jenny pleaded. "Come back. I didn't apologize." She called, "Excuse me," into the air.

Too late. The woman had vanished—walked away or flew away—

That long climb, six flights, left me giddy, Jenny decided. Or maybe one cup of coffee—nothing else since morning—that's why I'm weaving, like a sleepwalker.

At that moment something wonderful happened. She was sure it *was* all a dream; for, with rising excitement, she clearly and joyously saw herself.

"It's me," she cried. "Look! I can see myself."

A man turned and stared at her. It didn't matter. He didn't matter; not actually. Actually, he wasn't there.

She turned and laughed at his retreating back. "Hey, you, mister —I'm making you up. I'm dreaming you!"

She smiled and went forward eagerly, feeling quite detached as she watched herself walk slowly toward herself. Wasn't this exactly what she had figured out one morning after waking from a nightmare: that she could always tell it was a dream if she could see herself?

Sick with relief, Jenny wondered how much was part of this particular nightmare? The Doll? Everything since the Doll? Agreeing to pose for the portrait? Had she only dreamed Alice Molland and Mrs. Keefer came to the club a couple of weeks afterwards and—

She almost bumped into a glassed store front that jutted out onto Forty-third Street and came face to face with her own image. For a moment she swayed, then began to run as if she were being followed by that crazy creature in the window who had been yelling at people that they were walking in her dream. Had she really been that crazy creature? Having nothing in her stomach was making her act as if she had nothing in her head. She shuddered to think of the peculiar things she had done in the few minutes since she had left Lou's office building. She wouldn't blame anybody for thinking *she* was peculiar.

Luckily, she knew herself a lot better than they did. She could always explain and make them understand that she was perfectly all right.

Feeling fortunate to have such a good friend who could be counted on to take her part with strangers, she walked herself into a drugstore, hoisted herself up on a stool, and gently reassured herself: You'll be all right, Jenny, just as soon as you get something to eat.

She ordered a milkshake for Jenny, and a tuna fish sandwish, and watched her in the mirror behind the counter. Only a normal person, she reasoned, would know that's a reflection. Only somebody who wasn't would mistake it for a dream. —It was disturbing to realize she herself had made that mistake, but it had lasted only a couple of seconds and happened only because she had been so hungry. She was feeling better now.

I'm as clear-thinking as I ever was, she told herself confidently, and made up her mind then and there to buy three dolls.

If they were perfect (she would, of course, have to examine each of them carefully for pins first), then maybe the one Mr. Conner made for her wouldn't count as much. She swallowed the last of the milkshake, gulped the rest of the sandwich, and left the drugstore.

She shouldn't have told him that when she was a kid she never had a doll. If she hadn't, he wouldn't have made her that one and painted her face on it. He wouldn't have come to the club to give it to her. Funny how seeing him there had upset her so, yet a couple of weeks later, when she came out on the floor and spotted Alice Molland and Mrs. Keefer at a ringside table, she had thrown in an extra grind for good measure. It was like thumbing her nose at them—like saying, You came to get a look? Get a good one. Suffer.

Afterwards she had draped a long satin cape over her costume and joined them. "Well," she had said, "so this is the kind of thing you girls do on your night out."

"They water down the liquor here," Alice Molland grumbled.

Jenny nodded agreeably. "If you say so. Mind if I join the party?"

Between drawn lips, Mrs. Keefer managed to squeeze out, "It's you we came to see."

"If you say so," Jenny said again.

It could have been an excuse. These two wouldn't be the first to come to the club in pairs and minus escorts. Sometimes the women seemed to get more out of the show than the men. They laughed hysterically at the comics, and once the girls came out on the floor, "the girls" in the audience kept their eyes glued to the line and didn't miss a trick.

"How'd you like the act?"

For answer, Alice lit a black cigar while Mrs. Keefer carefully massaged her summer stretch gloves. There was unspoken and obvious censure in the gesture.

Jenny flourished her cape. It said better than words: Don't try to insult me: I'm thick-skinned.

Mrs. Keefer's knuckles showed through the crocheted nylon covering her fingers. You're jealous, Jenny decided; you'd like to have half of what I've got. And if it was as good, you wouldn't worry so much about hiding yourself. As for your pal—

She looked at Alice, overflowing and surrounding the chair with her enormous buttocks. The huge arm cushioned on the small table was bigger and more rounded than one of Jenny's thighs.

If I'm thick-skinned, Jenny wondered curiously, what about Jelly Belly here?

Once she had read that everybody has seven layers of skin. If Alice Molland's individual layers were no thicker than hers, then each one must be filled with some kind of soft creamy stuff to plump them up like that.

"Don't judge the act by the audience," she said. "The audience at the early show is always half asleep. A few drinks"—she grimaced in Alice's direction—"even watered down, and they wake up."

Mrs. Keefer sat straight and stiff, watching her companion puff at the cigar. There seemed a silent agreement between them to let Alice be the first to speak; only Alice wasn't in any hurry. With eyes lit with unnatural brilliance, she studied the cigar end.

She's doing it deliberately, Jenny thought, to find out how long I can take it. I'm on to her. Stubbornly, she settled back in her own chair and waited. After a while she couldn't stand it any more, the three of them just sitting around the table, staring at the gray ash growing longer.

I lose, she admitted to herself. I give up. "O.K.," she said with forced cheerfulness, "what do we do now? Join hands and see if we can contact the spirit world?"

Without a flicker of a smile changing the expression on her face, Alice said, "She's laughing at me again."

Mrs. Keefer turned to Jenny and gave her a look that beseeched: Deny it, please, Mrs. Frye.

Jenny answered with a look of her own: The hell I will! I am laughing.

"Not out loud," she heard Alice say. "But I can hear her just the same."

And Jenny felt a twinge of uneasiness. Every once in a while, this Weirdo did seem to know what she was thinking. If she read my mind before, Jenny thought uncomfortably, and saw a picture of herself as a great big seven-layer cake, I wouldn't blame her for being sore. —She shrugged. So what if she was? What could she do to her?

"I could help her," she heard Alice say. "But she won't let me. I told you that before. I told you we shouldn't have come. It's a waste of time."

"I don't want more trouble in my house," Mrs. Keefer mumbled. "It's my house."

"Then you should have gone yourself and not bothered me. It's going to happen anyway. I showed you the cards—a fair girl and a dark man."

"So that's what's still bugging you—me and Mr. Conner. That's what this little visit's all about."

"I didn't think it wise to discuss it in your room, Mrs. Frye. The walls are thin. He could have heard."

"And just how much have you heard, Mrs. Keefer, with your ear plastered to his door? I've been tripping over you for weeks— every time I leave. You ought to thank me. I'm always careful not to open the door too fast."

Maybe that was a slight exaggeration. Maybe she hadn't exactly tripped over her, but somehow whenever she left the studio there was Mrs. Keefer either going down the stairs or moving quickly and quietly down the hall. It happened too often to be a coincidence. It made her nervous, and posing was making her nervous enough.

Sitting still for a long time, not even moving her head, wasn't easy. She'd get an itch and be afraid to scratch it, for fear of changing her position. Then her neck would feel stiff, or her leg. Mr. Conner never let her sit more than twenty—maybe thirty—minutes without giving her a rest, but every day it seemed longer. Once, at a break, she went to the shelf to make sure the little clock was still ticking. It was. It had only seemed longer.

To be perfectly honest, she was always glad when he would say, "That's enough for today, Mrs. Frye."

Without waiting for a second invitation, she would jump down from the high stool. It wasn't only that she was glad to be able to move again; it was because then he would come back from wherever he had been. Jenny couldn't explain it, but whenever he painted he would get that inside-himself look she used to catch when she passed him on the stairs, and it didn't take much to remember how she used to move a little closer to the banister and turn her head the other way.

After a while she began to wish the portrait was finished. She didn't have the nerve to wish it had never been started. After all, hadn't it been her own idea? Well, hadn't it? Sometimes, lately, she wasn't so sure of that either.

She heard Alice let out a raucous spurt of laughter. "Go on, thank her for not opening the door too fast and letting you fall in flat on your face."

"I haven't heard a thing," Mrs. Keefer said in awkward defense. "It's all been very quiet, Mrs. Frye."

Jenny surprised herself by becoming suddenly both angry and grateful—angry because these two were interfering once more in something that was none of their affair and grateful because seeing them side by side, a pair of harpies, made her remember all the nice things about Mr. Conner she had almost forgotten: the way he had been so appreciative of anything she had done for him while he was sick—how interesting he had been to listen to, once she got him started—and how interested he had been whenever she had talked.

Perhaps, if she wanted to be perfectly honest, she wasn't so much nervous as disappointed in this posing business. She had looked forward to something other than the silent figure behind the easel who could let hours slip by without saying a single word, who couldn't be coaxed into conversation, who looked at her as he might look at a piece of furniture—and tried to hide his impatience if the furniture dared come to life and make conversation. "Please, Mrs. Frye," he would say, cutting her off politely, but with unmistakable finality, and go back to work.

Jenny didn't doubt for a minute that he was working hard. Hadn't she said to him once, "You're an artist? I think that's great. I really do. I admire people with talent."

Fine way she had of showing admiration or respect for talent— wanting to disturb his concentration.

I ought to be ashamed, Jenny thought. And this particular portrait must be doubly hard for him. After all, it's the first he's done in three years. Maybe he's even forgotten a little. Maybe it's not like driving a car. Once you get behind a wheel, no matter how long it's been, it all comes back. Painting may be different.

She looked first at Alice, then at Mrs. Keefer, and said with a sweetness she knew would be unexpected, "I'm going to tell you a secret about me and Mr. Conner."

She waited for a greedy look of anticipation. Mrs. Keefer obliged immediately. Alice only blew another cloud of smoke. Behind it, Jenny was certain, she was looking just as greedy. Jenny took a deep breath of satisfaction and prepared to throw them both a curve.

"You say you haven't heard anything, Mrs. Keefer, because we've been so quiet in there? Well, now I'm going to tell you why. I'm having my portrait painted and Mr. Conner doesn't happen to like conversation while he's working."

As she said it she determined to stop trying to interrupt that work with chatter. She'd let him get on with it—get the damned thing over and done with. And she wondered what made her think of it as a "damned thing."

The reaction to the information that she was having her portrait painted wasn't quite what Jenny had hoped. Maybe they didn't believe her.

"Give him your body," Alice Molland said, her eyes fixed on hers. "It's nothing much."

Jenny answered furiously, "It's something to me."

"A body," Alice told her—it was more a pronouncement than an opinion—"is only outer clothing we put on in each life to cover our souls. It's never worth the time or the effort most people waste to keep it clean. In the end, all our bodies rot and stink away." She rocked toward Jenny and waved the cigar directly under her nose. "But your soul, little dear, that's something you mustn't let him take."

Jenny waved away the smoke. "Who says he's taking my soul? All he's doing is painting my picture."

"Let someone take your image," Mrs. Keefer said knowingly, "and it's the same as giving part of yourself to a stranger." She looked for affirmation. "Isn't that so, Alice?"

Alice Molland gave an angry start and turned on her. "When did I give you permission to call me that?"

Mrs. Keefer drew back. "I won't again if you don't want me to."

"I don't let anyone call me by my first name." She turned in anger again, but this time it was directed to Jenny. "I gave you permission." Her voice shook with controlled fury, and with it the loose folds under her chin. "And I offered," she continued bitterly, "to read your cards—for nothing."

"It wasn't polite of you to refuse her, Mrs. Frye," Mrs. Keefer said.

"I didn't mean to hurt anybody's feelings. It's just that I don't believe in that stuff." Abruptly Jenny stopped, and realized for the first time that she hadn't thrown either of them such a curve after all. They had known about the painting.

"So you weren't just listening at the door, were you, Mrs. Keefer? You were peeking through the keyhole. Didn't anybody ever tell you *that's* not polite?"

"Tell him you changed your mind," Mrs. Keefer coaxed. "You don't want to take chances, do you? Don't let him finish that thing. You're a smart girl. You can think up a good excuse to get out of it."

"How do you know I want to get out of it, Mrs. Keefer?"

"Tell her what happened to the last model," Alice Molland suggested.

"He told me himself. He had nothing to do with that girl getting killed."

"The police," Mrs. Keefer said, "never found the one who did it. She nodded toward Alice. "We've got our own opinions, haven't we—" she hesitated, then added respectfully, "Miss Molland?"— and was rewarded with a half-smile.

"You saying he did it?" Jenny demanded.

"We know he put the stamp of death on her," Alice said softly.

"And you know all about that, too!" She wrapped her cape closer. "I wish I could have seen the painting."

"Do you? Do you really wish it?"

"He probably imagined the whole thing, probably had been working too hard or something. Your mind can play tricks when you're overtired, make you see things that aren't there at all. It's happened to me."

"Show it to her, Miss Molland." Mrs. Keefer was excited. "She says she wants to see it."

Alice Molland lowered her voice and said even more softly, "It isn't difficult to find the death's-head. Where the girl's arm bent is the top of the thing, and the curve in her hand makes up one of the big hollows for the eye sockets. And where her dress folds, you can see the jaw of the skull—"

Frightened in spite of herself, Jenny said, "But he burned it!"

"That what he told you? He lied."

"No, wait—he said all but one."

"All but the last," Alice told her, "and I have that. I bought it from him, paid more than it was worth probably, but it's mine now. Mine to show you if you want to see it badly enough. Study it, Jenny, so you'll know what to look for when he finishes yours."

"I don't want to see it!"

"Afraid?"

"Just not interested."

"That's not what you said before," Mrs. Keefer reminded her. "Remember the cards? You saw them, Mrs. Frye: ten of pentacles, a dwelling—my house, Mrs. Frye; and in it, a fair girl—a dark man—"

"So what?"

"You wouldn't stay to hear the rest. You should have, Mrs. Frye. Do you know what else Miss Molland saw? I recognized it, too. It's not pretty—not something you forget once you've seen it. I saw it in the cards Miss Molland laid out for me three days before my dear departed husband passed away. The Death card, Mrs. Frye."

Jenny jumped up in a rage. "Why don't you kids dance? Toss a coin to see who leads. Forget the check. That's for helping me pep up the act." She was trying hard not to attract attention, but couldn't help raising her voice above the music and almost screaming at them. "Stick around for the next show and see the improvements you've made. Tonight the customers will get a few extra shakes for no extra charge. You think it's nice, getting me all nerved up like this?"

"Little dear," Alice said slyly, "do you want to know what I think? I think you were nerved up long before we came. You've been a little uneasy since the first day he picked up the brush and began the portrait."

Tell her it isn't true, Jenny ordered herself, go on—tell her. But she couldn't.

"And you're getting more uneasy, more frightened the closer he gets to finishing it." She squashed the end of the cigar in the ashtray and moved it around and around the glass circle, grinding out a mixture of words that turned Jenny's stomach. "Black is the color of the Devil's own magic. Black is the color of the Devil's own mass."

She stood up to face her and Jenny stumbled backwards. Before she turned and ran, she heard Alice rasp, "Can't you tell looking at his color that he's filled with the black bile of the Devil himself?"

"Mrs. Frye."

"What is it, Mrs. Keefer?" Instead of turning, Jenny kept leafing through the magazine that came for her that morning. Sooner or later it had to happen. No matter how much trouble she took making sure the coast was clear before running down to get her mail,

9

she couldn't go on avoiding the landlady indefinitely. It was over a week since Mrs. Keefer had come to the club with Alice Molland.

And I'm still, Jenny thought, trying to get over that. —It wasn't easy.

At her elbow, Mrs. Keefer was saying, "I'm sorry."

"About what?" suspiciously.

"That's all that came for you. You never get much, do you? Not like some of the other tenants."

"Don't waste sleep over it." She waved the magazine. "The truth is: this is just what I wanted. I've been looking forward to it."

In a way it was true. She did look forward to *House and Garden*. It was the only magazine she ever subscribed to. Charlie used to kid her about that, but she liked reading articles written especially for "those who appreciate the best." What did it cost to appreciate?

She enjoyed looking at "breath-taking interiors—inspired by the elegance of tradition." Nice to know some people had bathrooms with crystal chandeliers. —Who needs money?

Fun looking at ads for gold muffin splitters. "Now you, too, can split a muffin quickly and beautifully." —Just what she wanted!

"Turn your living room into an outdoor garden." —The mosquitoes already had. Turn the page: "How to fit a Cadillac into any budget." —Any? Now, *that* could be interesting. She planned to go back to her own room and find out how, if Mrs. Keefer would only get out of her way.

"Can you spare a minute, Mrs. Frye?"

Jenny played it straight. "I wish I could, but I've got to read about one hundred ways to add unfailing gaiety to my outdoor living." For proof, she held open a double-page spread. "Look, Mrs. Keefer, a poolside cabana in bold zebra stripes. Couldn't you just die for it? And see? A magnificent focal point for my garden—a plastic birdbath."

"Mrs. Frye, this is important."

"As important as a stone fountain with a cupid, reusable water and no pipes? Which reminds me," she said, "as long as we're on the subject of water, what about that leak in my ceiling?"

"I'm going to have it fixed."

"I believe you. Don't think for a minute I don't." She tucked the magazine under her arm and moved toward the stairs.

"That leak!" Mrs. Keefer said in a restraining voice. "That's what I wanted to discuss with you."

"Really, Mrs. Keefer?"

"Really, Mrs. Frye."

That was different—as long as they kept away from other subjects, one in particular.

"O.K.," Jenny said, "let's."

"I don't blame you for being annoyed."

"You're very understanding."

"You don't know how difficult it is these days—getting repairs done. Labor is so high, and they're so independent. Not like the old days. In the old days—"

Jenny cut her off with: "Never mind the old days. What if it rains tomorrow?"

"Be reasonable. I'm trying, but I may not be able to have it done overnight."

"I'm reasonable. Just tell me when."

Mrs. Keefer twisted her mouth and appeared to be nervously biting the inside of her cheek. "You tell *me* when, Mrs. Frye."

Jenny frowned. "When what?"

"I'll have it fixed as soon as possible, but it may not be done before—" She took a deep breath. "You still planning on leaving next month?"

So that's it, Jenny thought. And I walked right into it. "Yes," she said, "I'm still planning to. And won't you and Miss Molland be glad? You won't have me to worry about any more."

"How long does it take to paint a picture of a person? I don't know much about things like that. Will he have time to finish it before you leave?"

"I suppose so."

Mrs. Keefer moved closer, lowering her voice. "Make him take his time about it, but do it so he won't guess you are. Tell him anything, only make it take longer. That way you can get away before it happens."

"Before what happens, Mrs. Keefer?" she asked acidly.

"Once he finishes it, Miss Molland says it'll be like it was before. Two faces will show on the canvas. And I'll have your room to rent again, Miss Molland says—but not because you'll be in Texas with your husband."

She came even closer and was caught in the light that illuminated the stained glass on the door. Her face was a mottled peacock green. "Why do you refuse to believe you're in danger?"

"Why," Jenny threw back, "does it bother you if I am or if I'm not? You really care?"

"It's my house," the landlady said, exactly as she had at the club. "I don't want any more trouble in my house." This time she added, "It's the only thing I have left to remember my dear departed for."

Now, if I could only read cards like Alice Molland, Jenny thought, it might be fun to look into her past and find out how dear her departed was—

It was a jarring thought; not the possibility that Mrs. Keefer had gone to her husband's funeral just to make sure the poor guy was dead, but the admission to herself that maybe old Alice could, possibly, read somebody's past in the tarot cards. Or somebody's future, perhaps?

Mrs. Keefer was quick to recognize interest in Jenny's face, and even quicker to take advantage of it. "Listen," she said, running her words together before she lost that interest, "he's not all there, that man."

"Are you saying he's crazy?"

"I'm saying you are if you let him finish that thing, after knowing what happened to his last model."

"All I know is he had nothing to do with her getting killed."

"I was sure nothing good would come of those two—always screaming and tearing at each other. They were like wild animals." Almost maliciously she kept Jenny waiting before she said, "Oh, you didn't know about that? That she was more than just another model to him? Well, she was. Don't take my word for it. Knock on any of the doors. Ask any of the other tenants. They'll tell you— how I had to go up there one night because they were all complaining about the screaming, the name calling. I was in time to see her rip the side of his face with her nails before she ran down the stairs. He didn't have a beard then."

So that explained why he had one now! He was covering up something ugly. What right had she to feel he had been hiding something else from her by not telling her about it? No right, Jenny told herself, no right at all.

"But she came back," Mrs. Keefer clacked. "She always came back. Maybe she deserved what she got."

"You make me sick," Jenny said, but her voice shook and she knew Mrs. Keefer noticed it. "I don't want to listen to any more of your stories. You hear me?"

"You think I'm making it up?"

"I just know I don't want to listen any more."

"They made quite a thing about it in the Sunday papers. Jinx artist, they called him. I've got it all pasted in a scrapbook if you're interested."

"Well, I'm not." She sidestepped and started up the stairs.

"It might," Mrs. Keefer suggested from the bottom, "give you a little something to think about next time you're posing."

"I've got better things on my mind," Jenny told her.

Somehow, though, after that it began to be the only thing on her mind during those times she sat on the high stool in the studio, not moving and hardly breathing. It wasn't that she wanted to think about it. She tried hard not to, but no matter what else she started with, somehow it always came back to that.

She would begin innocently enough by saying to herself: After today's sitting I'll go next door and wash my hair. Brush it dry at the open window. Good sun today. Wish I had a drier. I could buy one. It would be convenient. I could sit right under it and do my nails at the same time—

The next thing she knew, her mind would jump to: She must have had very sharp nails, that girl, to be able to rip the side of his face, rip it deep enough to make a scar, because I'm sure there is one under that beard. I wonder if she was white? Mrs. Keefer didn't mention that. None of my business. Poor girl. What difference did her color make after she was dead—?

Another time she began with Miss Quint, one of the Day People, who lived on the first floor. Jenny had seen her three mornings in a row at the mail table.

"Summer cold," Miss Quint explained. "You know how hard they are to shake."

Jenny had agreed, and agreed that the best thing for it was lots of juices—and a lot of rest.

"Rest is the most important. You work nights, don't you, Mrs. Frye?"

Jenny said she did.

"That must mean you sleep during the day. How do you manage? So much noise in the streets. How do you stand it?"

When she went back to her room she had carefully shut the door, so it made no sound at all.

Must be a bug on noise, Jenny decided, later that day while she was posing, and before she knew it she was thinking: Miss Quint was probably the first to complain to Mrs. Keefer that night three years ago, about the noise up here in the studio, about the screaming and the name calling, while Mr. Conner and the girl—like two wild animals, Mrs. Keefer had said— Don't think, don't think about it.

And she would switch to safer ground: Charlie. He hadn't telephoned again, not since that night he had needed her. Did it mean he didn't need her now? Of course not. He was working hard getting everything ready for the big opening. He wanted to wait until he had something definite to tell her. That was it. Next time he called would be to give her a definite date to leave. She leaned back, as if she were already on the plane. No smoking. Fasten your seat belts.

"Please, Mrs. Frye, you changed your position."

"Sorry." She pressed forward. "Better?"

"Yes."

"Will it be much longer?"

"Are you getting tired?"

"No," she answered. "I've got things to think about." She went back to thinking about the trip to Texas.

Charlie would be at the airport to meet her. "Well," he would say, "say something." That would be like him. "O.K.," she would answer, "I told you so, didn't I? I told you you'd make it this time." That would be when he would kiss her. He'd wait for that moment and then he would say, "I hate people who say I told you so. In your case I'll make an exception." Jenny smiled to herself. How long would it be before that happened? "How long," Mrs. Keefer had asked, "does it take to paint a picture of a person? I don't know much about things like that. Will he have time to finish it before you leave? Make him take his time about it, but do it so he won't guess you are. That way you can get away before it happens." Damn—damn—done it again. Every time her mind took a pleasant side road, it ended back at the same dead end. Dead.

"Mr. Conner!"

"Mrs. Frye?"

"You were right before. I am getting tired." She slid off the stool. "And I just remembered an important telephone call I have to make: my agent. I forgot about it."

"All right. Tomorrow then." He saw her hesitate. "You can't make it tomorrow?"

"It depends. That call I'm expecting, I may have to go down to see my agent. You understand."

"Of course."

"If I'm not here," she told him, "you'll know I'm not here." She laughed foolishly. For some reason, that sounded so stupid, like saying: if I'm not here start without me.

He had put down his brush and was looking intently at her. Deliberately, she reached for the cigarettes she had left on the table, and lit one. Why was it she was having such trouble lately—looking people straight in the eye? She had never in her whole life had that trouble. But with Alice Molland, for instance, she was afraid of being snapped up in eyes that were like jaws, snapped up, chewed up, and swallowed.

Mrs. Keefer's eyes were different. They made her nervous because of the way the pupils kept shooting back and forth like little black pellets, trying to keep up with the voice. —And Mr. Conner, with eyes that she could easily get lost in, or drown in, if she let herself.

"Is there anything bothering you?" he asked.

"No. I mean, nothing important."

"You're sure?"

"Yes," but she made sure not to tell him what it was.

"Has it anything to do with the portrait?"

"No," she answered quickly, and wondered if he guessed she was lying. When he began to clean up, stand his brushes in the jar of turpentine, and not question her further, she was reassured. Well, it hadn't actually been a lie. Her own portrait wasn't the one on her mind. Not really. It was mostly the other girl's.

She was conscious of trying to keep her voice steady when she paused at the door and said pleasantly, "I'd like to see it sometime though." And she was conscious that he was taking an awfully long time before he got around to answering. "Well," she persisted, "how about it?"

He stood before the easel, looked first at it, and then at her. "No," he said finally. "I don't think so."

"Why not? Isn't it any good?" She was baiting him now. "Why waste my time, Mr. Conner, if it isn't any good?"

"I'd rather not show anyone unfinished work," he answered, unmoved and unmoving.

She shrugged. "If that's the way you feel. It's your work."

It wasn't until she had returned to her own room that she thought resentfully: But it's still my face. I should have insisted. One of these days I will.

Then the day came when she felt she couldn't stand it any longer. She couldn't put off seeing that portrait any more than she could stop thinking about that other one. She had even given up trying. Sooner or later she always came back to it. No use thinking about anything else or anyone else. Not even Charlie. So cut out Charlie. Cut out the middleman. Get right to it. Think about her. Think about that poor girl who was murdered. Jenny had begun to think about her so much that drop by drop she got the feeling she *was* the other girl—that everything that was happening was simply happening all over again.

"I'll bet," she said, one day for the sake of hearing her voice in the big room, "that I know every inch of that wall by heart." When he didn't answer, she jerked her head back and shouted, "Don't you ever hear me when I'm talking?"

"What's that?" he asked, startled, as if he had forgotten she had a voice.

She stretched her arm to the wall. "I said—I bet I know every inch of that by heart."

"Don't change your position, please."

She obliged him by resuming it. "Is that all you've got to say for yourself?"

He nodded wordlessly.

"Sorry," she said pointedly. "I didn't hear that."

He looked confused.

"I want to talk, Mr. Conner."

"As soon as we've finished."

Jenny sat straighter. "You mean all finished?"

"For the day. Are you disappointed?"

She didn't want to tell him that she wasn't. She was relieved. All she wanted to do was see it, before he went any further. "I wonder," she said, "if the coffee's still hot." She went to the stove and put her hand to the side of the pot.

"Mrs. Frye," he said, upset, "if you could just go back up for a minute. I've not finished yet."

She gave him a smile, as forced as it was bright. "I am." She clutched the pot handle and stood with her back to him almost daring him to order her to return to the stool.

"Never mind," she heard him say quietly. "If you're that tired."

"I'm not tired. I'm just bored, Mr. Conner."

"Is that all? Just bored?"

She poured coffee into two mugs and handed him one. He took it from her and said, "The last few times you've been more of a stranger than you were the first time you came to this studio and brought me other coffee."

She climbed back on the stool, hooked her high heels on the top rung, and raised her knees closer to her chin. When she bent her head over the mug, her hair tumbled over her forehead. That way he couldn't see all of her face. She hadn't denied what he had said. In some ways she felt more of a stranger. She was even beginning to feel like one to herself—as if she were another girl altogether.

She astonished herself by saying, "I'm worried, Mr. Conner," and added falteringly, "about my husband."

The lie made her feel slightly out of breath. She sipped the coffee. "He promised that if everything panned out in three months, he'd come back for me. Maybe he'll send for me. Either way, Mr. Conner, that's not too far away."

"And you're wondering if he will come for you?"

"He'll come." She was conscious of sounding almost desperate.

"I'm sure he will."

"Or—send me a ticket."

His only answer was: "This coffee's cold. I could make it fresh—"

"Don't put yourself out." She drained her mug, and added, "That wasn't a nice thing to say."

He looked surprised and waited for her to explain.

"It isn't nice to say that maybe he was only handing me a line."

"Mrs. Frye, I never said that."

"You were thinking it," she accused him.

He shook his head, denying it.

Jenny managed a smile. "Well, I wouldn't blame you if you were. It wouldn't be the first time he built up my hopes to a big"—she shrugged—"nothin'."

"This time it'll be different."

Gratefully, she said, "That's what I told him—practically my exact words, Mr. Conner." She looked suspiciously at him. "Say, are you sure you didn't overhear it?"

"Yes. I'm sure."

"Could you hear what was being said in my room, if you wanted to? If you put your ear to the wall?"

"I wouldn't go to the trouble of finding out," he said.

Now he's insulted, she thought. Now he won't let me see the portrait, even though this is the day I made up my mind I'd make him show it to me.

"Of course not," she said soothingly, "any more than I'd just leave without saying good-by to you first."

Still holding the coffee mug, he returned to the easel and addressed himself to the canvas on it. "We have a lot to do—before you say good-by."

It made her uncomfortable having him talk to the portrait as if it was as alive as the model who posed for it. She hopped off the stool and rinsed out the mug.

She needed the excuse to run cold water over her wrists. Sometimes that made her head feel better. "Did you ever," she asked him casually, the way she would have inquired after the time, "have the feeling your head was beginning to shrink?" Abruptly, she turned off the tap, reached for the towel, and dried her hands up to the wrists.

"I've got some aspirins," he offered.

"I'd rather have a cigarette. I forgot mine."

"Aspirin will help more."

"I said I'd rather have a cigarette," she answered, deliberately defying him. That time she didn't look away; instead, she looked directly at him.

He was dressed all in brown today, open-necked shirt, brown slacks. Yesterday it was navy—all navy. She had never really been aware of anything he wore. Funny, how she began to be, after Mrs. Keefer told her that girl had been more than just another model to him.

He was leaning against the wall. There was strength in being able to still so big a body. To be able to have that kind of control over it, Jenny thought, is to be able to have it do anything, almost anything, he orders it to.

"Forget it!" she ordered herself, and realized as she did, that she herself didn't even have the control to keep down a few lousy words. She had let them slip out for him to hear. Close to tears of frustration, she repeated, "Forget it. I've got my own cigarettes, in my own room. You can keep yours. I'll get my own."

She started for the door, and he stopped her simply by moving, shifting his weight from one long leg to the other. "What's really wrong, Mrs. Frye?"

"I told you. I've got a headache, and you won't even give me one of your damn cigarettes."

Without saying another word, he reached into his shirt pocket and took out a pack. Her throat tightened and she stiffened. He hesitated before tossing the pack deftly in her direction.

She caught it in mid-air, shook out one of the cigarettes, and lit it from a book of matches on the table. She was embarrassed because she had been so rude, yet she couldn't put into words exactly what it was she had done to be rude, unless it was that he had known—without saying it—that she would rather not take anything from his hand.

"What do you want that ugly beard for?" Instantly she knew she had asked it not just for the sake of something to say, and saw his hand go swiftly to the side of his face. "You got a reason, Mr. Conner?"

"Do I have to have a reason?"

"Maybe you just want to look like a Greenwich Village character, that it?"

"I've got a scar. This covers it."

She narrowed her eyes. He wasn't telling her anything she hadn't guessed. "I don't suppose you want to tell me how you got it." It was more of an attack than a question.

"It wouldn't interest you," he said shortly, and moved back to the easel.

"Well, if it doesn't bother you to look like a character—"

He was addressing the painting again, when he said, "I haven't been fair to you."

"Meaning what?"

"Posing for me when the light is still good hasn't given you a chance to get much sleep."

"Don't worry about my sleep, Mr. Conner," she advised him tartly. "I get plenty. And I never dream either. Can you prove I do?"

She wished she could remember the dream she had had that morning. All she knew was that a man had walked with heavy foot through it. His heavy foot was still pressing on her chest, making it difficult for her to breathe. In all fairness, could she swear it had been this man?

"I can prove you're not getting enough sleep," he was saying, "just by looking at you. You come home late—"

Jenny corrected him. "Early, you mean."

"After doing three shows a night," he finished. "It can't be easy for you." There was unmistakable concern in his voice.

"God," she said, "how I hate those toads who come into the club." She said it with a sudden and welcome return of the old feeling she used to have when she was with him, that this was someone who cared to listen. "What holes do they crawl out of, Mr. Conner? Great mayor we've got in this city. Great sanitation department! Why don't they fumigate the city and get rid of the toads? The way they look at me—"

She covered her face with her hands. They smelled of turpentine. There must have been some on that towel she had dried her hands on. He must have used the same one, and it occurred to her that if his hands were on her face, this was exactly what she would smell.

"You'll be out of it soon," Jenny heard him say. "It'll be all over soon."

Her own hands fell heavily to her sides. "That's what I started to say before," she said nervously, "but I got sidetracked. This awful headache. What I started to say was: if my husband comes before you finish that, well—you just won't be able to finish it, will you? It won't be anybody's fault. Just one of those things."

"It'll be finished," he told her confidently.

"You—that close?"

"Practically done."

"Then I want to see it. Now."

"You'll see it when it's finished."

"Why do I have to wait?"

"I told you. I don't like to show unfinished work."

"It doesn't matter."

"It matters to me."

He moved to the easel and stood protectively in front of it. To Jenny it was obvious that he was testing his strength against her determination. The only way she could win was to try another approach.

She smiled pleasantly. "Such a silly attitude to take, Mr. Conner. I mean—if it's almost done anyway—I probably wouldn't know the difference. What do you think I am, an art critic or something?" She even managed a coy laugh. "Maybe I just want to make sure you're leaving out the circles under my eyes. I wouldn't want to give my husband a picture that showed circles under my eyes."

"I said *no,* Mrs. Frye."

She was past pretending now. Past being polite. "Listen," she said, "if that picture is of me— It is, isn't it?"

He frowned. "You know it is."

"Then I've got a perfect right to see it—rare, medium, or well done. And you know why? Because if a person lets someone take that person's image, it's like giving part of yourself to a stranger. And when you come right down to it, I don't really know you, Mr. Conner. I've never known anyone like you—in my whole life. You could ask my grandmother—only she's dead."

"Where did you get all that?"

"All what?" she asked, confused, wondering how much she had told him.

"Giving part of yourself to a stranger. It doesn't sound like you. Sounds more like Alice Molland. Has she been at you?"

"Why didn't you tell me she had that other painting?" Jenny asked resentfully. "The one you didn't burn?"

There was no trace of emotion in his voice as he asked, "Have you seen it?"

"She offered. I refused." She shook her head in disbelief. "How come you didn't burn it with the rest? How come you sold it to her?"

"I needed the money."

"But to her—of all people. Why Alice Molland?"

His voice was as carefully controlled as his body. "I remembered," he said, "how my grandmother once told me that to give

something evil to someone who is evil is like giving evil back to itself, and at that particular moment I wanted Alice Molland to take
the thing from me."

"That doesn't make sense," Jenny said. "It was crazy."

"I think I *was* crazy that day, Mrs. Frye," he admitted. "Half
out of my mind— Afterwards I tried to buy it back, so I could destroy it. She wouldn't give it up." He looked steadily at her. "You
sure you haven't seen it?"

"Positive. But I want to see mine. I don't care if it isn't finished.
I don't care."

In an instant he was on his feet again. She was sure he was going
to stop her, but all he said was: "If you're that curious, take a
good look." And he stepped aside.

What Jenny saw was an unfinished painting of a girl who was
beginning to look a lot like her. Nothing else. Yet she couldn't
take her eyes off that canvas. She kept looking—and searching.

"Mrs. Frye!" It wasn't that he said her name so loud, but it
was as if he had put two fingers in his mouth and whistled right
into her eardrum. She thought her head was coming off.

"Mrs. Frye, you're not afraid of me, are you?"

That was when she realized she was backing away from him.
There was a packing case behind her and she stumbled, lost her
balance, and fell. When she looked up she saw long legs standing
over her and she couldn't have got up again if she had tried. She
kept moving along the floor, crawling and whimpering, until she
got to the wall. Then she leaned her head against it, closed her
eyes, and waited for something to happen.

The slashing of the knife when it ripped the canvas seemed to
tear the room in half.

At first she didn't know what the sound meant. Then she opened
her eyes again, realized what he was doing, and felt that knife as
if it were going into her. He kept swinging his arm up and down—
up and down—hacking away at the portrait.

His work, Jenny thought numbly, all his hard work. He was

tearing it to ribbons, and he was crying, not making any noise, but crying just the same.

The next thing she knew, she was yelling for him to stop. Her arm was on his arm, going up and down too. She knew it was too late whether he stopped then or not, but she kept hanging on anyway, and she was crying too. After a long time he dropped the knife on the floor and turned his back on her.

"I'm sorry," she said, and said it over and over. "I'm sorry. I'm sorry."

"Tell me what you thought you'd see, Mrs. Frye," he asked softly, "or do you want me to tell you? It's a painting of a girl. Did you find that other face you were sure was there? Maybe it just wasn't so easy to see at first. Didn't you find it? The hollows for the eyes—the bones for the shape of the skull—"

Jenny shook her head. "It wasn't there."

"I shouldn't have started it. I should have known better."

"Please—" she said, wanting him to turn around and look at her, but not daring to ask him. More than she had ever wanted anything, she wanted him to turn around so she could apologize to his face. When he did, she apologized the best way she knew how by saying: "We'll do it over again. This time it'll be right."

"No!"

"Please, or I won't ever forgive myself."

"If the only person in the world who cared that I was running away from myself runs from me in fear, then I'm better off letting my own demons chase me into hell."

"I was wrong. I'm admitting it."

"I'm not your concern, Mrs. Frye. I never should have been. When you come right down to it, you don't even know me. You've never known anyone like me—in your whole life."

He was giving her own words back to her. She cringed at them and remembered others. "That night I called you hoodoo, I made you feel some of the old shame you lived with when you were a kid. You can't quit now, Mr. Conner. Don't you understand," she said, "if you quit now, there'll be two of us carrying around little invisible bags filled with chicken feet and razor blades and— what else was it?—dust from a fresh grave."

The only thing left to say would have been: And that will mean she's won. It will mean the Glob beat both of us. Somehow she couldn't bring herself to go that far. She wasn't even sure that would make any impression on him now.

He just kept shaking his heavy head back and forth. No, it said, I won't do it. That portrait was the one I did. It will be the only one.

Jenny went to the canvas and knelt down next to it. "It can't be fixed, can it?" she said miserably. "And I was going to get a fancy frame for it and give it to Charlie as a surprise. There's still time. Tomorrow we'll start again. If you don't say yes, I'll be sick. I feel sick now."

"Please, get up," he said. "It's all right."

"We'll do it again?"

While she held her breath, he went to a small wall mirror. The answer he gave her was less than satisfactory. It only avoided answering. "It's not a pretty scar, is it?" He rubbed the beard. "Maybe this is worse. It is a very ugly beard."

He was telling her he wouldn't do it. She was sure of it now. "I feel," she said, getting up and looking down at the canvas, "as if I had killed someone."

"You didn't do it. I did."

"It's terrible to see myself looking like that. Just terrible."

"That isn't you, Mrs. Frye. It never was. All it ever was—was canvas and paint. Canvas doesn't bleed and paint doesn't cry."

She remembered how he had cried in his own way while hacking at the picture. There was no sign of that in his face now, any more than there was much left of the portrait.

"It looked just like me," Jenny said regretfully.

He took her completely off guard by announcing: "The next one will be more interesting."

"We'll do it over?"

"If that's what you want. It's still what you want?"

"Oh, yes," she said, but wished he hadn't changed his mind quite so suddenly. After shaking his head "no" that many times, to say "yes" without preparing her for it was unnerving, to say the least. But it was what she wanted, wasn't it?

"All right then." He was smiling broadly now, and there was an excitement in the way he went to the ripped canvas, the way he bent down and swept it up with his large hands. "This will be thrown out later with the trash." There was fresh energy and enthusiasm in the way he said, "Tomorrow we'll start again. Tomorrow—all right?"

Jenny didn't answer.

He stopped smiling. "Are you changing *your* mind? If you are, just tell me."

"It's just—" she began.

"Just—what?"

"We're going to have to go through the whole thing all over again. I'm going to have to keep staring at the same wall. That's the only thing that really bothers me, Mr. Conner. Do you know there's a leak? The one in my room is on the ceiling. Yours is here. See?" She went to the wall and ran her fingers over it. "It must have wet the plaster, because when it dried this funny squiggly stain was left. Boy, if you knew the crazy things that stain kept turning into—a dog with horns, and once a black cat hung upside down—"

"We'll turn the stool around. You won't have to look at it any more."

"Thank you. I would appreciate it."

"It'll be better next time." He smiled at her.

Jenny smiled back. Sure it would. It would be much better. And at that moment she believed it.

He came over and stood next to her. "Show me. I'm curious. Where do you see it—that black cat hung upside down?"

She traced it with her fingers. "I know it's crazy, but it frightens me."

"As long as I don't," he said. "I don't want you to be afraid of me, Mrs. Frye."

"I'm not, Mr. Conner," she said.

And at that moment she even believed it.

"White," Jenny declared flatly. "I prefer white."

"That one on the form? With the ruffles?"

"That one, please."

The saleslady took her in quickly with practiced eye. "Size thirty-six." Without waiting to be told she was right, she slid a lucite

10

box from the shelf, lifted out a blouse, and spread it on the glass counter.

"Is it wash-and-wear?" Jenny asked. "If I like it, I'll buy it anyway. I just wondered."

"The label says it is." She lowered her voice in confidence as if the manufacturer could overhear. "But I always find it needs a little touching up with a warm iron." She nodded toward the fitting rooms in the rear of the shop. "Why don't you go in and try it on?"

Jenny didn't know what made her tell her. "I'm having my portrait painted."

"Are you? How nice! Is that why you're buying this?"

"Yes. Do you think it's a good choice for something like that? In your honest opinion."

"It should be extremely flattering. Off the shoulder always is."

"And the ruffles," Jenny reminded her.

"Extremely gay."

Suddenly critical, Jenny held the blouse at arm's length. "Fussy?

That what you mean by gay? Because I wouldn't want anything fussy—you know—cheap looking."

As if she were in danger of seeing a cash sale disappear into the ruffles and being lost forever, the saleslady said with a conviction too intense to be completely honest, "Feminine was actually the word I was searching for: extremely feminine."

"O.K., I'll take it. And I won't bother to try it on. It's my size. No reason why it shouldn't fit."

Actually, she was delighted to have found exactly what she wanted so quickly. Only that morning she had decided to go up to Broadway to shop for it. It was while she was having her first cup of coffee. She had dipped the sugar cube into the scalding liquid, watched it slowly stain itself brown before letting it slip from her fingers, and thought about the portrait he had destroyed the day before.

Correction, Jenny. The one you made him destroy. Never mind. Never mind. Don't think about that. Gone. Thrown out in the trash by now. Just remember the good part—how well it had been done—little spots of yellow in the eyes, for instance, to make them seem to light up from behind. He hadn't, she recalled, pleased, painted in any circles under them either! And he certainly had a way of doing hair, a real knack for it, if that was the word. You could almost reach out and feel it. Soft.

The only thing she hadn't liked was what she had been wearing. That hadn't been his fault. It was hers. The pale-blue sleeveless shirt with the V neck may have been comfortable, but it sure hadn't done a thing for her. Maybe it's just as well he's doing it again, she thought, I'll wear something prettier this time.

She was sure now that the only face on that canvas had been her own. She had proved it with her own eyes, and one thing she knew she had besides a thirty-six bust was 20/20 vision. She began to look forward to having him finish the new one, so she could buy that fancy frame. Fancy. That didn't mean fussy.

She paid for the blouse and left the shop. The saleslady had warned that wash-'n'-wear didn't necessarily mean no touching up with a warm iron. Nothing unusual about that. And she had said, "How nice," when Jenny told her about having her portrait painted. She hadn't pleaded with her to "tell him you changed your mind. You don't want to take chances, do you?"—Of course not, because there was nothing so particularly unusual about having a portrait painted either.

What happened the day before in the studio was too bad for the painting, but good for her. I needed that, Jenny decided, to bring me to my senses.

She had needed the ugly sound of a canvas being slashed and senselessly destroyed to drown out the echo of ugly words: "Black is the color of the Devil's own magic; black is the—" Sick words. Forget them. "Let him have your body. It's nothing much. But your soul, Jenny—"

"Shut up!" she said out loud and glanced around quickly to see if anyone had overheard. No one seemed to have. —I said forget it, she told herself sternly; only someone with a sickness in her own soul could even talk like that.

As she ran up the front steps of the brownstone, it occurred to her that the last person to mention that word to her had been her grandmother. Her grandmother was *big* on the *immortal soul* bit, and Jenny had an uncomfortable moment, just before she started the long climb to three, of wondering whose side her grandmother would be on in this: Alice Molland's or Mr. Conner's.

The arm holding the box containing a white blouse with ruffles remembered almost being torn from its socket as she was yanked to the other side of the street to avoid passing another man with a beard.

O.K. So her grandmother hadn't liked colored people! That didn't mean she would have liked the Glob, did it? Even thinking such a thing was like spitting on a grave. I'm sorry, Granny, she said silently. And I'm sorry I didn't like you. I really am. —Somehow that had bothered her more and more lately.

Halfway to the landing of her own floor, she heard Mrs. Keefer say: "Fill in the neckline, let out the seams, and I could wear it to church."

Jenny froze, and instinctively moved quickly to the wall and began inching her way up slowly. Unless she was mistaken, what she had just heard came from the left of the hall—from her room, to be exact. And unless she was mistaken again, Mrs. Keefer wasn't talking to herself. Her next words proved it.

"This isn't like robbing the dead, is it, Miss Molland? I wouldn't want to do that."

"She owed you rent, didn't she?"

"That's true."

"Then what's hers is yours by law."

What the hell was going on? They were in her room. No doubt about that now. Through the half-open door she could see her dresses strewn all over the bed and across the backs of chairs. The bureau drawers spilled over with her underwear, her stockings, her nightgowns. Everything was exposed to the harsh August sun. For some reason she couldn't explain, Jenny felt more undressed than she ever did in the club spotlight. These were her things. All hers. All personal. She put them against her body and hooked and snapped or pulled them on. Seeing Alice Molland pick up a lacy brassiere and then toss it aside to look for something else made Jenny feel worse than undressed. It made her feel raped.

The nerve of those two! The gall! Only Mrs. Keefer had the passkey, so she must have been the one to open the door; but the idea of breaking in in the first place smelled much more like Alice Molland. Jenny felt just mad enough to be just strong enough to rush in, take them by surprise, and then heave them both out. Yes, she thought indignantly, even the Glob.

"Oh, my," she heard Mrs. Keefer exclaim, "this is nice, isn't it?"

Cigar smoke rolled around the corner of the door and out into the hall. It held her back for a moment and gave her a chance to reconsider. Barging in on them now wouldn't put her room to rights. That unpleasant job would be hers later and she would use all the four-letter words that didn't rhyme with sweet violets while she was doing it!

But break up their little party now, and she wouldn't have a chance to find out whose birthday they were celebrating. What had Mrs. Keefer said? "This isn't like robbing the dead, is it?" O.K., then, whose funeral!

Jenny played with the idea of concealing herself behind the swung door and listening to find out what it was all about. Since it was her room, could anybody call it spying? If they did, she wouldn't give a sweet violet about that either.

She crossed the hall as quietly as her own shadow, and flattened herself again the dark-red wallpaper.

Mrs. Keefer had wrapped herself in a Spanish shawl that Jenny had forgotten she still owned. It had a red rose embroidered on the back and was hung with thick black silk fringe. Some of the fringe looked a little ratty. Mrs. Keefer was trying to straighten the hopelessly knotted tassels.

Lots of luck, Jenny thought. Alice, she saw, had given up the drawers for the jewelry box that stood on the bureau.

She scooped up beads and earrings, dumped them to one side, and kept scrounging around with a hand that reminded Jenny of a huge cat's paw. It was on the tip of her tongue to say, You're wasting your time. What you're looking for is underneath. You have to lift up the top shelf. Ah, that's it. That's what you wanted, isn't it?

Alice let out a smile of satisfaction, and with it a pleased hiss. She took out the brooch and turned to Mrs. Keefer. "That shawl becomes you." Jenny had never before heard her address her disciple with such warmth.

Apparently Mrs. Keefer was surprised, too. "You think so, Miss Molland?"

"I won't mind if you call me Alice from now on. We've known each other a long time."

"Six years," the landlady said, delighted. "That is a long

time . . ." She hesitated before adding, "Alice"; then twisted her face and began nervously to chew the inside of her thin cheek.

Alice only smiled. Then she let the palm of her hand fall open and showed the brooch nestled in folds of fat. "She let me borrow this once."

"You warned her. No one can say you didn't warn her."

"My conscience is clear." She looked hungrily at the brooch, then up at Mrs. Keefer again, and waited for her to say something.

"It wasn't your fault she didn't listen to you. Now she's lying dead in some alley."

Outside the door, Jenny thought: *That* isn't what she wanted you to say. And who's lying dead in some alley? Me? Where'd you two ghouls ever get a crazy idea like that? Oh, I get it! A tarot reading this morning, I bet! Well, this time the cards goofed; and in just about one minute, ladies, you're going to find that out.

"She let me borrow it for one of my parties," Alice said, returning to a subject that really interested her. "Everyone admired it." She peered over several chins to attach it to her dress. "I wore it here." She let an impatient moment pass before adding pointedly, "You like it—Mildred?"

With sudden inspiration, Mrs. Keefer said, "Why don't you keep it?"

Brilliant, Jenny thought, amused in spite of herself. You don't need a brick wall to fall on you.

"Oh, now—" Alice said, as broadly as the bosom that wore the brooch. "I wasn't hinting."

"As if you would!" Mrs. Keefer chided. "But it's mine to give, isn't it? You don't think there could be any mistake?"

"If she owed you rent? Of course not."

"I meant about her being dead."

Jenny was all prepared for Alice to reproach her with: Have the cards ever been wrong? They're not wrong this time! It would be interesting to watch Mrs. Keefer's reaction when she found out that they had been—this time.

Her own reaction when she saw what Alice did then was one of shock. She saw her go behind the armchair and bring out the canvas that had been hidden there. She saw her hold up the mutilated portrait as if it had no weight at all. Mrs. Keefer shuddered. Jenny shuddered, too.

"Poor unfortunate girl."

"Poor stupid girl!" Alice said.

"When I found that thrown out in the trash," Mrs. Keefer said, pulling at the fringe on the shawl, "I refused to let myself think what it meant. Then, just a few minutes later, *she* left the house."

"Walking fast, isn't that what you said? —Walking fast, as if she knew she was being followed?"

Jenny wanted to cry out: That's not the reason. I was in a hurry to get to Broadway—to buy a blouse. —But she couldn't say anything.

"And right at her heels," Mrs. Keefer continued, "oh, she couldn't have got further than the corner, I saw *him*—looking so pleased with himself."

"You didn't tell me that. Really pleased with himself? With what he was looking forward to, more likely. Black devil! When I told you what must have happened, you didn't want to believe it."

"I still don't want to, but you're probably right."

So that was it. It had nothing to do with the cards. I left the house, Jenny thought; then, for reasons of his own, so did Mr. Conner. Mrs. Keefer had already found that—picture—so they put two and two together and came up with an unlucky thirteen.

"What other reason could he have for slashing this the way he did, unless he meant to do it to her next?" Mrs. Keefer moaned and rocked back and forth.

At the mirror, Alice was saying, "It's all over now. You can be sure of that." She tilted her head, admiring the brooch. "Only one of them will return to this house tonight."

Jenny wanted to burst in on them. She should have done it in the first place. Now her knees felt unhinged, and she would have to wait a moment more.

She heard Mrs. Keefer announce: "I'm going to the police."

"What's your rush? They'll be here soon enough. They'll identify her and find out where she was living—*when* she was living. Never go to the police, Mildred. Always let them come to you. Keep away from them as long as possible. I've always found it pleasanter that way."

"Her husband," Mrs. Keefer seemed to remember suddenly, "asked me to look after her."

"You didn't promise."

"Just the same, I hope he doesn't accuse me of being the least bit responsible. I did what I could. Not that I got much thanks for it. Still, I won't hold that against her." She raised her eyes through the leak in the ceiling in the direction of heaven and murmured, "I just hope she knows wherever she is—wherever she is—that I did try."

That was what finally tightened the hinges in Jenny's knees. She wasn't where these two thought she was and it was time she let them know. She kicked open the door all the way, glared at them, and said, "This may come as a big surprise to you, Mrs. Keefer, but this is my room."

The landlady gasped and fell weakly against the disordered dresser as if she were seeing a ghost. The only surprise her partner registered was to raise thick eyebrows slightly and only slightly widen her eyes.

"Except for the crummy furniture," Jenny stormed, "all the personal belongings belong to me. I pay rent to keep it here."

"I—we—" Mrs. Keefer stammered, trying to compose herself "—you're not paid up for next month, Mrs. Frye—and it's in advance. You know the rules."

"It's not the first yet."

"I—we—didn't figure you'd be here to pay it."

I know damn well what you figured, Jenny thought. She wanted to make her squirm just a little before she threw them both out.

Mrs. Keefer turned helplessly to Alice. "You were so sure—" she began; then, without waiting, started to stuff things back into

the dresser drawers and bang them shut. She hung dresses lop-
sidedly on hangers and shoved them into the closet.

Jenny let her work, even though she knew she'd have to do it
all over herself. "Cute pair of vultures you are," she said, screwing
her hands into fists and jabbing them on to her hips. "Now suppose you get out of here."

Losing neither her dignity nor her composure, Alice Molland
told her, "If it's of any interest to you, Jenny, I didn't take anything. Mrs. Keefer gave me this." She unpinned the brooch and
reluctantly put it back in the jewel box.

Mrs. Keefer, frantically tossing hats up onto the shelf, seemed
to realize with a start that the shawl was still draped around her
shoulders. She grabbed a handful of tassels and yanked. Even more
reluctantly than Alice had parted with the brooch, she gave up the
shawl, folding it before laying it neatly on the bed.

"Oh, cheer up," Jenny consoled her. "If Alice played her cards
right in the beginning, you'll get it back soon." Now that was a
dumb crack to make, she told herself, even in a joke.

"You don't have to believe this, Mrs. Frye," Mrs. Keefer said,
"but when I thought you were lying in some alley, all cut up, I
felt a little sorry for you."

Jenny pretended to notice the painting for the first time. She was
glad now she had been standing out in the hall. If she hadn't been,
discovering it now might have thrown her. This way she could put
on an act—pass it off as if it weren't important. All she hoped was
that neither of the two women noticed her hands trembling when
she picked up the canvas.

"I got a real pain in my stomach when I found that in the trash,"
Mrs. Keefer said. "I've always had a delicate stomach."

"Did you know he had done that to you, Jenny?" Alice asked.

Jenny forced herself to look down at it indifferently, even though
forcing put a sharp pain behind each eye. She hoped her voice
wouldn't give her away.

"I was there when he did it." She surprised herself by managing a controlled little laugh. "It isn't me anyway. It never was. It was just—"

"The part of yourself you had given to a stranger." And Jenny knew she hadn't fooled Alice Molland, not for a minute. "You just stood there, Jenny, and watched him do it?" She seemed astounded that anyone could have acted with such deliberate stupidity.

"I tried to stop him," Jenny told her. "I asked him to stop it—"

Stop it! Stop it!—she told herself, clenching her teeth. Don't explain anything to her! Not to her!

"Look," she said, "I've got an appointment." She was drained suddenly of any desire to tell them off for making such a shambles of her room. All she wanted was to get them out—and fast. "It was a lovely wake," she said, "and the corpse apologizes for coming back and taking all the fun out of it."

Better—much better. Make a joke of it. She went to the bureau, got the brooch and offered it to Alice.

"This is for your trouble."

Alice's face widened even more with greed, and she made a grab for it. "To keep?"

"I meant to give it to you before. Just never got around to it."

Alice looked skeptical.

Only it's true, Jenny thought. After Mr. Conner said it was cheap, somehow I never enjoyed wearing it any more.

Out of the corner of her eye she saw Mrs. Keefer gaze with undisguised yearning at the shawl.

Impulsively, Jenny draped the thin tired silk around the thin tired shoulders. "And for you, Mrs. Keefer."

Mrs. Keefer's mouth fell open and hung. "For me?"

Jenny smiled grimly. "That's because you were a little sorry when you thought I was dead. That was something. It wasn't much, but it was something."

"Oh, I wouldn't dream of taking it—" stroking the fringe. "I couldn't—"

"Strain yourself, but don't rupture." She was relieved to have regained her sense of humor.

When it came right down to it, her sense of humor was the only thing she owned that she really wanted to keep. Health? Maybe she had that now, a strong heart and a stomach so hard she could bang it like a drum; but health was too much of an iffy thing. The way she figured it, if God wanted everybody to be healthy, there wouldn't be so damned many people in hospitals. And money? Love? Forget it! The only way to enjoy either of those was to use them; and once you did, they were gone. At least that had been her experience. So all she had ever hoped to hold onto—when the money was gone and the love was lost and the day came when maybe she'd feel too rotten to lift her head—was to find something to laugh about. Maybe it wasn't much, but it was something.

"It's very generous of you, Mrs. Frye," Mrs. Keefer was saying, overwhelmed. "So generous."

"Everybody's friends again. O.K.? No hard feelings." She opened the door wider. All the way. "See you around."

Moving quickly and with surprising buoyancy for someone her size, Alice sprang to the door, closed it, and planted herself against it.

"I told you," Jenny said, "I've got an appointment."

"She wants to be friends, Mildred." But it was Jenny she was looking hard at. "Isn't it nice? She wants to be friends—"

Mrs. Keefer seemed as bewildered as Jenny at first, but she was faster at adapting herself to the situation, quicker to follow the other woman's lead. She nodded agreeably and waited for Alice to finish "—because, you see, Jenny, that's what we've wanted all along—" before she picked it up and continued: "Your husband asked me to look out for you. You heard him yourself. 'You'll take good care of her for me, won't you?' That's what he said. As if you were a little girl."

"Now, wait a minute—" Jenny began.

The two women were pushing her back into the room. They

stood on either side of her, boxing her in.

"If anything happens to you," Mrs. Keefer was saying, "I'd want to be able to look him straight in the eye and say, 'I did my best, Mr. Frye.' "

"Nothing's going to happen to me," Jenny warned, "except that maybe I'm going to lose my temper." And if she wasn't careful, her sense of humor.

Alice pressed closer. "Just tell us why he did that to the painting. Only a madman would have carved it up like that—stripping off the skin."

"It's not skin. It's canvas and canvas doesn't bleed and paint doesn't cry." Somehow, those words had sounded better when Mr. Conner said them.

"Why did he do it to you?"

"How many times do I have to tell you? It isn't me!"

"Looks like her, doesn't it, Mildred?"

"It's not so easy to tell the way it is now," Mrs. Keefer obliged, "but I'm sure it did once."

"Why?" Alice asked. "Why did he take a knife to it?"

Strange, so strange to feel lost in her own room. —She had forgotten where the bed was until the back of her knees hit against it: then she sat down. That was a big mistake.

They were standing over her now. Jenny cast her eyes about wildly. She had cut off any escape. She had no freedom of movement left. All she could do was sit helpless and let herself be cross-examined. Alice didn't need a rubber hose. Her tongue cut deeper.

What a damn fool I was, Jenny thought bitterly, letting myself be cornered like this.

She tried to get away by turning her head. Immediately her chin was clamped tightly between a broad thumb and forefinger and her face sharply twisted front again.

"Hey," she said indignantly, "that hurts."

"Answer me. Why did he take a knife to it?"

"I said that hurts, damn you!"

Alice released her.

"All right," Jenny said, rubbing her chin, "he did it because I wanted to see it and he—didn't want me to." She looked from one to the other and slowly stopped rubbing. The pain that was left was very little compared to the realization of how lame that must have sounded. It even sounded lame to her. "He—Mr. Conner—doesn't like to have anybody see unfinished work."

"And for that," Alice said in broad comic disbelief, "he picked up a knife and—" She lowered her face still closer and Jenny had an overwhelming urge to spit in it.

That was something she had never felt like doing to anyone—never in her whole life. She fought the impulse by jumping up so suddenly that it startled the women enough to make them move back and give her room to stand and defend herself.

She was ready to defend Mr. Conner, as well, if she had to. "All right, he did it because I was looking for that other face—that face you had me believing I'd find. Are you satisfied?"

"And did you find it?" Mrs. Keefer asked.

"It wasn't there."

And from Alice: "You're positive?"

"Positive."

"How long did it take him to start hacking away at it before you had a real good look? A long look?"

"It wouldn't have mattered how long I looked. There was nothing to find."

"He made sure, didn't he, that no one will find it now. I might have been able to."

"Was he," Mrs. Keefer wanted to know, "very angry?"

"No, he wasn't," Jenny threw back at her. "All he was—was just —sad."

Alice picked up the cigar she had put down in the ashtray, inhaled, pushed a smoke ring out of her mouth, and followed it with: "He has a violent way of showing sadness, hasn't he?"

"You don't even begin to know him," Jenny told her.

"And you do?"

"I know he wouldn't hurt anybody. I know that much about

him. He doesn't have it in him. He's—too—gentle."

Alice tossed her head back and snorted. "Would you say," she asked, nodding at the portrait, "that this was done by the hand of someone who's gentle, little dear?"

As soon as Jenny said, "He won't do it to the next one; he'll have no reason," she regretted it; not for telling them, because sooner or later they would have snooped and found out anyway, but for telling them now when she wanted to get rid of them. It was practically an invitation for them to stick around and talk about it, and one of her headaches was coming on. What a dope I was, she thought.

"What a fool!" Alice was saying. "You really agreed to pose for him again?"

Defiantly, she said, "I even asked for it."

Mrs. Keefer's lips were moving, forming words without sound. It's enough to make a person nervous, Jenny decided, nervous enough to imagine that the words are the same ones the landlady used once before when she talked about his last model: "She came back. She always came back. Maybe she got what she deserved."

"If you've got anything to say," Jenny ordered sharply, "say it out loud."

"I was saying that Alice might still be able to help you if you ask her."

"I won't ask her, so forget it."

"I offered to be your friend once," Alice Molland reminded her. "Do you think so little of me, Jenny, to think I would withhold that offer now when you really need it?"

"I don't think of you at all."

Alice smiled and took no offense; and Jenny, her head beginning to throb, knew it was because she had guessed, suspected, or perhaps read in the cards that it wasn't true. She did think about her: a lot.

"You have a headache," Alice said. "Haven't you?"

"No," Jenny lied.

"I know a remedy." Heavy lids fell and she chanted, "Knot on the right and arrange flat in regular bands; on the left a woman's diadem: divide it twice in seven little bands; gird the head of the invalid with it—"

Jenny interrupted. "Aspirins are all I need—washed down with lots of black coffee." She stopped, realizing it had been an admission.

"Do you get them often?" Alice said solicitously, but she was grinning broadly.

Jenny managed a smirk in return. So the old witch had known about the headache. What did that prove? Only that she had taken the trouble to look. It always shows in the eyes. "I hardly ever get them," she lied again.

"Perhaps," Alice conceded, "aspirin and coffee can keep it away —for a while. But don't try taking them to keep back the Devil or his demons."

Jenny couldn't restrain herself. She hooted at that, but stopped immediately when Alice drew the cards from her deep pocket and began to shuffle.

"And I'm not in the market for those, either," Jenny said, fascinated in spite of herself by the brilliance of colors rising and falling.

"I've already seen you in them," Alice told her. "Think of me when it happens, and ask yourself if, perhaps, there was anything I might have told you that could have stopped the tide from coming in"—she raised mountainous shoulders, let them fall again slowly and finished—"or stopped the tide from going out."

"She's our friend," Mrs. Keefer said. "Didn't she give you that brooch and me this shawl?"

"I do know of one or two things that have helped others in the past. Make her ask me."

Mrs. Keefer appealed to Jenny. "Please."

"Will you two get out of here?" Jenny said impatiently.

"She gave you such a pretty brooch," Mrs. Keefer reminded Alice reproachfully, and was rewarded almost immediately: "Spirits do not always appear the same. They must find a body to appear in. Lucifer, when angry, appears red; Beélzebuth, when angry, vomits fire; Astoroth appears black, and always in human shape."

This time Jenny yelled, "Get out!" but Alice, eyes closed, big head lolling from side to side, didn't seem to hear her. She continued in voice startlingly masculine and frighteningly full of masculine authority: "This is from an ancient tablet! If he comes near, you must cry out: 'Hearken to my prayer. Free me from my bewitchment. Loosen my sin. Let there be turned aside whatever evil may come to cut off—' "

Before she went any further, Jenny cut her off. "That's as bad as all that hoodoo jazz."

Alice's eyes flew open. They shone with excitement. "Hoodoo? So he told you about that!"

That must mean, Jenny thought with surprise, that he's told her as well. And there I was under the impression that he told it just to me—that it isn't the sort of thing he goes around blabbing to everybody—especially to this woman he once called a hag of hell. Maybe he isn't so ashamed of having it in his past after all. Maybe he's even proud of it.

"How much did he tell you?"

"More than I cared to hear," Jenny told her shortly, resenting the two of them at that moment—her *and* Mr. Conner.

"I don't blame you, little dear. It couldn't have been very pleasant listening."

It hadn't been: little bags with chicken feet—and broken razor blades—

"Tell me," Alice said soothingly.

"He told me about the love potions," Jenny began; then changed her mind about going on with it.

"So he gave her one of those first, did he? Now, that's interesting."

"Love potions," Mrs. Keefer said. "To have such goings-on right here in my own house—"

Jenny frowned. Suddenly she had the uneasy feeling that they weren't talking about the same thing. "Gave who a love potion?"

"Come on. Come on," Alice urged. "You've already told me more than he would that day."

"What have I told you?"

Without warning, she pushed up a purple sleeve and uncovered her upper arm. "Here," she said, poking into soft flesh and making a well that plumped out again as soon as she released her finger. "Here is where he grabbed me. Look closely. Can you still see the mark?"

Jenny drew back.

"It was that day I went in to bargain for the portrait. It was then I saw the dolls and guessed right away what he used them for. All those little heads. I asked him if he had painted *her* image on one of them first before he transferred it to the canvas." She rubbed her arm in memory. "He hurt me," she recalled bitterly.

Dismayed, Jenny thought: We *haven't* been talking about the same thing! He never did tell her what he told me—like the reason he had for running away, for instance. I got it wrong—all wrong. She's talking about—

"Voodoo dolls," Alice said triumphantly. "I knew it as soon as I saw them. So I was right."

"I never said so," Jenny denied hotly. "You just heard what you wanted to hear. As for those dolls: that's the way Mr. Conner makes a living, painting faces on them."

"So he says. And you believe him?"

"Unless you like the police," Jenny said, remembering how Alice had discouraged Mrs. Keefer earlier from going for them, "then you better get out of my room now, because I'm going to call them." She started for the telephone, and Alice swept past her to the door. She waited for Mrs. Keefer to open it.

"Mrs. Frye," Mrs. Keefer said, before she did, "I'm glad you're all right. We were worried."

"Oh, I could tell." Jenny still held onto the phone as a threat. "The minute I walked in I could tell. Don't think I didn't appreciate it."

"You're really going to let him do another portrait?"

For an answer, she started dialing. Mrs. Keefer opened the door.

As they left, Jenny heard her ask, "What are voodoo dolls, Alice?"

"*They* make up a doll," Alice Molland answered, "to look like the person they want to see dead—"

The door closed. Jenny hung up, rushed to the door and locked it. "Then what?" she heard Mrs. Keefer ask.

"Then they doom the absent victim by thrusting thin needles into their wretched bodies—little—tiny—pins. . . ." Her voice faded as they went down the stairs.

A cold draft seeped under the door and into the room. Jenny turned on the flame under the coffee pot and reached for the aspirin bottle.

She swallowed two tablets with water, and when the coffee was ready, poured it into a cup and gulped it down, still black and scalding. She blew and gulped and, when she had finished, drew the shades and fell face down across the bed.

The remedy wouldn't work immediately, but lying perfectly still

11

sometimes made it happen faster. This particular headache was worse than usual. Was it any wonder after what they had just put her through? And she had felt so good when she awoke that morning—so good, and so happy afterwards finding the blouse, exactly what she had wanted. Damn those women. She should have taken three aspirins.

Maybe, Jenny thought, the directions only say to take two because what they really want is for headaches to hang on and not go away. Then people will be forced to take two more later. Damn the aspirin companies, too. I don't trust them anyway. One ad says they're all the same because according to law the ingredients have to be the same and other ads say it's a big fat lie because there definitely is a difference and you should get down on your knees and thank God you live in the United States of America where you're free to pay for what you get and get what you pay for: Quicker—Faster Relief.

"Oh, my head," she said aloud. "I should have taken six. There's a regular band across my eyes. What is it Alice said before? Arrange flat in regular bands—on the left, a woman's diadem— What the hell is a diadem? Right now I'd try anything."

Some sunlight the shade hadn't been able to push back made a square on the ceiling and touched the dark patch caused by the leak. The only spot of pure light in the room sat gently on the disfigured little patch and soothed it.

How nice of the sun, Jenny thought, to be sorry for that, and she closed her eyes and wished it would come down and sit on her—just for a minute.

Thinking of the light, she slid into the dark. She could see herself clearly, lying face down on a beach, close to the shoreline.

She could feel water pulling the sand from under her, and threw out her arms and spread her hands to grip it when it returned. And it did, but no matter how she clung to it, she wasn't able to hold it. It swept away, leaving her fingers to grip mud.

With nothing covering her, Jenny felt colder and lonelier than ever in her life. Completely exhausted, she let her wet cheek press against sharp wet pebbles and refused to admit to being the loser.

"Next time," she cried, "I'll find a way to hold you." But as each word left her, she heard it being swallowed whole by the sound of the water that was coming closer and would soon wash over her and then leave—dragging with it more of her strength.

"Do you think, little dear, that you can stop the tide from coming in—or going out? Maybe I know a way. Ask me." She looked up. From that angle, Alice Molland took on almost mammoth proportions. The hem of her dress was drenched. It hung in uneven points and dripped purple dye.

Jenny got up and ran so fast she was afraid her heart would burst and fall into the water and be carried away, leaving behind a bright purple stain.

And, suddenly, there was Mr. Conner. "Mrs. Frye, were those two boys bothering you?" His voice was full of concern and she laughed into the wind with relief. "They're not bothering me now."

"Good. Come see what I've done. Tell me if you think it has your face."

She looked down and saw a head rising from the sand. "Go on. I'm not half as pretty as that. You think so?"

The next thing she knew she was screaming, "The water! Oh, God, the water—" And she had to stand by helpless while it fell on top of the face that was so much like hers. When it retreated, she knew it would pull away some of the sand, leaving the features disfigured.

"It's terrible," she told him, "to see myself looking like that— just terrible. And I was planning to get a fancy frame for it."

She ran from him crying.

It wasn't easy to run wearing high heels, but she didn't want to stop to take them off, so she kept on running and thought: How funny it was that high heels could make a noise on sand—because she heard them plainly under her—tap—tapping—

Jenny sat up dazed. The tapping was coming from the next room. She slipped off the bed, stumbled uncertainly to the wall and, leaning her still throbbing head against it, tapped a return to let him know she had heard.

Aspirins hadn't helped much this time. As far as she could tell they hadn't helped at all. She went into the bathroom and splashed cold water over her face. Better. She let it rush full force on her wrists. Much better.

What did water remind her of? Something she had dreamed? She couldn't remember.

Never mind. Not important. More important to remember to change into the white blouse quickly. It was after three o'clock. Mr. Conner had expected her long before this. She must have slept longer than she realized.

As she lowered the wide ruffled collar over her head, she looked up. There had been sun on the ceiling, not much, just a small bright square. Gone now. Never mind—not important. His studio would be flooded with sun.

Before leaving her room Jenny glanced quickly into the mirror, wove a few more hairpins at the nape of her neck to tidy flyaway strands, and thought how many years it had been since she went to a beach.

Now what made her think of that all of a sudden?

She had never seen him so cheerful and wondered why that should irritate her. She watched him move about the easel, squeezing colors from fat tubes onto the square palette and collecting clean rags to put alongside the brushes on the table. He didn't stop humming and, after letting her in, didn't look at her.

And he didn't mention my new blouse, Jenny thought resentfully. That's probably what's bugging me. I bought it for this. It isn't the kind of thing I'd have any other use for and he hasn't even mentioned it.

Annoyed she asked, "Are you planning to keep that up all day?"

"What did you say, Mrs. Frye?"

"If there's one thing I can't stand, it's humming. Drives me nuts. That—and anybody cracking gum."

"Was I humming?"

"Didn't you know you were?"

"No," he said, and smiled at her.

"Feeling pretty good today, aren't you?" she said sarcastically, but he didn't seem to take either notice or offense.

"I'm feeling glad."

"Any special reason?"

"Because the light is good—"

Something in the way he said it made Jenny feel sure he was going on. She waited. When he didn't, she pressed on herself, sure of only one thing now: she wanted him to stand still for a minute more and talk to her. He used to talk to her.

"That the special reason, Mr. Conner?"

"It's something to be glad for. I'm starting a new project and even the sun approves. Would you mind taking your place?"

She wanted to shout: Wait, can't you? What's your hurry?—but all she did was hesitate.

"I've given you a different view," he said.

"I noticed."

"You can look out over the city. It'll be nicer for you than staring at that cracked wall." He nodded encouragingly and she surprised him by going not to the high stool but to the easel.

She looked down at the palette. "Those colors are awfully dark."

"They'll be fine."

"You'll never get blonde hair with colors like that."

"Is the model becoming the teacher? Wait until it's finished, then you can be the critic."

"I don't claim to know anything about art. I told you I can't even draw a straight line. But I do know those colors won't give you my hair—or this either." Pointedly, she flipped the ruffle. "Do you like this? I bought it for the new portrait."

"I'm sorry. You shouldn't have gone to the expense."

"Six-ninety-five won't break me. What's your opinion? Will it look better than the other?"

"It really won't make any difference. It's the face that interests me."

"You mean you're not going to paint it," she asked indignantly, "after I paid—"

"Don't worry about it," he said. "Everything that should be there will be."

"It's a white blouse."

"I can see that."

"Well?"

"Well, what?"

She glanced questioningly at the palette once more, then shrugged. "Maybe you do know what you're doing."

After a moment he said, "You trust me, don't you?"

She tried to answer, but only made a vague gesture.

"Do you trust me, Mrs. Frye?"

Nervously she combed her hair with her fingers and confessed, "I'm a little upset today, Mr. Conner."

"I understand."

Oh, no, you don't, she told him silently, not unless you were standing in the hall outside my room a few hours ago and eavesdropped the way I did.

She was certain he hadn't. He would have mentioned it.

He lowered his voice as if he were afraid someone was eavesdropping on them now. "I told you I was starting a new project. Are you listening to me?" He waited for her nod before continuing. "I've forgotten what happened here yesterday. There's nothing to be upset about. The stars are all in the right places today."

"No, they're not," Jenny said. "The sun is out—" and felt foolish because she knew that wasn't what he meant. To tell the truth she didn't actually know what he did mean.

"Your star is in the right place," he insisted. "You can't see it, but it is."

It made her uncomfortable to have him say things she was supposed to understand but didn't. That was one of the things about Alice Molland that made her uncomfortable.

"Try to forget about that other portrait," he said. "It's on your mind, isn't it?"

She didn't answer.

"It won't do you any good to remember what happened to it— or think the kind of things you did. Do you understand?"

"Talking about it isn't doing me much good either, Mr. Conner," she snapped.

He shrugged and Jenny couldn't help feeling sorry for him. She knew he was honestly trying to find the right words to make her feel better.

"Perhaps," he suggested, "if you just remembered that when this is over, it will be the end of it for you. I'll be able to go on without you."

She was on the verge of nervous laughter, but managed to restrain it.

"All right?" he asked.

She nodded, not daring to answer; then went to the stool and sat down.

It was so pathetic it was almost funny. If he had tried he couldn't have found a better way of making her feel—worse.

It reminded her of the time she had the miscarriage. Charlie had come to the hospital after it was over. The first thing he had said was: "Listen, hon, I wasn't so hot on the idea of having that kid anyway. I don't really like kids, so don't feel bad."

And she had turned her face to the wall, and bit her lip until she tasted blood, and cried for a little baby that not only never had a chance to live but whose father didn't care one way or the other. Poor Charlie. She was sure now that he hadn't meant it. He had only tried to find the right words to make her feel better. It had been the same just now with Mr. Conner. But what words he had found!

Men, she thought with fond indulgence, and was startled to find herself thinking of him as a man. Well—wasn't he? From all reports, his last model had thought so.

"Mr. Conner," she said sharply, "don't you want to get that mirror out of the way first?"

"I want it there."

"I never noticed it before."

"Probably because it wasn't there before. I bought it this morning."

And you left the house a few minutes after I did, Jenny found herself thinking. —I was walking quickly as if I knew I was being followed, and then you came along practically right at my heels—oh, I couldn't have got further than the corner.— I know, because Mrs. Keefer saw you. You were looking so pleased with yourself, she said; with what you were looking forward to, Alice said.

She held her head and wondered what she would have to do to shake out the words they had put there earlier.

He was blending the colors with the flexible flat end of the palette knife, spreading them like soft butter one into the other—and appeared to be looking through her rather than at her when he said: "This will be a much more interesting portrait than that other one. You have my word."

"I thought we weren't going to talk about that, Mr. Conner."

He put down the knife. "Wouldn't you like to see yourself both the way you look to me and the way you look to a mirror?"

"Not particularly. Besides, I didn't agree to anything like that."

"What difference does it make to you?"

She shrugged with uncertainty. "I don't know. Maybe it would make a lot of difference. How do I know?"

He was rubbing his crisp black beard exactly as he had the day before when he looked into the small mirror over the washbasin and had agreed with her that it *was* a very ugly beard.

That's probably, she decided, when he got the bright idea for this. Well, I don't think much of it and I'm going to let him know it.

She took a deep breath and ordered: "Take this thing away, or let's forget it."

"Mrs. Frye," he said, disturbed, "it won't make posing any more difficult for the model. If it's more difficult for anyone, it will be for the artist."

"I don't know," she said again, but she knew she was being unreasonable. Actually, did it make any difference to her?

"I want to give this my best," he said. "Please—let me."

She was being more than unreasonable. She was being ungrateful. Face it, she told herself, he *is* the one who's going to have to work harder, and all because he wants to give it a little extra for no extra charge.

She let her hands relax into her lap and lifted her chin as she had during all those other sittings. "All right," she said, and prepared to start memorizing what she could see of the world beyond the window.

He said, "Will you let me have your hair?"—and brought her abruptly back into his world.

"What?"

"I didn't mean to startle you. I only meant it the way I would have said 'Let me have a smile'—or 'Let me have one shoulder turned toward me.' —You have pretty hair, Mrs. Frye."

Jenny didn't deny it. Nobody could confuse a pure statement of fact with conceit and she had always been proud of her hair. It was pretty. It had been one of the first things Charlie had noticed about her. "Does it glow in the dark?" he had asked. "Let me turn off the light and see if I can read." But after he had turned off all the lights, somehow he hadn't been much in the mood for reading.

Charlie had been a real nut about her hair! After they were married, he wouldn't let her cut it. It just kept on growing until finally she had to pin it on top of her head. "That's O.K. with me," he had said, "as long as I'm the only guy who ever watches you take out the pins."

"To see your hair reflected in the mirror would be lovely."

"Yes," Jenny murmured, then realized Mr. Conner, not Charlie, had said it.

"You'll do it then?"

"Do what?"

"Let it down."

"Sure," she said, thinking of how much more Charlie was going to like this picture. She lifted her arms and remembered with a start that no other man but him had ever seen her like that, hair falling down to the middle of her back. Her fingers froze, and she couldn't move them.

"Anything wrong, Mrs. Frye?"

She didn't know how to put into words that with her hair down she would feel more undressed than she ever did on the club floor. Asking her to take the pins out of her hair was almost like asking her to take off her clothes and pose in the nude. It was crazy to think like that, but she couldn't help it—any more than she could help the headache that was tying a band over her eyes again.

"Don't you want to know why I was so late?" she asked, her hands still on her hair.

"It doesn't matter as long as you're here now."

"I had a migraine headache. I've still got it. There are bumps all over my forehead from it and I'm feeling a little sick."

He surprised her by saying, "We could start again tomorrow."

"You won't mind?" she said eagerly, and jumped off the high stool before he had a chance to answer.

"The sun will shine again tomorrow."

"And nothing will stop that. It would be like trying to stop the tide from coming in or going out. Isn't that what you said?"

"I never said that, Mrs. Frye."

"Who did then? Oh—Alice Molland. Just today." She was anxious to get back to her own room so she could swallow more aspirins.

"I didn't think you were going to have anything to do with that woman," she heard him say.

"I gave her my brooch." Why did he keep her there talking? He offered to let her go—until tomorrow. Why didn't he? "Giving her my brooch wasn't my idea," she told him crossly. "It was yours."

"Did she like it?"

"Wild about it. I gave Mrs. Keefer something, too. Christmas is early this year."

"It's up to you, Mrs. Frye," he said slowly, "but I wouldn't encourage either of those two as friends."

Something like a fist seemed to hit her at the base of her skull. She clenched her teeth and took it. "I don't think you should pick my friends for me, Mr. Conner."

Learning to ride with pain was like riding a wave. Once you got over the crest it wasn't so bad, and she found herself thinking again about a beach. It probably meant she needed a vacation. It was years since she had had a real one. Being at liberty isn't a vacation. Ask anybody in the business! She wondered if they had beaches in Texas. Swimming pools would do as well! Well, why not?

"I said it was up to you," he said.

"What was?"

"The people you choose as friends."

Was he still on that kick? "You bet it is," she said almost angrily. "They mean well." She thought about it for a moment. That had just slipped out. She hadn't intended to say it, but it was true.

When you get right down to it, she thought, they do have my best interests at heart. They don't want anything to happen to me and that isn't just because I gave them presents.

"They honestly like me," she said.

He began to gather the rags on the table, and didn't answer.

At the door she said, "Well, good-by, Mr. Conner."

"I hope your headache is better, Mrs. Frye."

"Thanks." She watched him screw the caps on the big tubes and added apologetically, "I'm sorry you went to all that trouble for nothing. If you don't use the paints you squeezed out, what happens? Do they dry up so you have to throw them away?"

"Don't worry about it."

"I still think the colors were wrong."

"They would have worked out. I knew what I was doing."

"Yes," she said, "I'm sure you did."

Her hand was on the doorknob when she told him, "Once I had a costume made of peacock feathers."

"Did you?" He sounded surprised.

And it isn't, she thought, because I had a costume made out of peacock feathers, but because I mentioned it. Why did I? "In show business," she heard herself explain, "that's supposed to bring bad luck. But the act was a smash. I was held over."

She smiled at more than the memory. She was glad she had realized without having to think about it too much, and thinking never helped a headache, just why that had come back to her suddenly and kept her from going. Just as suddenly she knew she wasn't going to leave.

"It was probably a very good act," he said.

"It was O.K.—nothing sensational, I only did it on a dare."

"I don't understand."

"Peacock feathers are supposed to be bad luck. I wanted to prove it." Her hand dropped from the knob. "I did, and won a fiver into the bargain. —And I'll tell you something else: I always whistle in a dressing room. Sometimes I do it deliberately. That's supposed to be bad luck, too. Do you know what else? I'll sit on an empty trunk and won't give it a second thought, if my feet are tired and there's no place else to sit."

"That supposed to be bad luck, too, if you're in show business?"

"Say, listen," Jenny said, "if there were no superstitions, show people would invent them. They're like that. I was always a little different." She felt her head and smiled.

"Your headache," he said. "I hope it's better."

"It's practically gone."

And it was, along with all the excuses she had been inventing to keep him from starting the new portrait.

She had tried to get him to put it off; at first, by making him talk to her—about anything—had wasted more time quarreling about the colors, as if she knew more than he did—and finally, had made her headache worse by getting herself all worked up because he paid her a compliment and said she had hair nice enough to paint.

If I'm honest, Jenny thought, all those excuses did have something to do with my hair, figuratively speaking. Alice Molland was in it earlier today.

Hadn't she been fine until Alice had set her off, telling her the canvas wasn't canvas at all, but skin; and that he had done a thorough job of carving it up so no one would find that other face?

A face that wasn't there, Jenny told herself again. I'll never believe it was, any more than I believe he's a jinx or a hoodoo or anything else he called himself, just the way I don't believe in tarot cards or peacock feathers.

"What about stepping on rainbows?" she asked. "Have you ever heard of that as a superstition?"

"No," he said.

"It's something I never do. Remember I told you?"

"I remember."

"You said you don't either."

"That's true."

"I'll walk under a ladder and on a crack. Ever heard of 'Step on a crack—break your back'? But I'd never step on a rainbow I find in a street. Wouldn't it be awful, Mr. Conner, if I found out after all this time that it's supposed to be bad luck?"

"Why don't you ever step on them?" he asked her.

Without hesitating she answered: "Because I'd hate to spoil anything—nice—for no reason."

He smiled, "That's not a superstition, Mrs. Frye."

"I guess not," she said, relieved, and came farther into the room. "As long as my headache's gone, and as long as I'm still here, why don't we get started?"

She hadn't waited for his permission to get off the stool. She didn't wait for it when she hoisted herself up on it now. "There's an old lady at a window across the street," she said, as she removed the pins and freed shining hair to glide over her bare shoulders and cascade over the white ruffle. "Do you think, Mr. Conner, when you look at people, especially old ones, that they were ever cute little babies?" She laughed and shook her hair loose. "You think Alice Molland ever was? I doubt it." She realized he was staring at her and said, "What's the matter?"

"Nothing—I mean I didn't realize it was so long."

"Didn't you? Say, I bet I've got enough to make wigs for all those." She pointed to the little doll heads lining the shelves around the room. "Voodoo dolls," Alice had said. "I knew it as soon as I saw them."

"Let's get started," Jenny urged him quietly, "while I'm still in the mood, because a person has to be in the mood to sit still and stare out of a window."

He picked up his brush and began to work.

Sometimes she worried about the mirror, a large old-fashioned oval balanced uneasily on wooden claws. Tall as it was, he had mounted it on a huge crate. Jenny was always conscious of glass she couldn't see, standing behind her and locking her reflection within its walnut frame.

12

Once, when she jumped down too hurriedly and too hard, the mirror trembled. "You're positive," she asked nervously, "that it won't fall on my head someday?"

He assured her it wouldn't, unless she deliberately backed into it.

"Don't worry. I don't like it well enough to get that close to it." She stood at a distance and looked back at it with distaste.

"What don't you like about it?" he asked curiously.

"It's so ugly."

"It's out of style, and I don't think it was a particularly good design even when it was fashionable." He narrowed his eyes and squinted at her as he often did when she was posing. "But you, of all people, should like it, Mrs. Frye."

"Why?" stiffly. "Is that what you think of my taste, Mr. Conner?"

He studied his day's work. "You should like it because it's making your portrait so unusual."

Absent-mindedly Jenny pulled a length of hair forward and began to chew the end of it. It was newly washed and smelled like sweet

172

grass. She let it fall over the rise in her blouse and said, "I wonder which one of me I'll like better."

He was still deeply preoccupied with the canvas and didn't seem to hear her.

"You said you were going to show me the way I look to you and the way I look to a mirror," she reminded him. "I've been thinking about that. Why should there be a difference?"

"Because there always is. I know that the face I see in the mirror isn't the same one other people see. To different people, Mrs. Frye, I have a different face."

She couldn't argue that. She didn't know exactly what he saw in the mirror, but she did know that he looked different to her than he did to Alice Molland—or Mrs. Keefer.

She caught herself wondering how he had looked to the model he used before her. Did his face seem less black, or hadn't it mattered to her? Jenny dismissed the thought with a rude tossing back of the hair she had been chewing.

It's not a thing, she told herself, for me to even think about. Their relationship was one thing; ours is strictly another.

She raised her voice louder than necessary to cover up thoughts that might somehow turn to solid words and take on sound. "I've never thought about it, but you're right. All those cracks about people being two-faced—say, that's nothing, is it? I wonder how many faces I have."

He asked, "How many people do you know?"

She shook her head. "Confusing, isn't it? The only face I'm absolutely sure of is the one I see in the mirror."

"You're sure of that one?"

"Oh, I don't kid myself. Say, I know what I look like, Mr. Conner."

"Do you have a lipstick?" he asked suddenly.

"Sure. Why?"

"Get it."

She opened her handbag and found the gold tube. "What do you want me to do with this?"

He motioned with his head towards the mirror over the wash-basin. "Stand in front of it and draw—as best you can—the outline of your face."

She laughed self-consciously. "You know I can't draw."

"It doesn't have to be perfect. Just as nearly as you can do it—trace what you see of yourself."

"Well," she said, "tracing's something else again. What I mean is—a person doesn't have to have any real talent to trace. But what will it prove?"

"You'll find out."

She shrugged agreeably, went to the washbasin, and leaned over it—the lipstick poised like a pencil in her hand. She hesitated. "You really want me to mark up your mirror?"

"Soap and water will wash it off. Go on, follow the contour. Close one eye. It will make it easier to do."

She leaned forward and, running her tongue over her lower lip, rimmed the face close to her in the glass with a thick red line. After a while, she said, "O.K., what did I just prove?"

"That you don't even know the size of the face you see in the mirror. Stand back and look at it."

What Jenny saw was an oval, crudely and unsteadily drawn, but nevertheless easy to recognize as the shape of her own face. What she found impossible to recognize, or accept, was the size.

She gasped in amazement. "Why, it's so tiny. I don't understand." She moved closer and her face slipped back into the crimson frame. She moved away, and once more it became the size of a large egg, one she would have no trouble at all holding in the palm of her hand. "Is this some kind of trick mirror, Mr. Conner?"

He shook his head. "The same would happen to you in any mirror."

"I don't understand. What made it happen?"

"It's an illusion. Sometimes, Mrs. Frye," he told her softly, "I wonder if perhaps that's what all of us really are—illusions."

It was like looking at a shrunken head of herself. Over what she had drawn she could see the reflection of doll heads on the shelf behind her.

She snatched up a sponge, soaped it frantically, and scrubbed the glass. "It's hard enough for me to know what I'm really like on the inside. I mean—what I feel—and all that—" She was talking as she polished the glass with a dry towel and spoke in panting little breaths. "But to find out now that I don't have any idea what I'm like on the outside—that I don't even know how big my face is—or how small—"

She worked at it furiously until the mirror was clean again, except for the doll heads and the tall man at the easel. "I thought you'd find it interesting," he was saying.

I didn't, she thought. I found it creepy, and I have no intention of thanking you for showing it to me.

"I'm going to make some fresh coffee," he told her. "Join me?"

She gave her answer to his reflection. "No, thanks. I don't have the time today." She waited until he moved to the stove before she turned. "I'll see you tomorrow." She left the studio quickly, returned to her own room, and warmed up coffee made several hours earlier.

While she waited she went to her closet and took down a shoe box from the top shelf—one Mrs. Keefer and Alice had somehow overlooked that day they ransacked her room.

She lifted out the doll he had made and looked at it. It certainly had her face. She had known that from the beginning. "What I didn't realize," she told it, "is that close up in a mirror my face turns into the size of yours."

It was terrifying.

The next day he made no reference to the incident. Neither did she. She took her place in front of the big mirror and looked out again on other people's lives in other people's rooms.

In one room a crib had been added overnight. Silly, she knew, but she was glad for whoever had put it there. In another room a short-sleeved young man sat at a desk and pounded a portable typewriter. A cigarette dangled from his lips. Every once in a while the ashes probably dropped, because he would remove the cigarette just long enough to blow on the keys, then he would start puffing and typing furiously again.

For all I know, Jenny thought, impressed, I'm watching a best-selling novel being written, or maybe a big Broadway hit.

The old lady was still sitting at her window—looking out. Every once in a while she and Jenny would look at each other. Doing the same thing, Jenny thought; nothing—just nothing.

Then she remembered that she wasn't doing "nothing." She was posing for an artist. She sat a little straighter and thought what a pity it was the young man at the typewriter didn't know she, too, was taking part in something creative.

But the old lady just sat. Maybe that's all she has to do, Jenny thought. It's very sad. I'll bet I know why a lot of old people die. It's because they've got nothing else to do. Or maybe it's the only way they have left of getting other people to pay any attention to them.

One day the crib was moved out of sight to the other end of the room; the young man became discouraged and deserted the type-writer; but the old lady stayed on. That didn't change, any more than moving the stool had changed what Jenny thought of as the "inside-himself look" Mr. Conner always got when he painted.

He neither smiled nor talked, and most of the time kept his head slightly to one side, as if he were listening to somebody invisible standing beside him. Sometimes he'd even move his lips as if he were answering somebody she couldn't see. She tried not to let it bother her, but it did. And too often he seemed to be staring past her rather than at her, almost as if he were painting one girl and looking at another. Once she even turned her head sharply to the right and tried to catch the ghost of that other model. There was nothing there, of course, and she shuddered and thought, God, this is turning me into some kind of a nut.

Something else was bothering her: a rotten habit Mrs. Keefer had developed of leaving her door open on the first floor. Jenny was certain it was left open for her benefit. Whenever she left the brownstone, or returned to it during the day, she could count on seeing the landlady in a big rocker, upholstered in royal blue velvet, facing the vestibule, and watching her go up or down the stairs. Mrs. Keefer never said a word. She just watched and seemed to be waiting.

A thing like that can make a person nervous, Jenny thought angrily, especially since I haven't been feeling too hot lately anyway.

It was those headaches. More and more when they came on she had the feeling her head was beginning to shrink to the size of the head she knew actually existed for her in the mirror.

Any mirror. She had proved that to herself one night in the dressing room at the club. She came early, intentionally, before any of the other girls arrived and, taking a soft eyebrow pencil, closed one eye and, even more carefully than she had the first time, traced the outline of her face.

What she saw afterwards no longer surprised her, but it still shocked her. She let it stay on the glass and applied her stage makeup within the penciled oval. It was the most peculiar sensation. Knowing how small it was made her feel she was painting a doll's face, pasting miniature false eyelashes on little eyes, painting a brilliant spot of color on little lips, rubbing shading rouge onto little cheeks.

"And soon," she whispered to it, "some little girl will go to sleep holding this head that frightened Jenny so."

One day when she finished posing she lit a cigarette and pretended to concentrate on the flame of the match as she said, "I know how you feel about unfinished work, Mr. Conner, but it would be extremely interesting for me to see this in stages. You know what I mean?" She was trying hard to sound offhand and casual about it. The truth was she had spent a long time planning exactly how she was going to ask him. "It would be very educational for me to see the way you—progress, so to speak, little by little until you end up with a whole picture." She tossed the burned-out match into the nearest ashtray and finished, "Unless, of course, you feel strongly about it."

"I'm afraid I do, Mrs. Frye."

"You don't want me to look at it at all?"

"When it's finished, you can look at it as much as you like. When it's finished," he said almost indifferently, "it's yours." He surprised her by adding, "You won't hurt my feelings if what you choose to do is burn it."

"Why should I want to burn it?"

"I only meant you would be free to do as you pleased with it."

"I told you what I'm going to do. I'm going to get a fancy frame for it."

He smiled at her. "There's time to worry about that."

Jenny didn't really blame him for refusing. He didn't want to risk what happened last time, and—the only way she could convince him she trusted him was by not insisting.

"All right," she said, and didn't know what made her ask, "Have you seen Mrs. Keefer much lately?"

"Not often. Why?"

"Does she leave her door open when she hears you coming down the stairs, and does she just happen to have it open when you go up again?"

"No," he said, puzzled. "Is it that way with you?"

"Yes. And I'm getting pretty sick of it. I know exactly why she's doing it, too."

"Why is she, Mrs. Frye?" He looked concerned and lit a second cigarette for her. She had nervously ground out the first unfinished one.

"Because she wants to get my goat—wear me down."

He looked more puzzled than before. "I still don't understand."

"She's deliberately trying to get under my skin. Doing a good job, too, I can tell you. I'm beginning to feel crawly and for all I know she's doing it under orders."

"Orders?"

"From Alice Molland."

He didn't say anything until he had lit a cigarette for himself, then he said, "I'll speak to her about it if you want me to. To both of them."

"No!"

"It's foolish to let them upset you and do nothing about it. Why should they want to anyway?"

She knew she couldn't tell him, so she didn't answer, and he interpreted her silence for ignorance: "They wouldn't need a reason, not those two. Why won't you let me put a stop to it?"

She looked up at him and remembered that this was the same man who had come to her rescue on the stone steps leading to the boat basin. He was offering to do it again.

"Thank you," she said simply. "Thank you very much, Mr. Conner, but I can handle it myself. All of a sudden I'm even looking forward to it."

She wasn't sure exactly what she would say. Certain speeches were best left unplanned. Somehow, the perfect words would come to her. —They always did when she was mad enough and knew she was in the right.

All those times she had read the riot act to Charlie, for instance; pure masterpieces some of them—and every one unrehearsed.

She could hardly wait to find out what particular words would occur to her when she came face to face with Mrs. Keefer later that evening on the way to the club.

It was disappointing to find the door closed for the first time in almost two weeks.

Wouldn't you know it, Jenny thought, disgusted. I was just in the mood to tangle with that one.

That one was entertaining a dinner guest who didn't sound particularly appreciative of the menu.

"Take that slop away," Jenny heard Alice Molland order. "I don't like stew."

"It's beef casserole." Mrs. Keefer apologized and Jenny could imagine her inside the apartment, wringing her hands—drops of sweat mustaching her upper lip.

"It's stew," Alice said. "Take it away. Nobody serves me garbage. It's an insult. What else do you have?"

Jenny left the brownstone before she heard the answer, and let the door slam. She knew what *she* would serve the old witch!

Mrs. Keefer's door was still closed when Jenny returned at four o'clock that morning, but then it always was at that hour.

It was closed at noon the next day as well, when Jenny left for the cleaner's. She saw the landlady arguing with one of the tenants near the mail table in the vestibule. The tenant, one of the Day People, was doing most of the arguing.

"God damn it, that letter was important," Jenny heard him shout as she came down the stairs.

"Is it necessary to raise your voice, Mr. Snyder?"

He shouted louder. "You couldn't take care of the postage due until I came home tonight? Would it have been so much to ask?"

"The letter," she answered coolly, "will be brought again tomorrow. Now that you know, if you'll leave the money with me—"

"I came all the way uptown on my lunch hour to get that letter."

"I'm sorry you went to the trouble."

Pausing halfway down the first landing, Jenny didn't think Mrs. Keefer sounded very sorry. Not that it was any of her business, but she wondered how much the postage was.

"Three cents!" Mr. Snyder exploded. "You couldn't see your way clear to laying it out for me?"

"If I were to do it for you, I'd have to do it for the others, and I cannot make a habit of things like that, Mr. Snyder. Whoever sent that letter should have been more careful. That's all I can say."

If she had any more to say, she stopped when she saw Jenny. Mr. Snyder was just beginning. Jenny didn't wait to hear any more that time either. She left the house again.

The day before, old Alice had lit into the landlady. Today, it was Mr. Snyder. Maybe later it'll be my turn, Jenny thought. It's open season on Mrs. Keefer; and just as she was about to feel sorry for her she remembered the letter that must have been pretty important to Mr. Snyder or he wouldn't have come all the way back uptown on his lunch hour to get it.

Jenny shook her head. Postage due: three lousy pennies. What a crab!

The vestibule was quiet again when she returned from the cleaner's fifteen minutes later—so quiet she could hear the squeak the rocker made as it rolled gently back and forth over uneven floor boards. And as she had grown to expect to see it, the door was open.

O.K., Jenny thought belligerently, move over, people. My turn.

She pretended to start up the stairs, then made a sudden surprise move and walked straight into the landlady's apartment. Immediately Mrs. Keefer stood up.

A few well-chosen words and there would be an end to this "bird watching" bit. You can get yourself another canary, Jenny thought, and decided maybe that wouldn't be a bad way to start the conversation. It would confuse her, throw her off balance. Then she would tell her off and polish her off.

It was the other woman who confused *her* by jumping up, smiling with colorless lips and saying, "I knew you'd come for it sooner or later." She went quickly to the door and closed it. "You're a good girl. What you do for a living doesn't make you bad. —I thanked you for the shawl, didn't I?"

Jenny was too surprised at her reception to do anything other than nod and wonder what it was Mrs. Keefer thought she had come for.

"I treasure that shawl," Mrs. Keefer told her warmly. "Isn't it funny, Mrs. Frye, the way some things just take your fancy? Would you like to see the way I fixed the fringe? If you knew the hours I spent just working out the knots. It was a labor of love."

"Not now," Jenny told her. "That's not what I came for."

"I know," she confided softly. "I know." She went back to the rocker and lifted the plump cushion. Under it was a family album. She held it out. "The first part's all personal, pictures of when I was married—things like that. I put a marker in the pages you want to see."

For some reason she only vaguely understood, Jenny reached for the scrapbook. It floated toward her in Mrs. Keefer's arms and the next thing she knew she found herself holding it in her own.

"That's a good girl." Mrs. Keefer walked out into the vestibule and waited with almost maternal protectiveness at the foot of the stairs while Jenny started up.

At the first landing, Jenny turned for a moment and tried to say something, but the words she had counted on to serve her when she needed them, the scathing words to tell her off, sarcastic words to put her in her place, the pure masterpiece, the pearls—somehow, they hadn't been there.

Bewildered, Jenny thought, What happened? What am I doing with this scrapbook? She looked down.

The older woman sent a secret little smile back up to her, then returned to her own apartment and locked the door.

By the time Jenny reached the third floor she managed to convince herself that she had accomplished, rather cleverly, exactly what she had originally set out to do. Taking the scrapbook without argument had been very clever. Why waste breath on her, Jenny told herself, if it's easier this way? She won't bother me from now on. All she wanted was to unload this. Now she's happy and I don't have to read it. Nobody says I have to read it.

She didn't—for several days.

Then one morning, as the city was getting light, she pulled a chair up to the window and laid the album across her knees. She yanked it almost savagely from the top of the cold radiator where she had put it. Letting it sit there on the peeling silver ribs had given it a snub that rather tickled her and she had been prepared to push the snub further by ignoring it altogether.

She would have if the radiator hadn't suddenly and for no reason seemed to become the largest object in the room. She admitted finally to being curious about the pages where Mrs. Keefer had placed the marker.

If I'm the least bit curious, she reasoned, and don't look at it, it will be the same as admitting I'm afraid to read three-year-old clippings. Besides, there won't be anything in them I don't already know.

Once she had made up her mind, she forced herself to put it off by undressing slowly and filling a bowl with cornflakes the way she always did after work. She even placed what was left of a doughnut on a plate in case she was still hungry afterwards.

If I rush it, she told herself, it'll make me seem anxious. —She wouldn't admit to a growing excitement at the prospect of finally opening the album.

When she did, an orchid, thin as parchment, cracked and pale, fell into her lap. Jenny shook it off her nylon robe, as if it were a lifeless moth that had fallen there.

"If there's anything I hate," she said aloud, "it's dead flowers."

It probably had a sentimental meaning for the landlady to have kept it all that time—years, from the looks of it. Gingerly, knowing it could crumple in her fingers and leave her holding dust, Jenny picked it up again, put it on the window sill and let the album fall open at the marker.

Having the story take place in the house she owned was probably the biggest thing that had ever happened to Mrs. Keefer. She had saved all the newspaper accounts, including the one from the *New York Times*, which wasn't much, not more than a very short paragraph.

It's almost an apology, Jenny thought, for taking up any space reporting the murder of a single person, when so many are being murdered in bunches all over the world. The only way they would have thought her death worth more space, she decided, was if the girl had had a publicity agent while she was alive to let everybody know who she was. It was unfair—but only up to a point. Even publicity men can't pull strings and get a client more space in a cemetery.

Mrs. Keefer had been right about the coverage in the Sunday supplement, though. They sure had "made quite a thing of it"—

gave it the full treatment—and spread the whole thing on with a trowel.

The heading "Death Stood Beside Him"—was blazoned across a double page—and in the illustration a seminude girl, breasts exposed, long legs outstretched, posed for an artist that Jenny didn't think looked a bit like Mr. Conner, except that he was a Negro and had a beard.

She sneered down at the drawing. In it, the artist wore a smock and a beret! How corny could they get?

Mr. Conner probably could have had a good laugh over that if he had been in any mood to laugh at the time. According to the story that followed, he hadn't been.

> After she was brutally murdered, Conner went half insane with a sense of guilt-ridden remorse and tried to convince the police, in spite of all evidence to the contrary, that he was responsible for the killing. Yet, perhaps in some macabre way, without his knowing it, he had been a partner with Death.

It was written that way, from first sentence to last; and all of it, Jenny thought, for cheap thrills. She bet it sold a lot of papers.

She slipped the orchid back into the front pages and deliberately slammed the album shut.

"And that," she said, "is that."

She had been right the first time. There had been nothing new or startling in it for her to discover.

Only the illustration disturbed her. After she got into bed and closed her eyes she could still see it clearly, even more clearly somehow.

Standing next to the artist, holding another paintbrush, had been the tall, shrouded figure of Death, dressed in a long black hooded cloak. Jenny fell asleep remembering how Mr. Conner always seemed to be listening, when he worked, to somebody she couldn't see.

When she awoke much later that morning, the first thing she noticed was an envelope that had been shoved under her door.

She was out of bed in an instant and, even before she read what was on the slip of paper inside the envelope, knew who had written it. And that was crazy, really, to guess old Alice would have handwriting like that—so fine, so flowery, so delicate—so very different from the way she looked. Still, Jenny was positive it was from her. After reading it, she knew she had been right.

> *I can help you if you'll let me. Memorize this Babylonian Incantation from the ancient tablet of Assurbanipal: "Hearken to my prayer. Free me from my bewitchment. Loosen my sin. Let there be turned aside whatever evil may come to cut off my life."*

It wasn't signed. It didn't need to be. Furiously, Jenny took a match to it, but as the corners of the paper curled in flame she found herself frantically trying to memorize the words before they were lost.

Jenny wondered what would happen if she were to call out to the old lady at the window: "Don't feel bad. I know you're there."

But she didn't, so day after day the old lady sat and waited to die or be noticed. Someone must have paid some attention to her —once. "I wonder what she thinks about."

13

Mr. Conner wouldn't answer.

She was past expecting that of him. It had taken a while to get used to talking to a person who was there, but wouldn't answer back. It was only, she realized, because he wasn't really there to hear her.

"Who?" he asked, which told her he was on his way back from wherever it was he went when he worked. It also meant the day's sitting was over.

She stretched her arms until she sent shivers down her back and made tiny bones crackle. "Good! I was beginning to get stiff." She remembered she hadn't answered his question. "That old lady across the street."

"What do *you* think about while you're sitting?"

"I try not to. That isn't easy, but I try, because if I let myself—" She sprang lightly from the stool and as lightly told him: "For the last ten minutes I've been thinking how nice it would be to have a cigarette."

He watched her shake the last one from a pack and asked, "Why do you smoke so much?"

"Because I like to. Think of a better reason if you can, Mr. Conner." She was annoyed with him, not for asking that particular question, but because of the other one. Did he really care what she thought about up there day after day? What an awful hypocrite he was. If he honestly cared about her feelings, would he have let her pose for a second portrait?

"Are you satisfied with the way it's coming out? Most of the time you look so pleased with yourself."

"It's a good likeness."

She started over to the easel, then remembered. "I promised not to look at it until it's finished."

"You've been very patient." He wiped paint-stained hands on a rag.

"Can I at least ask you about it?" There was a fascination in the way he could stand so still, not moving a muscle, and give her the impression he was running.

"You're going to ask if I like it as much as the other one, aren't you?"

The fingers that held the cigarette trembled and she stiffened her hand to steady them.

Stop it, she ordered them silently, but they kept shaking.

She regarded them crossly like disobedient children who refused to do as they were told. Ridiculous not to be able to get those thin little things to obey. She was bigger than they were.

"Stop it," she said, aloud this time.

"I'm sorry," he said. "I was the one who said we shouldn't talk about that first portrait, wasn't I?"

Jenny frowned. "What?"

The powerful figure with grizzled hair was so blurred, she could have been looking at him through a wet pane of glass. It was probably the sleeping pill she had taken at six o'clock that morning. For the first time it hadn't had any effect, unless it was beginning to now. She had to strain her eyes to get him back into focus. "Oh, yes," she said, "that's right. You were the one, Mr. Conner."

"Are you all right, Mrs. Frye?"

"I'm fine. I'd like some coffee though."

He offered to make some.

"No," she said, "I need it faster than it'll take to perk. I'll boil water and make instant." She filled the kettle, carried it to the stove, and turned a high flame under it. "I took a sleeping pill that didn't work." She glared at him. "And don't tell me I take too many of those."

"I didn't know you took them at all."

"Well, I do." She exhaled a stream of smoke and a long sigh escaped with it. "The truth is, Mr. Conner, I have thought about that other painting—a lot."

"I shouldn't have brought it up."

"It's all right. I mean that. I'd even like to talk about it now, if you don't mind."

"Why don't you just forget about it?" he advised her. "It's gone."

"Maybe," she said shortly.

"What do you mean by that?"

She took a cup and saucer from the cupboard. "You want some?"

He shook his head. "I only want you to explain what you meant."

She leveled a teaspoon of powdered coffee from the jar and dumped it into the cup. "For all I know, Mrs. Keefer still has it— or Alice."

He stared blankly at her. "What are you talking about?"

"They picked it out of the trash."

In a choked voice, he cried, "Stupid!"—and the spoon she had been holding clattered to the floor. "Leaving it for those bitches to find!"

He followed the words with a piercing shriek that made her clap both hands over her ears; then she realized the sound hadn't come from him at all. It was only the kettle whistling. She ran to turn it off.

When she finally found the courage to turn and look at him again, she saw that he had lit a cigarette for himself. It seemed to compose him; and his voice, when he spoke, was calm.

"How do you know they did?"

She was on the verge of telling him to forget it, but the expression on his face hadn't changed and she didn't dare. "They showed it to me."

"What did they say about it? They must have had something to say about it—especially the old witch."

"I guess so. I don't remember."

He knew she was lying, of course. She had always been a lousy liar. She carried the steaming kettle to the table, poured boiling water into the cup and wondered why she always did things the hard way.

Why did she always make it tough on herself? She should have done it the other way around and brought the cup to the stove, just as she shouldn't have told him what she had. Now she would have to pay for not thinking, by bringing the kettle back to the stove; and she would have to talk about something she really wasn't in any mood to discuss. But it was her fault. She couldn't deny it.

"I want to know what they said about it."

She spun around. "I said I don't remember."

How can I tell him, Jenny asked herself, that they wanted to know why he did that to me—stripped off my skin? Could even he, honestly, say that had been done by the hand of a man who is gentle?

Or could she honestly say she had never, in the early mornings when she had trouble sleeping, never once asked herself if maybe old Alice had been right?

"It isn't nice to call her a witch."

"Didn't you tell me she'd be the first to agree and be proud of it?"

"The way you say it doesn't make it sound like much of a compliment."

He showed white teeth in a stiff humorless smile. "It wasn't meant to be. There was a time when I thought you agreed with me about her. Have you changed your mind?"

"She's nobody's fool. Don't make that mistake about her. You'd be amazed at some of the things she knows."

He answered coldly. "I wouldn't be the least interested."

"In many ways she's an extremely intelligent person. And you should see her handwriting. Beautiful. A lot better than mine, I can tell you. Nobody who's ignorant could have handwriting like that."

"All I want to know about her is what she said to you about the portrait."

"And I want to know," she cried, frightened at having heard herself defend Alice Molland, "why you're giving me a headache— for no reason."

"You have a headache, Mrs. Frye?"

In a biting voice, she mimicked, "I have a headache, Mr. Con- ner."

She dropped her eyes and began to make tight fists, closing them hard to let sharp nails dig—then opening them again and looking down with curious detachment at the tiny half-moons imprinted in the soft palms. All the while she was thinking: What a miserable person I am, really. He's concerned because I have headaches. That day we began the new portrait, all I did was mention, in passing, that I had a migraine and he immediately said we should start the next day. He was perfectly willing to throw away all the new paint he had squeezed out of the tubes. He didn't try to talk me into staying. The fact that I did afterwards was strictly my own decision.

She opened and closed fists again and thought: He's concerned about me now, and what a snippy answer I gave him! I'm just not a very nice person. It's a wonder anybody likes me.

Mrs. Keefer, for instance, sitting and waiting for me day after day, making sure she wouldn't miss me by keeping her door open and all because she wanted to let me borrow her personal album, which is probably extremely precious to her. The fact that I didn't want the damn thing is secondary to the thought. It's the thought that counts. Always.

And Alice Molland—offering to read my cards for nothing. She said she doesn't do that for everybody. I believe her. It wasn't polite of me to refuse. Mrs. Keefer did have a point there—

When she came right down to it, Jenny decided she hadn't acted very appreciative of either of those two women. All they had ever wanted was to be her friends—give her things.

Mr. Conner had given her a bowl—filled with the colors of the rainbow. She kept it on the table in her room where she could admire it. She wouldn't dream of putting it on the floor! It wasn't a superstition, but she wouldn't step on a rainbow and destroy it—for no reason. It would be a pity.

She stopped making fists and let her hands fall open. "That wasn't a nice answer I gave you before, Mr. Conner."

"It doesn't matter."

He smiled and she returned the smile. Hers was slow and apologetic.

"Feeling better?" he asked.

"A little."

"I'm glad."

He meant it. She was sure he meant it. They were all her friends here in this brownstone she had hated so in the beginning. She had almost moved out of it, found another place to live. That would have been a terrible mistake. Where else did a person like her find three such good friends? Alice—Mrs. Keefer—Mr. Conner—three people who cared about her. And that was something, too, because they liked her better than they liked each other.

She knew what the two women thought of *him*. They had made that clear enough—and Alice did everything but spit right in Mrs. Keefer's face. If she ever actually did, Jenny was sure the landlady would let the spittle dry there and say it was just what she always wanted. Underneath, though, Jenny suspected Mrs. Keefer liked old Alice about as much as vice versa. Oh, she had great respect for her, but she probably hated her guts.

Yet all three of them, Jenny thought almost humbly, care about me!

She wished she could say the same about her own husband. Not a word from Charlie, not a letter, not a phone call since that one— how long ago had it been?—in the middle of the night when he needed her to hold his hand long-distance. He hadn't really wanted to talk to her! He only wanted to talk about himself! He hadn't really wanted to find out how *she* was making out. All that had been important to him was how *he* was going to make out. Once she told him, he hung up and forgot about her. What a bastard he was really. The hell with Charlie. She didn't need him anyway. She had friends now. Good friends.

Mr. Conner proved it now by saying: "You haven't touched the coffee, Mrs. Frye. Don't you want it?"

"I forgot I made it." She went to her handbag, took out a little bottle and held it high, almost gaily. "I'll bet you think these white pills are sugar substitute. Well, you're wrong. They're aspirins."

She swallowed two with water, then carried the cup to the high stool and got up on it. She sat there swinging her legs and sipping the coffee.

"You get a lot of headaches, don't you?"

"More lately, somehow," she told him. "And it's funny, because I used to have them and then they stopped—about a year ago—a little while after Charlie walked out. At first, I was so busy picking up the pieces—" she had stopped swinging her legs and let the cup and saucer rest in her lap while she continued quietly—"so busy putting my life back together again. —But after I got through doing it, I realized something funny: I hadn't had one headache. Not one. When Charlie was around, I had them regularly." She interrupted herself. "How'd I get on that subject? I don't think it was nice of you to pry into my personal affairs, Mr. Conner—make me tell you all kinds of personal things about me and my husband."

"Drink your coffee."

"I don't want it. I don't like powdered coffee, especially if it's lukewarm." She swiveled around and carefully placed it on the crate behind her. "You asked me what I think about—sitting up here hour after hour, Mr. Conner? I'll tell you. Sometimes I think how nice it would be to go through a whole day without once feeling my head start to shrink—down to the size of that shrunken head I see in the mirror—or go one whole night being able to lie down and not hear the buzzing."

"Buzzing?" he repeated.

"Like someone left the phone off the hook. So I get out of bed, and check the phone. But it's always all right, so then I know it must be in my head."

"I'm sorry," he said. "I'm very sorry."

"So I take a sleeping pill." Her shoulders relaxed and body slumped—remembering: "After a while the buzzing gets softer and my head gets lighter. Then after a long time, too long, it's morning again and I'm so glad to wake up." She straightened as if coming out of a deep sleep. "I even look forward to the headache again. You don't understand, do you?"

He was frowning. "No, I don't."

"Because it means the night is over," she explained patiently. "I don't have to dream any more."

"What kind of dreams do you have, Mrs. Frye?"

She jumped down from the stool and glared at him. "Alice Molland wanted to know that, too. It was none of her business, Mr. Conner. It isn't any of yours either, even if you are in them sometimes."

"You dream about me, Mrs. Frye?"

"You've got no right to ask such personal questions." Nervously, she combed her hair with her fingers. "No right!"

He nodded in the direction of the portrait and said quietly, "That's what's doing this to you, isn't it?"

Tired as she was, Jenny found the energy to shout: "If you slash it again, rip the skin off the canvas—God damn it, I won't go through it a third time. I've had enough."

"Yes," he agreed, "I think you have. Come here."

She was having difficulty getting him into focus again. "What?"

"I said come here."

"What for?"

"I want you to look at this."

She was not only having difficulty getting him into focus, she was even having difficulty breathing. "It's not finished, is it?"

"Just about."

"You didn't want me to look at it until it was," she reminded him. "You made me promise."

He went to the easel and stood beside it. There was room for her beside him. "I won't hold you to that promise."

Jenny didn't stir from where she was standing. "What if I want to be held to it?"

"Mrs. Frye." His voice may have been gentle, but she was sure there was something closer to loathing in his eyes that made her know he despised her. At that moment she seemed to know something else, too: that he wasn't gentle and he wasn't her friend. He never had been. Otherwise would he try to force her to do what he was now—now when she was so tired?

"You're afraid to look at it," he accused her. "You are, aren't you?"

"I just don't like to break promises. It's as simple as that." She gave him a smile she hoped was disarming. "I'll look at it when it's done. I'd rather."

He studied the canvas. "If you look at it before it's finished, maybe it never will be. All right—"

It was as if he had said it was all right to start breathing normally again. She started to inhale deeply, but the next moment her breath was cut short halfway through her lungs and she couldn't push air from it either up or down. She heard him say: "You'll look at it next time. There's only one more sitting."

"Only one more? Doesn't it take longer? Say, if I'm paying for it —and I insist, don't forget that—I want you to do a good job."

"You won't have to take it if you don't like it."

Jenny watched him study it again and had the distinct impression that he himself didn't very much like what he saw. "It may not be anything you'd want to frame."

"Why not?"

"It just may not," he answered briefly.

"I've got to go now." She waited for him to stop her.

"I hope you'll be feeling better tomorrow," he said.

The long hairpins were in the pocket of her dress. Jenny decided to let them stay there until she returned to her own room. "I still don't know how you got blonde hair with colors like that. Did it come out all right?" Not wanting to see the painting—just yet—didn't stop her from being curious.

"It came out," he told her, "the way I planned it. It's all coming out—the way I planned."

"Chalk one up for you, Mr. Conner," Jenny said wearily. "You're one of the lucky ones." She went to the door and opened it. "Nothing ever came out the way I planned—in my whole life."

The shelf of doll heads extended to the door. She reached out and stroked one of the little faces. "They all look the same, don't they?"

"I just turn them out. Yours was different."

"Was it, Mr. Conner?"

"You know it was. I took special care with yours. I wanted it to look just like you."

Alice had said that *they* made up a doll—to look like the person they want to see dead and then—

"If you look at the portrait before you go," he said, "it's possible you won't dream tonight."

"No! I mean I haven't the time. This posing business has really cut into my time, Mr. Conner. I've got to run."

Once she closed the studio door behind her, she did run—away from him—and an unfinished portrait he had openly admitted might not be anything she would want to frame. She was sure he hadn't intended to admit that. It must have slipped out; but she had heard, and it would give her something else to think about—or dream about.

Jenny hurried down the hall and promised herself that in spite of him she wouldn't dream. Simple! All she had to do was stay awake. She had forgotten how to sleep anyway. That was the reason the pill hadn't worked. She was groggy, but grateful, because she had forgotten how to sleep.

She hurried faster. There were benzedrine tablets in the bathroom cabinet. Those would help keep her awake if she weakened and fell.

The next thing she knew she did fall—against a dark-purple nightmare. It smelled of stale perfume and had a voice like Alice Molland's.

"Your hair, Jenny," it said; "letting him have your hair. Don't you know any better?"

Mrs. Keefer was a thin shadow behind her. "Didn't I tell you, Miss Molland? Isn't it the way I told you? I looked in and saw for myself. Such a shock. With her hair down, there's a definite resemblance."

"I've got things to do," Jenny stammered. "This posing has really cut into my time." She knew she was repeating the words she had used a moment ago for him. Never mind. It was the best she could do. She was so tired. If she could just get to the bottle of green pills.

"I have to get by," she said desperately.

"You've been avoiding us," Mrs. Keefer said reproachfully. "Don't you know we're your friends?"

"And you need friends, little dear."

Jenny felt a long length of hair being lifted and held for a moment—before it was released to fall in a spray over her shoulder.

"You don't know anything about hair, do you?" Alice asked.

Standing that near to the banister, Jenny could look down the spiral to the ground floor. It was the only escape from them, but she couldn't find the courage to jump. She swayed, then looked away.

Alice's face, so close to hers, was fuzzy, as Mr. Conner's had been earlier. It softened coarse features—made the heavy-lidded eyes appear even paler. The mouth, flabby and clay-colored, moved. "What do you know about hair?"

Jenny had to fight both exhaustion and fear to remember that the only way she had ever been able to hold her own with the Glob had either been to laugh at her—or defy her. She couldn't laugh. Like sleeping, it was something she had forgotten how to do. But she could still stand up to her if she tried hard enough.

"I know this is mine," she raged, grabbing a handful of her own hair. It was like holding silk threads from a hundred unwound spools. She twisted them into a blonde rope and clutched it jealously to her. "It belongs to me, Miss Molland. I don't like to have it handled. Not by you! You're dirty. You smell dirty. Your hands are filthy. Look at your nails. Disgusting!"

When Alice Molland answered, Jenny could find no hint of resentment in the voice. And I insulted her, she thought, amazed. What's she grinning about?

"That doesn't really belong to you, little dear. Don't you know that? Don't you know it lives a life apart from your body—that it will continue to grow after you die?"

If it was true, it was terrible. Jenny had a fleeting mental horror. She saw closed coffins and inside, hair growing wild—like untended weeds.

"I don't believe you." She took a step back to put more space between them; but in doing that, no longer saw her as an indistinct blur. The face became clearer and sharper. The voice was clearer and sharper, too. As always, it made Jenny feel childlishly ignorant, overwhelmed by Alice's immense weight and the weight of Alice's immense knowledge.

Hadn't she herself told Mr. Conner not to underestimate this woman?—that this was nobody's fool?

"All the Ancients," Alice Molland was saying, "knew that Satan took hair as a deposit on the contract he made with them."

O.K.! So she's nobody's fool! That doesn't mean, Jenny reminded herself sternly, that she still isn't what I first thought she was—a Kook and a Weirdo!

"This happens to be today," Jenny scoffed. "Not the dark ages."

Triumphantly, Alice said, "You're right, little dear. Let's talk about today." She prepared herself by first swallowing a full draught of air, then she let it out slowly. Within one breath came all the words: "In this civilized year of our Lord 1965, there are Turks who stuff their hair into walls—Armenians who hide it in churches or hollow trees—French peasants bury it secretly and mark the spot so they can find it on the day of resurrection. In Belgium, at this moment, good people are removing hair from the comb very carefully, to make sure it will not come into possession of a demon." She stopped only when the long breath had thinned to nothing.

She left Jenny almost gasping. "What's all this got to do with me?"

"Why did you show it to him? Why did you let him take it?"

"He's not taking it. He's painting it. He thought it would be interesting to see it reflected in the mirror. He said—he said . . ." Her voice trailed off as she recalled the way he had smiled and said, "Will you let me have your hair?"

"Those were his exact words?"

Hastily Jenny continued, "It was the way he would have said, 'Let me have a smile'—or 'Let me have one shoulder turned toward me.' "

That was exactly what he had said, too—and more than anything else in the world, she wanted to believe it.

"He wants to do a good job," she told them. "He knows I'm giving it to my husband as a surprise. He's taking special care with it. He wants it to look—" she was conscious of her own breath thinning as Alice Molland's had done—"just—like—me," she finished. She appealed frantically, first to one, then to the other. "That's what he said he did with the doll. Took special care."

"Doll?" Mrs. Keefer said. "What doll?"

And Jenny remembered that this was the woman who had waited for her day after day to let her borrow something very precious—and personal. This was her friend.

With quiet authority, Alice Molland said, "Show it to me."

And Jenny raised her eyes and looked into the eyes of the woman who had offered to read the tarot cards—for nothing. She didn't do that for everybody. She offered, because she was her friend.

"I want to see the doll, Jenny."

"It doesn't really look like me. I told him that the night he gave it to me. I told him I'm not half as pretty. So if it doesn't really look like me, it doesn't really mean anything."

"I'll tell you if it looks like you or not." Without another word, Jenny went to the door of her room and unlocked it.

They followed her in. One of them closed the door. Jenny didn't notice which one. She was too busy pulling the chair over to the closet, climbing up on it, and coming down again with the shoe box. "It's in here."

Alice reached for it, but Jenny held back. She carried the box to the bed and put it down.

"At the time I thought it was so nice of him. After all, I didn't do that much. I had to shop for myself anyway."

"Hurry up," Mrs. Keefer said. "Open it."

She removed the lid and lifted out the doll. "There's real fur on the collar." She stroked it gently and with one finger fondled hair so much like her own. "Take it!" she said suddenly, and thrust the doll into Alice's waiting arms. "I don't want to touch her. I don't ever want to look at her again."

She turned to the wall separating her from the bearded colored man who reminded her so much of the one who had come to the town where she lived many years ago—and frightened her poor grandmother. He was an evil man. He must have been evil to have frightened such a good woman.

"Tell me what you think. Tell me that doll doesn't really look like me."

"Turn around," Alice said.

"No!"

"How can I tell—unless you turn around?"

"She wants to help you," Mrs. Keefer said.

"Turn around, Jenny."

It was a command. Jenny did as she was told. She felt a cold small face press against her cheek. "The same," she heard Alice Molland say. "The same face."

Jenny watched her pick up the doll and pitch it violently to the bed. It fell face down, and the girl whose face it had, touched her own for bruises.

She watched the gross body bend over the fragile one on the chenille spread—and powerful hands split the dress with real fur on the collar—up the back, and rip tiny sleeves down the middle.

Jenny closed her eyes and listened to the familiar sound of slashing. For a moment she was back in the studio, crouching against the wall where she had crawled, feeling the knife as if it were going into her.

She opened her eyes again. His work, Jenny thought numbly, exactly as she had that other time. All his hard work! Now it was Alice Molland who was destroying it. He had cried while he was doing it, not making any noise, but crying just the same; she was laughing, not making any sound, but laughing just the same, almost wallowing in a savage physical enjoyment.

"Stop it! What are you doing? I said you could see it. I didn't give you permission to—"

"There must be a pin in this creature somewhere. There must be."

Jenny waited until Alice flung the doll over on its back and tore the dress down the front before she admitted, "There was. It stuck me."

Mrs. Keefer moaned and Alice tossed the doll aside. "Why didn't you tell me about the pin?"

"I didn't know what you were looking for."

Mrs. Keefer pressed forward. "Has he any idea you found it?"

"He was here when I did. He pulled it out."

Alice shrugged. "Exactly as he had put it in."

"How do you know? How do you know he did?"

"Oh, why don't you stop behaving like such a headstrong little fool? Is it because you don't like us? Because you think I'm dirty, and she's stupid? Well—you're right. But what of it?" Mrs. Keefer bristled and started to protest, but Alice waved her to silence. "You don't deserve it, Jenny," she went on, "but I still want to help you. Stop hiding things from me, not for my sake, but for your salvation.

Show me. Where was the pin? Show me exactly."

Jenny hesitated, then answered meekly by holding her hand over her breast. She could almost feel the wound the pin had left. Her heart was pounding so she was afraid it would jump out of her and back into the doll where it had come from. She held it down, so it couldn't, and the pressure made tears well up in her eyes.

In a way, she thought, they're tears of relief. It's all over. After so many months, it's over. I'm through fighting them. *Her* especially. She hasn't been wrong about a lot of things. And she likes me. She wants to help me. Wouldn't I be grateful to hide in a pile of dung if it meant my salvation? Would I care how much it stank?

She had willfully got herself into this trouble. The least she owed herself now was to listen—ask questions she should have asked long ago.

"Why would he want to hurt me? Just because I was afraid of him once? Would he hold that against me?"

"There's more to it than that." To the landlady, Alice said, "You were right, Mildred. With her hair down this way, there is a definite resemblance."

"Of course the color was different. More on the auburn."

"Tied it back with a ribbon, didn't she?"

"Or let it fall loose—like hers is now."

"Who?" Jenny said, terrified because she already knew the answer.

"You're playing the fool again." Alice sounded as if she was losing patience.

"That other model, of course," Mrs. Keefer said.

"The last girl, whose portrait he did the way he's doing yours now—and cleverly worked in the death symbol as a warning of what he planned to do afterwards."

Half to herself, Jenny remembered, "It's coming out the way he planned. That's what he told me—just the way he planned." She shivered and covered her shoulders with hair he had said was so pretty he wanted to paint it twice. That was something else she was forced to admit now. She had had such a feeling about that big ugly mirror, from the first. It frightened her. She didn't know why. —"*Let me have your hair. Let me have your hair. To see it reflected in the mirror would be interesting, don't you think?*"

"Do we really look alike?" she asked them.

"I gave you my scrapbook, Mrs. Frye. Didn't you bother to read it?"

"I read it."

"Then you must have seen the photograph in the Sunday Supplement. Didn't the resemblance strike you? It's so obvious."

Jeny shook her head.

"You're lying again," Alice accused.

Jenny swore she wasn't. It was true. At the time, she had been much too disturbed by the illustration showing Mr. Conner and the shrouded figure standing beside him to pay much attention to the photograph.

"Where's my album, Mrs. Frye? Open it and look again."

"No," Jenny said, with a brief return to her old obstinacy.

"Forget the album," Alice said. "I have something better than a newspaper reproduction of a photograph."

Jenny knew what she had in mind. "I don't want to see it! Please —I don't want to—"

"Get the portrait, Mildred."

"You'll be wasting your time. I won't look at it."

"Afraid to see what she looked like?"

"I already have—in the scrapbook. So she had long hair, too. What of it?"

"Perhaps," Alice Molland agreed, "you won't think there is much of a resemblance."

"That's what I've been telling you."

"But you're not telling me the real reason you don't want to look at it. You're afraid to have me trace the death's-head with my fingers. You are, aren't you?" She waited for an answer. When none came, she ordered briskly: "You know where it is in my room, Mildred."

"They were like wild animals, Mrs. Frye. Remember I told you how I had to go up there because the other tenants were complaining?—how I was in time to see her rip the side of his face with her nails before she ran down the stairs? It was after that he grew the beard. Remember, Alice? He looked better without it."

"Just different." The two words were saturated with such hate the left her lips moist. "Why are you wasting time? Don't you know there's not much left for her?"

When they were alone, Jenny asked softly, "How much time is there left for me?"

"It depends. When will he be through with the painting?"

"One more sitting." She stared at the wall that hid her from him and tried with final desperation to convince herself: "There was no other face but mine in that first one. You can't tell me there was. I looked for it. That's why he destroyed it—because he knew I was afraid. There was nothing wrong with that painting."

"And there's nothing wrong with the doll, except that it has your face on it. Take an oath, Jenny, that he never made one with *her* face on it."

She tried, but couldn't.

Alice held the doll at arm's length and let it dangle upside down by one leg. Its clothing hung in ribbons and it was naked to the waist. "And there's nothing wrong with the body of this thing either, except that it has the color of your body. It's the color *hers* was once." She let it fall into the box and replaced the cover, before dropping it to the floor.

Jenny wondered how long a person can live without air. "Do you think he wants to kill her all over again? Is that what you think?—that he's got her all mixed up with me?"

A glint of satisfaction flickered across Alice Molland's eyes. "Then you do believe he killed her now?"

"I don't know," Jenny moaned. "I don't know."

"You just said it."

"Did I?" confused. "Did I really say that?"

"Now he's doing another portrait, the way he did *hers*. Take an oath, Jenny, that you won't find a death's-head stamped on yours."

She couldn't do that either.

Mrs. Keefer returned, breathless and carrying a canvas. "I had such a scare. He almost saw me." She held onto the table for support. "I have a pain—an actual pain in my chest."

Jenny stared at the back of the canvas.

"The knob on his door turned—at the very moment I passed his room. Then he must have changed his mind about leaving. Do you realize what would have happened if he had caught me with this? I know what he is when he's—violent."

"Never mind all that. Let me have the painting."

At first Jenny couldn't find what she was looking for; then, it leaped out at her. Where the arm bent was the top of the skull—and the curve in the hand made on one of the big hollows for the eye sockets. Where the dress folded, she could see—

"The jaw," Alice said. "See the way he worked it in as part of the design."

"Couldn't it have been an accident? He told me he didn't mean to put it there."

"And you believed him?"

"Yes."

"Look at this again and tell me you still believe it."

Instead of looking, Jenny closed her eyes and once more was back in his studio—this time holding a print she had bought to show him. She was saying: "The artist must have had to work very hard to make it come out like this; to draw one face and have you see two. Don't you think he had to plan it very carefully, know exactly what he was doing?"

"Yes," Alice agreed. "Very carefully."

Jenny opened her eyes and knew she had said it aloud. "I'm freezing," she murmured. "I'm freezing, Alice."

"Poor little dear. You've been so stubborn—so stubborn." Huge hands on her shoulders were strong, but unexpectedly gentle.

Jenny yielded and relaxed under them.

"Why did you fight me when I told you I liked you? It was more than that. I had a feeling about you from the first. I knew we were destined to touch each other's lives."

Mrs. Keefer's voice seemed to be coming from a great distance. "Trust her. She's never been wrong with me. Never."

Alice Molland's voice was more than close. It was all around her—terrifying and caressing.

"Life," it said, "exists on two planes—the visible and the invisible. One is no less real than the other. Each has its own laws. Learn the law before you grow colder than snow—and turn as stiff as a puppet of wax."

It was a drowsy voice—a slow voice. Even time seemed to have stopped for it. "There are remedies. Call them foolish—call them false. They run through the dark undercurrent of all the ages and all the cultures of man. Deny them and you are lost. There is more than one formula for invoking the Devil. More than one spell for banishing his demons."

Jenny felt an almost irresistible hunger to turn completely into the purple warmth for shelter and protection. She had a need to half-suffocate into the depths of the heady, stale perfume. Only recognition of the need, the unspeakable horror of it, made her recoil.

"Go to hell!" She jumped up and ran past her into the bathroom. Once she got there she remembered the pale-green pills, and determined that she wouldn't be sick for the same reason she wouldn't sleep. There were more important things to do.

Benzedrine on top of a sleeping pill would probably fill her brain with red ants. Never mind. She swallowed it. It didn't matter as long as it would keep her going long enough to get away.

When she returned to the room, both women were standing exactly as she had left them. Mrs. Keefer looked about to faint.

"Where are you going?" Alice asked tonelessly, watching her take the long hairpins from her pocket and with practiced fingers twist and pile the blonde hair on top of her head. "Don't bother going to the police. I'm the only one who can help you—now."

Jenny finished putting up her hair. "You're wrong." She took her coat from the closet. "There's somebody I almost forgot about. Somebody I've always been able to count on. Best friend I've got in the whole world." She walked up to Alice Molland and forced herself to stand face to face with her. "And you're looking at her! I don't need spells to banish demons. All I need is a one-way ticket out of town!"

To Mrs. Keefer, she added, "You two better not be in any hurry to divide the loot. I'll be back for my things."

———

She didn't blame Lou. Nobody wants to get involved in other people's nightmares.

She stopped short at Fifty-ninth Street. The Huntington Hartford Museum was white against the darkened sky, and the New York Coliseum was brilliantly lit. The big clock over Columbus Circle told her it was 60 degrees and almost eight o'clock. Had she actually walked that far and for that long?

She shifted the large shopping bag to the other arm. Except for finding the dolls, she had wasted precious time going over everything that had happened since that day Alice Molland had asked her what kind of dreams she had—Charlie had asked her to wait three months for him—and Mr. Conner had asked her to get out of his room.

He had warned her to get out.

It seemed colder than 60 degrees. She belted the trench coat tighter and hailed a cab. When it came, she got in and gave the driver the address of the brownstone. Then she leaned back and remembered how Charlie used to clown around with cabbies—all the time. He'd hop in after her and say crazy things like: "Moscow and ride like the wind," or he'd cross his eyes and wiggle his ears and squeak: "Take me to your leader."

Remembering, she began to laugh silently. She kept on laughing until she realized tears were rolling down her face. "Oh, Charlie," she sobbed, "it's three months and I waited. I waited, because I promised."

Gabby New York cabbies! Charlie Frye had forgotten how some of these clowns expect a passenger to play straight man and join in the act. They sure expected a lot; free entertainment and a fat tip besides. The size of the one he had just tossed into the kitty should have made up for the way he let it be known, clearly, that all he

14

had wanted during the long ride from Kennedy Airport to the brownstone on the West Side was time to think. That buffoon sure hadn't given him much of a chance to think, and he needed more time.

He shouldn't have been so generous with the tip. Too late now; the taxi he had been in moments before was rounding the corner past the One Way sign. Instead of 'One Way'—it should have read 'Condemned.' He put down his overnight bag and glanced up and down a street that seemed even grubbier, more squalid—"sordid" was actually the word he wanted. No, he decided, it hasn't changed. I have. Places don't change. People do.

It was an interesting observation. Too bad Jenny didn't think he was capable of deep observations. She wasn't like someone else he knew, someone who was probably crying her eyes out, right that minute, knowing where he was and why. Poor kid.

He had been honest with her from the beginning—told her all about the wife he promised to go back for—in three months. No one could ever accuse him of stringing her along.

She had been the last to leave the club on opening night. He could get drunk reliving that night! It didn't cost anything and there was no hangover—only a nice warm glow inside remembering how there weren't enough tables to accommodate the crowd. They stayed anyway, practically stood on each other's shoulders. They stayed and snapped their fingers to applaud, and didn't want to go home to their own—or anybody else's—bed.

There was a sort of chemistry at work. Nobody can explain these things, but the minute the doors opened it was obvious that everybody loved everybody, especially Charlie Frye who had given them *the* new place in town to go if you were anybody who was anybody and you damn well better make reservations in advance.

She had been the last to leave. It was five o'clock in the morning. He found her sitting at a table all alone—and she was crying. It was beautiful the way she said, "I suppose now that the club's a success, you'll go back for your wife."

Just like that! So simple—so beautiful. He remembered the way a tear rolled down her cheek and plopped into a drink. Beautiful, like something in a movie.

He hadn't answered. "You're not the kind of man who would go back on your word," she said. "You're too honest, Charlie, too nice a person."

It was like she was sending him back. It killed her, he could tell that, but she was doing it anyway. That's the sort of person *she* was.

Not that he wouldn't have gone anyway. He had promised and Jenny was a good kid, too. Maybe not such a kid any more. Thirty-three pretty soon. Actually, this other one needed him more. She leaned on him, looked up to him, turned to him for advice.

Jenny, on the other hand, thought she knew everything. He wasn't knocking her, but he faced facts. That was one trait his wife had he didn't like. That, and a miserable habit of throwing the punch line of every joke before he got to the finish.

This other one, though, never had heard any of the jokes. That was especially true of the blue ones. She was so innocent, it was beautiful.

And the night before he left Texas, that night in his place: it had been almost a spiritual experience. Nothing, as some people might say—carnal about it. Still—no need for Jenny to find out about that.

He had been so gentle. She even acted grateful afterwards. Poor kid. A baby, really. Only nineteen. Because a girl is only nineteen and has a rich daddy doesn't make her any the less sensitive. It doesn't mean she cries less when she's hurt and hopelessly in love. He hadn't ever known anyone like her—a girl who could wear a simple little dress and have an invisible price tag scream "expensive."

He looked up to the third floor and wondered if Jenny was still partial to sequins. Once she had even bought a little gimmick that punched the damn things out. Punched them on everything. When he kidded her about it, she had punched a few gold ones onto the seat of his shorts. He couldn't understand now why he had laughed and thought it was so funny.

He wondered if she still had so much hair. When she took the pins out, she looked like Lady Godiva. He frowned and seemed to remember he had been the one who talked her into letting it grow. Maybe he liked long hair once.

She wore hers short and casual. When she saw him off at the airport, she had tied a silk kerchief around her head and told him she intended to stand and wait until she couldn't see the plane any more.

Well, he couldn't stand on this street all night, looking up at the third floor. It was too—sordid.

How did Jenny live like this? It was typical of her! She could lounge around reading *House and Garden,* but be perfectly satisfied to call a slophouse home.

He picked up his suitcase and pushed open the door to the vestibule. The landlady must have noticed the change in him right away, because she nearly dropped her teeth.

"Mr. Frye," she stammered. "You are Mr. Frye, aren't you?"

He fingered the hand-painted tie and came to the conclusion

that the reason hand-painted ties hold a better knot is because they're made out of better material. Would anyone go to the bother of hand-painting a piece of rag?

"I guess you didn't recognize me right away, Mrs. Keefer." He smiled winningly.

He was always nice to older girls, since he had discovered that it's the Menopause Millionaires who control most of the big money in these United States. He didn't have anything to gain being Charming Charlie to Mrs. Keefer, but it was second nature to him now.

"I hope you took good care of my girl."

She whispered, "I tried. I did everything I could."

"Thank you, Mrs. Keefer." Then deadpanning it, he added, "You know it's remarkable. You haven't changed, not one little bit." It was an inside joke. He didn't mean it as a compliment, but she wouldn't know the difference. "Bell's fixed, I see. Just the same, I'm glad the door was open. I'd like to surprise her." He started up the stairs.

"You won't find her in." Suddenly she darted ahead of him. "I have a passkey. You can wait for her."

He thought it over. "Never mind. I know where she works. I'll surprise her there." Why not? It might be good for laughs. The owner of that particular nitery had once fired him.

I'll be a gentleman, Charlie decided, and give him a few pointers on how to run a club.

"You won't find her there either." She stopped a few steps above him, turned and took out her keys. "Better wait in her room."

"You don't happen to know where she is working, do you?"

"When she left here, she said she was going to get a ticket out of New York."

"Oh? Ticket to where, Mrs. Keefer?"

"I don't know."

"You sure she's coming back first?"

"She said so. All her things are still here." She pulled her shawl closer about her and Charlie remembered that when she ran past him before it was like a big wind had blown a rose up the stairs.

He and that rose were old friends. He reached out and fingered the silk fringe. "I can see that, Mrs. Keefer. Her things *are* still here."

She snatched it from him. "Your wife gave me this. It was a present. I liked it and she said she wasn't using it anyway."

"Sounds like my girl. She'll give you the shirt off her back. Just ask her."

"I didn't ask. It was her own idea. She gave Miss Molland something, too—because she knows we're her friends."

"Miss who? Oh—the gypsy queen."

"She offered to read your wife's cards for nothing, Mr. Frye. Don't think she does that for everyone."

"Oh, I don't," Charlie said soberly.

"But she didn't ask for the brooch, any more than I asked for this. They were presents."

"O.K.," Charlie said, "I believe you. Don't worry. I won't call the cops."

"They couldn't help anyway. Only Alice Molland can, but your wife wouldn't listen."

Charlie didn't have time to figure that one out. He was too busy trying to keep up with her as she took the three flights at a pretty good clip for someone her age. He didn't mind admitting that he, himself, was winded by the time they reached the top.

She ran out of gas in front of the door halfway down the long hall from Jenny's room—stopped cold, took a deep breath, then went quickly past it. Charlie followed.

It was a peculiar sensation coming into her room. He could have picked it out of a hundred other furnished ones and said it was Jenny's. There was the familiar oversized coffee pot on the stove, the copy of *House and Garden*—a few long gold hairpins on the floor.

It was more than any of that. Without them, he would still have known it was hers. He could feel her in it. And he missed her.

"Did I thank you for taking care of her, Mrs. Keefer?" he said.

"Because I appreciate it. I mean that sincerely."

"I told you I tried. I couldn't do more than that. I warned her."

He lit a cigarette and looked around for an ashtray. The one he found almost overflowed with stale butts, each used down to the lipstick stain on the tip—all the same shade of lipstick.

Another ashtray on the window sill was even worse. He never remembered her smoking so much. She was a regular chimney now.

"Warned her about what?"

She answered so softly, he had to strain his ears; but there was nothing wrong with his hearing. "To keep away from him."

So he had been wrong! There *was* something to gain by being nice to the landlady. He tossed the burned-out match over his shoulder into the sink. "Him, Mrs. Keefer?"

She pointed to the wall. "He lives there. I wish he had died there last time he was sick. It would have been up to me to make the proper arrangements, but I wouldn't have minded the inconvenience."

Cool it, he cautioned himself. Don't forget, Jenny gave her that spick shawl. Maybe to keep her from talking too much.

But the old girl had taken a fancy to him. He could always tell. If he played it cool, he could get anything he wanted from her, and all he wanted was information. He smiled apologetically. "I should have asked your permission. Smoke doesn't bother you, does it, Mrs. Keefer?"

She shook her head.

"Just the same, I should have asked." Almost as an afterthought he said, "I seem to remember hearing somebody with a bad cough —that day I was here. I said to my wife, 'It's almost as if he's right here in this room.' I'm curious, Mrs. Keefer," he asked almost jokingly, "has he been in this room? Much?"

"She's been in his—too much."

Disgusted, Charlie thought, It was too easy. She overflows, like bad plumbing.

For a minute he was sorry for Jenny who had tried to stop her up with a shawl. The next minute he was much sorrier for himself —remembering all he had given up to come back. It didn't pay to be a nice person. Decent.

I ought to walk out of here now, he thought bitterly.

Somehow, though, he couldn't. He had to find out more about the man on the other side of the wall.

"Tell me about him. What's he like?"

"Always pays his rent on time. I couldn't use that as an excuse to get him out."

"I meant what does he look like," he persisted. "Handsome? Young?"

She seemed astonished by the question.

"What's the matter?"

"Handsome? I always turned my face the other way if I could."

Charlie told himself that it wasn't vanity; still, he found it hard to accept the fact that his wife had replaced him with someone so damned unattractive. Positively ugly, judging from the impression he had just been given by the landlady.

Jenny had not only been unfaithful to him. She had been worse. She had been insulting.

"That beard didn't make him any better looking either," Mrs. Keefer was saying.

A beard! If the man next door really had one, he would have to be at least—

"Seventy," Jenny told him once. "When you're seventy, Charlie, you can grow chin whiskers." She had come to visit him in the hospital where he was feeling lousy, groggy from sedatives, and didn't care how he looked.

Under the bandage his right hand was all mashed up. His only consolation was that the bartender who lost the argument had come off much worse.

"I'm going to give you a shave," she announced. "You'll feel much better afterwards."

"Like hell you are," he said, and the next thing he knew she squished shaving lather from a push-button can into the palm of her hand and spread it over most of his face.

"Don't make me nervous, Charlie. This is a sharp razor and I've never done this sort of thing before. Think how lucky you are to have so many doctors and nurses around if you need them to stop the bleeding."

That was Jenny. That was his girl. He tried to talk her out of it, but she kept at it until she had her way. Afterwards he had to admit he did feel a lot better. He admitted, too, that for an amateur she hadn't done a bad job.

"You've got plenty of time to grow a beard," she had said, "when you're an old man."

Funny to remember that now. He was glad he did. This put an entirely different picture on the whole relationship between her and the man who lived next door.

"How old is this character, Mrs. Keefer?"

"I wouldn't care to guess. And I certainly wouldn't dare ask him."

The poor guy is probably sensitive about his age, Charlie decided. "How'd my wife get mixed up with him?"

"It wasn't my fault," she insisted.

"I'm not blaming you."

She seemed nervous. It could have been irritation at being questioned so much about something so unimportant. Still, she was the one who had made such a point of saying she had warned Jenny to keep away from him.

"I'm only asking, because I'm interested in anything that concerns my wife."

"It started when she bought groceries for him that time he was sick."

"So that's how come she was in his room."

"After that he wouldn't let her alone. We warned her—Miss Molland and me."

Charlie didn't need or care to hear any more. It was clear to

him now. "You know how it is with some people, Mrs. Keefer. Do 'em a good turn and they become pests. And that wife of mine wouldn't hurt anybody's feelings, even if it meant being bored to death."

Unexpectedly, Mrs. Keefer said, "Get her away from here fast, Mr. Frye. You better listen to me. Take her tonight. One way or another, whether she goes by herself or with you—she has to get out."

"Why is it so important?"

"Because I want her out."

"What's the matter? Have you rented the place to somebody else?"

She hesitated before she said, "Yes, that's it. The room's been rented."

When the door opened, they saw Jenny. They heard her let out a single word: "Charlie?" It was a question, and she spoke it softly.

"Hello, little girl," he said. "I was waiting for your mother."

It wasn't necessary to ask him if things had worked out. Just looking at him told her they had. He kept his promise, she thought, dazed, but I'm going to have to break the one I made Mr. Conner. I'm going to leave the brownstone without saying good-by to him. There just isn't time.

There was a crashing surf in her ears, making it almost impossible to hear herself think above the sound of the tide coming in.

With a stiff smile, Mrs. Keefer said, "Alice went out. I'll tell her about this later. She'll be glad for you, Mrs. Frye. She's not the kind of woman who would hold a grudge."

She slipped out of the room so quietly that neither one of them knew she had gone until they heard the door close.

Seeing him is a shock, Jenny realized, because no matter what I told Mr. Conner, I guess I never really expected him to come back.

All she could think of to say was "You look wonderful."

"It's great seeing you again." He had started to tell her she looked wonderful, too, but couldn't.

She reminded him too much of the pet she had bought herself once from Woolworth's—a scrawny canary with unblinking eyes stuck into its head like a couple of black apple seeds. The only sensible thing to do with seeds was either to throw them away or bury them in the ground. The stupid bird was smart enough to know how he felt about it, and those black seeds seemed to spit yellow whenever they met his. Once he had stuck his finger through the wire and damned if the thing hadn't pecked him with its beak and actually drawn blood. Jenny had come home to find it lying dead on the bottom of the cage. It had been disgusting the way she held the small clump of yellow feathers in her hand and cried. At the time he pretended to be sorry, but was only glad the tiny eyes were closed and couldn't ever accuse him.

He hadn't given the stupid bird another thought until now, and it made him uncomfortable to look at Jenny and imagine it had come alive all over again in her.

"You're awfully thin."

"You think so? They still look at me three times a night as if they thought I was O.K."

She stared at him with those unblinking eyes and he was dangerously close to confessing. I didn't mean to knock you off the perch. It was just a pencil. I didn't mean to hit you hard. He managed to stop himself in time and said, "I meant your face. It's smaller."

She laughed. "You have no idea how small it really is, Charlie. It would amaze you. If I could get my lipstick I'd show you—"

She took off her trench coat and tossed it over a chair. She wasn't wearing sequins. This was worse, an off-the-shoulder blouse—with ruffles! And under a trench coat!

"You look wonderful," she said, and frowned. Hadn't she just told him that? She wished she could think of other words. Poor Charlie. He deserved to have her say the right words to him. He had earned them.

"I'm not surprised your club worked out," she told him. "Didn't I know it would even before it did?" Better—much better. He was almost smiling. "Sooner or later you were bound to hit the right combination. Didn't I always tell you that? It's a matter of being in the right place at the right time. Some of the biggest dopes got there because they were in the right place at the right time. In your case, Charlie, you had talent and personality. That didn't hurt, did it?"

When he opened his arms wide, she pitched blindly into them. He felt her tremble against him and the ruffle fell over the back of his hand.

"New blouse?"

She jerked away from him with such suddenness that he staggered backwards.

"I hate it," she said. "Buying it was a terrible mistake."

He couldn't help being pleased to hear that, but was a little startled the way she tore it off, rolled it into a ball and threw it to the floor. She stood there wearing a lace brassiere above the slim fitting skirt.

With old desire, Charlie thought, maybe her face is thinner, but from the neck down she's still my girl.

"You're taking me with you this time, aren't you?" When she asked it, her eyes seemed to swallow the whole of her face.

"Why else would I be here? Nobody pushed me." For the moment, he was sure it really had been his own idea.

She gave an excited joyous cry, at the same time choking down a sob of relief. It was touching—her almost childish delight at the prospect of being with him.

He watched her wrest a heavy suitcase from the closet and start to drag it across the room. He took it from her and lifted it to the bed.

"Why didn't you ask? What am I here for?" He snapped open the lock.

When he turned back again, she had yanked out every one of the dresser drawers and was gathering an armful of underwear and sweaters—stockings rolled into nylon balls. She ran with it to the case and dumped it in; then she ran back in a frenzy and began to do the same thing over again. All the while she kept saying, "I've got to get away from here."

"What's the rush? Why can't we stay tonight and leave tomorrow?"

"No," Jenny said, "we can't do that."

He reminded her, "We've slept in a single bed before, and didn't think it was so bad."

"I said we can't stay here."

"Oh, I forgot. The landlady told me the place has been rented."

"What? Oh, yes, that's right. It's been rented."

"How long have you known you had to get out?"

"Today really." She squinted uncertainly at him because she forgot what he had asked her. Oh, yes, she remembered now. "It all happened today," she told him. "I knew I should have cut off my hair and hidden it in a church or a hollow of a tree, or buried it somewhere and marked the spot so I'd know where to find it on the day of resurrection."

"Jenny!"

"They do that today, Charlie—in 1965 . . . in different parts of the world. Isn't that interesting? I wish I had known before I took down my hair."

"You're talking crazy," he said. "Do you know that?"

She covered her face with her hands. When she dropped them, she saw his face and didn't like the way he was staring at her. "What's the matter?"

"I don't know. You feeling O.K.?"

With great effort, she said calmly, "I'm all right. I'll be fine just as soon as we get away from here."

"You had me scared, the way you were stuffing things into the suitcase. You were—like wild."

"I was just so glad to be going."

"And that loony talk—about wishing you had cut off your hair."

"It feels so heavy," she explained, "when I have a headache. That's why I said it."

"You still get headaches?"

"Sometimes, not often. Only once in a while." She found a paper bag and swept everything from the top of her dresser into it—a brush, lipsticks, hairpins, a perfume atomizer.

He thought he heard glass breaking. "That's no way to pack," he said. "You never were much good at it."

"Help me, Charlie. Please help me."

"Sure." Perfume from the broken atomizer was seeping through the paper bag. He dropped it, paper bag and all, into the wastebasket, then overturned the suitcase, throwing out what she had haphazardly thrown into it, and neatly began to fold her things. "This is the kind of dump people move out of at night," he quipped. "Not into! Why can't we stay over and leave in the morning before the new tenant arrives?"

"No," stubbornly.

"I don't dig this whole arrangement, Jen. Are you on a day-by-day basis? I thought you paid by the week."

"By the month," she corrected him dully. "And in advance. Those are the rules. I'm paid up to the thirtieth, so they had no right coming into my room while I wasn't here, did they?"

"Wait a minute. If you paid in advance, why do you have to get out? Just because you told her you were going to? Too bad about her. You'll leave when we get good and ready." He started over to the stove. "I'll bet there's coffee here."

She got it before he did, grabbed the handle of the percolator and deliberately tipped it over the sink. She watched the contents swirl down the drain.

"Why the hell did you do that?"

"Weren't you listening to me? I said I have to get away from here." Jenny knew he didn't understand. How could he? And there was no time to explain. "You see," she lied, "I hate this place. It's terrible, Charlie. I don't think I can stand being in it another night. That's the reason I asked Lou to get me a booking somewhere else."

"Maybe you're right," he agreed. "I've been thrown out of better places than this mud hole. We'll check into a decent hotel for the night and take a plane tomorrow."

"It sounds wonderful. Just wonderful." She pulled a turtle-necked sweater over her head and began to put on fresh makeup.

She looks better already, Charlie thought, and decided to forget to pack the blouse with the ruffle. She said she didn't like it anyway.

"When did you close at the club you worked last?"

"I didn't. As a matter of fact they expect me tonight." She gave a short dry laugh. "The toads will have to look at their own wives tonight, because Charlie's wife won't be there. Let 'em suffer."

"You mean you just quit?"

"I had a reason."

"Before a weekend?"

"All of a sudden you're talking like a boss. When you weren't doing the hiring details like that never bothered you."

"It just isn't like you, Jen."

"I said I had a reason."

"It must have been a good one."

"Lou thought so."

"What was it? I'm interested."

She remembered how Lou had been interested—right up to the point where she said, "There's a man who wants to kill me." Then all of a sudden he wasn't so interested any more.

She wet the eye-liner brush with the moist tip of her tongue and said, "The owner insulted me. Never mind the details."

There was a lot to be said for lying. It made life easier. It's a pity, she thought almost gaily, that I wasted so many good years being honest. It's my grandmother's fault.

"Made a pass, did he?" Charlie was asking.

"I don't want to discuss it." That, at least, was honest. "You wouldn't want me to work at a place where I was insulted, would you?"

"Of course not."

"So I decided not to go back and not to give notice either."

"Where did Lou book you next?" He was taking some of her dresses from the closet.

"Mike's—South Boston."

"That dive? I'd call *that* an insult."

"It was just a place to go. I didn't care."

"But Mike's—"

She turned a worried face to him. "I don't have to go there, do I?"

"You're going with me."

She breathed a long-drawn-out sigh of relief. "Remind me to call Lou, get him to cancel that booking. I owe it to him." She bent down to straighten her stockings. "I've got a rip. Did you pack the stockings?"

He tossed her a rolled-up pair, and brought another dress from the closet. "This case can't take much more. Anything in that shopping bag you want packed?"

She finished attaching the last garter—and let her skirt fall. "I don't know. What's in it?"

He shrugged. "You brought it back with you."

After a moment she ordered quietly, "Give it to me."

When he did, she reached in and took out three dolls.

Every once in a while since he arrived Charlie had had the distinct impression that something wasn't quite right, but Jenny always managed to come up with what could pass for an explanation, so he had let it ride. He wanted to see her talk her way out of this. What was she doing with the dolls?

She crooked her elbows until her hands met, and enfolded the dolls within her arms. He saw her blonde head above the three smaller ones. They were all smiling and expressionless. None of them seemed real and he was almost surprised that the largest one of them was able to speak.

"You think they look like me, Charlie? Look carefully. Your opinion is important to me."

He moved uneasily away from her.

"I asked you if you think they look like me."

"Since when do you play with dolls?"

"I'm not playing with them, Charlie. I don't even like them. That's peculiar in a way, since I never had one when I was a kid."

"I asked you what you were doing with those things."

She looked up at him and didn't answer at first, then she smiled brightly and said, "I bought them for Lou's little granddaughter." She was pleased to have thought of this fresh lie. "That's exactly why I bought them. Anything wrong in that?"

It sounded reasonable, but he wasn't completely sure any more. "I didn't know Lou was a grandfather."

"That's what he told me today when I was in his office." Lovely, lovely, she thought delighted, the way a person can slide from lie to truth so easily no one can see where the break comes. It's like sliding from dreaming into being awake. Hardly any difference at all. "He said being a grandfather was one of the reasons he didn't want to get involved."

"Involved in what, Jen?"

She tightened her hold on the dolls. "You haven't answered me," she told him peevishly. "Do I look anything like these? See—we've all got blonde hair."

He went to her then, took the dolls from her and dropped them back into the shopping bag. "That's right," he said gently, "you're all blondes and you're all dolls. I know what's wrong with my girl."

She seemed surprised. "Do you?"

"You've been working too hard and you're tired. That's all."

Gratefully she clung to him. "After I left Lou's office I walked and walked, and all of a sudden it was dark. But I had to buy three dolls, Charlie, three perfect ones—so it wouldn't matter about that other one."

"I understand. The kid broke the one she had, that it? Well, getting her a new one would have been a nice gesture. But you overdid it, hon. That's how you knock yourself out, wear yourself out. Letting the creeps in this house take advantage of you, for instance—the landlady and the gypsy."

"Alice can see around dark corners that aren't there."

"I'll bet," Charlie said. "Listen, if those two nuts have been getting in your hair, that's a good reason for wanting to cut it off. Can't you ever say no? And that guy next door. Mrs. Keefer told me all about him, how you shopped for him when he was sick."

At that Jenny broke away from him. "I need a cigarette." She was standing in front of the wall that separated her room from the studio when she asked, "What else did she tell you? I didn't want to say anything until we were far away. Then I was going to tell you the way it happened—from the beginning, but not until we were far away."

"I don't care to hear about him at all. We've got better things to talk about than some old duffer who—"

"He's not so old. Thirty-five—forty."

"That so?" Charlie said. "I thought he had a beard."

"You don't have to be old to have a beard, Charlie."

"Just how friendly did you get, Jen?"

"Please," she said, "let's finish packing. Remember the valpac you won in a crap game? I've still got it."

"I said just how friendly did you get? I'm a lot more interested in hearing about him than I thought. And maybe I don't want to be too far away before I do."

"There's too much to tell."

"I've got time."

Her eyes opened very wide again and she reminded him more than ever of that canary. They were spitting yellow, too. "I don't want to talk about it. Not now. There's not enough time. You can ask Alice Molland if you don't believe me."

He went to her and flattened his hands on the wall behind her, boxing her in, but not touching her.

"I'm asking you, Jenny, and when you answer, that's when I'll make up my mind whether to believe you or not."

Because she couldn't move, she twisted her face so she wouldn't have to look at him. With her cheek pressed so hard against the wall, she felt almost inside the studio behind her. She even imagined she could hear heavy breathing and she whispered, "He wants to kill me."

"Say that again."

"That's why I've got to get away from here. Now."

He dropped his hands and she was free to move somewhere else. Instead she remained where she was and heard him say: "A lot of things are beginning to make sense. That's why Mrs. Keefer is throwing you out!"

"Charlie."

"She told me how you're in his room a lot. How is it you didn't tell me yourself, Jen?"

"He was painting my picture."

"Now, isn't that nice," he said broadly.

"I was going to have it framed—give it to you as a surprise."

"I've had enough surprises for one night. Boy, this is the limit. There I've been breaking my back trying to make good for both of us—and here you've been getting friendly with all the goddam neighbors, especially the man next door."

He was as near to her as she had wished him all those times she had thought of him during the long months; but whenever she had wished it, his face was never like this. Anger made his skin blotchy and stretched his mouth thin. Poor Charlie. His cheeks were bloated, like a drunk who's just come to and realizes he's been rolled. They were swollen with nausea and self-pity. Jenny wondered fleetingly why she had ever found him attractive.

My fault, she reproached herself. I'm to blame for making him ugly. Why couldn't I simply have told another lie? I was getting good at it. It was easy. He would have gone on being handsome and gentle, helping me pack, making plans to take me away. And I had to spoil it all by telling him the truth.

It was frightening the way he had taken that truth and twisted it into such a terrible lie.

"You don't really think that, do you, Charlie?"

He was much too close and she was having trouble getting him into focus. She had had that same trouble earlier, first with Mr. Conner, then with Alice Molland.

She wanted to use both her hands to push him away, and didn't, only because she knew that if she did he would go far away. She would never see him again. "Tell me that's not what you think."

"Tell me what else to think."

She laughed. That was another mistake. His face turned redder and became even more blotchy. But it was so ridiculous! "He's never even called me by my first name."

"What does he call you? Mrs. Frye? I'll bet."

"As a matter of fact, he does, and I call him Mr. Conner."

"Oh, come on, Jen. And you've known him how long? Since when have you been so formal?"

"It's just been that way with us, Mr. Conner and me."

"O.K.," he said. "O.K., I'll buy it. You wrap it up and I'll buy it. Just tell me this: why does he want to kill you, *Mrs. Frye?*"

She shook her head. "I don't think you'd understand. I'm not sure I do myself."

"What kind of promises did you make him that you don't want to keep? You did promise him something. Come on. Let's have it."

"I said I'd sit for him," and she remembered how she had dared him to paint her picture.

"Sit for him, Jenny? Or lie down for him. Which was it?"

Right then Jenny knew Alice Molland had been right all along. Only a hoodoo's magic could have turned Charlie's mind so black against her. It hadn't been necessary, after all, to push him. All she had to do was tell the truth. She watched him move from her to the other side of the room and knew he was already a lot farther away than that. If she couldn't get him back, she would be alone again.

With deliberation she said, "I waited for you, Charlie—a lot longer than three months. It was for a whole year before that; but I waited—and just for you."

"When did you decide you wanted something a lot bigger and

much warmer than a good conduct medal to pin on you, Jenny?"

She told him to shut up, but told it to him in such a faint small voice she couldn't be sure he heard her.

"What does he look like? Your landlady doesn't think much of him. I guess you weren't too particular, Mrs. Frye. She says she turns her head the other way whenever she sees him. Is he that bad?"

"It has nothing to do with his face—not really. Only with the color of it."

That time she was sure he had heard her. "A dinge," he said hoarsely. "You mixed up with a dinge?"

"Don't call him that," she cried. "It isn't a nice word."

"I can think of a word for you, too," he flung back, "but one that's not half so nice."

Jenny went over to the bed and sat down next to the open suitcase. "I gave a brooch to Alice Molland," she told him, "imitation diamonds and bits of colored glass."

"And you gave the landlady a spick shawl. Never mind. All I want to know is what you gave the dinge."

"Mr. Conner said it suited Alice Molland," Jenny said. "He said it was cheap and that I wasn't. I didn't want him to see me at the club, but it wouldn't have made any difference because he doesn't think I can be cheap and dirty—not three times a night, not ever. Isn't that funny? He doesn't think I am—and you do."

She had taken a stocking roll from the corner of the case and began to toss it lightly into the air, and catch it when it fell.

He's never been anyone for me to lean on, she thought. I won't miss him now. "Go away, Charlie," she said. "Why don't you go away?"

"You mean that?"

"It's what you want, isn't it?"

"You think anyone would blame me?" he asked furiously. "Who would blame me?"

There was a new note in his voice, and Jenny recognized it immediately for what it was: relief. She walked slowly to him, turning the nylon ball over and over in her hands. A few minutes before she hadn't been able to get him into focus. Now she was seeing him too clearly.

"It's not Mr. Conner, is it, Charlie? It has nothing to do with him—not really. This is a way out for you, isn't it? You were the one who said we've got time. All right, I'm listening. Tell me about Texas. Did you leave a woman? Did she cry when you left? And were you sorry for her? You may not believe this, Charlie dear, but I'm a little sorry for her, too."

She didn't have to be an Alice Molland to tell him a lot more about some of the things he had been up to since she last saw him. All she had to be was someone who was married to him—once, a long time ago.

"One thing puzzles me," she said. "Why did you come back? Why did you even bother?"

"Because I felt I owed it to you," he said. "But I don't owe you anything—not now."

She opened the door for him. "Don't forget your bag. I don't want it. It's yours."

He glared down at her for a moment without speaking, then quickly took his bag. She made it easy for him by opening the door wider.

"That's right," he said, his jaw tight, "the sooner I leave the sooner you can get back to your friend next door."

Jenny leaned against the door and laughed soundlessly. "If I go in there," she murmured, "it's very possible I may never leave again."

He was holding the overnight bag with his left hand. She saw his right hand rise up. She heard a sharp slapping sound and knew he had hit her, because her head snapped back involuntarily. That was the only way she could be sure.

"I felt it more," she told him, "when I dreamed it—three months ago. Remember? I told you about that."

"So long, Jenny," he said.

She gazed up at the leak in the ceiling and crooned, "Dream of

beetles crawling on you and you'll have bad luck in money matters. So be careful not to dream of beetles, Charlie, because everything's coming up orchids for you. I'm so happy. It's been a long
time coming for us."

When she looked down again, she realized he was gone. She
hadn't felt it when he slapped her and hadn't heard him go down
the stairs. Jenny closed the door and went back to sit on the bed
beside the suitcase.

She was still sitting there when Mrs. Keefer returned.

"I knocked first."

"I didn't hear you. I'm sorry. You really ought to get that leak
fixed, Mrs. Keefer. It looks awful."

"I passed your husband on the stairs. I asked him what you
wanted to do about the big wardrobe trunk in the basement. He
didn't answer. He seemed in a hurry."

"Oh, he is," Jenny smiled. "He's a bright young man in a hurry.
He'll get where he's going, too."

"He had his bag."

She shrugged. "I didn't want it."

"He's coming back, isn't he?" she asked anxiously.

"Don't be silly, Mrs. Keefer. You know he isn't."

"But he's taking you away from here tonight. He promised."

"He made me a lot of promises, Mrs. Keefer, but he never
promised to keep them." She went to the window and looked out
into the dark. In the distance she could hear a horn honking. For
all she knew, it belonged to the taxi he was in.

I should feel something, she thought. It's not natural.

Being empty of any emotion gave her a strangely weightless
sensation that was not exactly unpleasant.

She turned to Mrs. Keefer. "Who's complaining?"

"I am, Mrs. Frye. You told me you were leaving here tonight.
You told us both."

"Did I?"

She went to the stove and shook the percolator. "Do you realize
it's the first time there hasn't been any coffee in this? On this par-

ticular night, would you call that an omen? Do you believe in omens, Mrs. Keefer?"

"Answer me! I can't stand this." She was nervously working her fingers, and Jenny stared fascinated at the veins that stood out on the backs of them, wriggly blue worms twitching miserably under the tight skin.

But they can't escape, Jenny thought sadly, they're trapped. Poor things.

"This is my house. I don't want any more trouble—here. Are you leaving or not?"

"You're being silly again, Mrs. Keefer. I can't go anywhere. I'm much too tired. I've been overdoing it again, knocking myself out for years. He wasn't worth it. Why don't you leave me alone?"

"I'll help you pack," she offered. "I'd be more than happy to—"

Jenny narrowed her eyes and advanced on her. Terrified, Mrs. Keefer turned and ran from the room.

It was very quiet after that. Too quiet. Jenny switched on the radio, twisting the dial until she found music.

Since I don't feel anything any more, she thought, kicking off her shoes, it would be interesting to find out what it's like to be weightless and dance.

It was lovely—lovely. She hadn't felt so free in years.

"Then I do feel something." She laughed out loud. "Free! I shouldn't have waited until now to get rid of him. I should have told him to go away long ago."

She was still dancing, spinning and twirling—making herself a prisoner within the dizzying circle that got smaller and smaller, until she was caught in the very heart of it. It was while she was rooted there, not able to move, that Mr. Conner knocked at her door.

From outside in the hall he told her, "I know you're there. I heard the radio."

She kept watchful eyes on the door she remembered—too late—was unlocked, at the same time taking quick padded steps backwards on stockinged feet until she reached the radio on the night

15

table. Without turning to look for it, she let her fingers grope clumsily for the knob. When the click came and the music was gone, she realized she had made a bad mistake.

If she had let it play on and not answered, he might have thought she had simply forgotten to turn it off when she left for work. He might have gone away. Now he wouldn't.

She heard him say, "Mrs. Frye? You are there, aren't you?"

Stupid, stupid to have let him know for certain she was. The valise on the bed gaped at her. Charlie was crazy! There was room for a lot more. She scooped an armful of costumes from the closet and stuffed them into the case, pausing only to notice how pretty they were and how the light sparkled on the sequins.

"Mrs. Frye, is everything all right?"

"Yes." She was annoyed because she couldn't stop even one simple word from quivering.

And her hands, her darn old hands, all reddened and puffy; she couldn't control those either, and she needed them to help her finish packing.

"I want to ask you something."

Her eyes were drawn unwillingly in the direction of the deep voice that wouldn't stay beyond the unlocked door. It crept slyly under it, flew in, and sat on her shoulder. She let out a strangled cry and brushed it off. What kind of man was he?

She remembered how his cough had had the power to cut through the solid wall and slip between the sheets with her. More than once she had sprung from her bed in the middle of the night to escape from it. What kind of devil was she running from?

Mrs. Keefer had been nice enough to offer to help her pack. —I should have let her, Jenny thought ruefully. I could have been far away from here by now.

Instead, she had dawdled away precious time dancing, like a fool, all by herself, twisting and writhing like those blue worms under the backs of the landlady's hands. Now she was trapped the way they were.

"Mrs. Frye, will you please open the door?"

She could picture him standing there, a tall shadow in the hallway, the light from the ceiling fixture casting a second shadow.

How can he tell, she wondered, which of the shadows is really him?

For a moment she felt sorry for him because life was probably much more difficult when your skin was black. "What did you say you wanted, Mr. Conner?"

"I want to ask you something."

"You have what? Something for me?" She found her shoes and sat down on the floor to put them on again. She couldn't go anywhere in her stockinged feet. "I don't want another doll," she cried. "You've already given me one. I said thank you, didn't I?"

She looked around for the shoe box and found it across the room on the floor. Lucky Charlie hadn't discovered it. What kind of lie could she have invented to explain a thing like that?

On her knees, she waddled to it, threw off the cover and picked out the doll, holding it as Alice had done, at arm's length. She couldn't honestly blame Alice for not wanting to hold it any other way. It was hideous.

Letting it dangle that way by one leg, she stood up and carried it with her. She flung open the door. "What kind of present do you call this?" she demanded; then she narrowed her eyes and wondered curiously who this stranger was. She was hardly conscious of his taking the doll from her.

"So this is why you sounded upset!" he said, and Jenny recognized the voice. "What happened to it?"

She shuddered. "Horrible, isn't it? Just horrible."

He stared down at it. "I don't understand."

She covered her face, and, dry-eyed, began to sob. Suddenly she didn't understand either. She tried very hard to remember exactly how it had happened; but couldn't. It was ridiculous, because a moment before she had known. All she was sure of was that it had something to do with Alice Molland.

"It was so beautiful," she said. "I loved it, Mr. Conner. How do you suppose a thing like this could have happened?"

"It looks as if a cat got at it."

She brightened, and showed her face again. "Why, that's right. The cat probably got it. Alice Molland has a cat—just like the cat that hangs upside down on your wall." It seemed such a reasonable explanation.

She was relieved he had thought of it. She had known Alice was somehow involved in the massacre. Memory began to stir in her— memory of big paws and filthy nails, clawing away at the doll as if the poor creature was real!—scratching with sharp, vicious nails for blood that wasn't there.

"If she wants to keep an animal," he was saying gruffly, "she ought to keep it in her own room. She has no right letting it loose to destroy other people's property." He smoothed the torn bit of fur, and stroked the blonde head where clumps of hair had been plucked, leaving tiny bald spots. "Don't worry about this. I'll have it repaired."

Jenny hardly heard him. She was staring even harder at his clean-shaven face than he had stared at the doll. "Mr. Conner," she gasped, "your beard."

He smiled. "You said it was ugly. I wondered how soon it would be before you noticed it was gone."

"Did you shave it off," she asked shocked, "just because I said it was ugly?"

If that had been his reason, she wished he hadn't. For some time she had known that the scar was there; but since it had been hidden, she could forget about it. Now she couldn't—not when it stood out, like this, raised and jagged and lumpy.

She stammered, "I feel as if I don't even know you at all."

"Does it make such a difference?"

"You're like someone else altogether," she told him, and realized why she had thought she was opening her door to a stranger.

He had done it to please her, and she couldn't bear the sight of his face. The scar sickened her. It was more than that. She knew that this way he must look exactly as he had looked three years ago when another girl sat and posed for him.

And, as she had once before, Jenny began to get the feeling that everything that was happening was simply happening all over again. A force stronger than Alice Molland had carelessly laid out the same cards: a dark man, a fair girl—and death, and had been too lazy to reshuffle and lay them out again.

"I had another reason for wanting to shave the beard," he admitted. "After tonight, I'll be starting fresh. I wanted to be clean for it."

She started to ask him what he meant by that, when he noticed the valise on the bed.

"Why are you packing?"

"I saw my agent today," she heard herself say. "He has a booking for me out of town."

"Oh? When do you open?"

"A week from Monday." Immediately she realized she had made another mistake, even more stupid than turning off the radio and letting him know she was there. She had just told him she could stay.

"Then you don't have to leave tonight."

She shook her head.

Satisfied, he said, "That's good. The portrait is about done. I want you to see it. One more sitting."

"There's no sun."

"I can turn on the light. Will you come with me?"

"Yes," Jenny said softly, too terrified to scream "no" at him. It was very strange the way she seemed to be standing two feet behind herself, watching things happen. It was sad, so very sad; she felt like crying.

She saw the man who lived next door lead her out of the room and thought, That poor girl. Who's going to help her now?

Then she remembered words in flowery script on a paper she had set a match to: "I can help you if you'll let me. Memorize this Babylonian"—no, maybe it was Assyrian—"Incantation." Jenny was certain the word had been incantation—"from the ancient tablet of—something—something."

She closed her eyes, stumbled once or twice as she walked down the hall ahead of him, moving her lips and trying to remember: "Hearken to my prayer." That much was easy. "Free me from my —something—something. Loosen my evil—no—my bewitchment—"

She opened her eyes and knew she didn't really want to remember. She had told the two women she didn't need spells to banish demons.

She had been humiliated enough for one night. Charlie had done his best. Was it right to abuse herself further by repeating gibberish and expecting it to help her?

In the studio, he made her go up onto the platform for the last time. For the last time she took out the pins and let him have her hair. There was a nervous excitement in waiting for the inevitable. Instead of exhaustion, she felt a terrible kind of exhilaration.

"Do you suppose," she asked, "that she's sitting there in the dark, the old lady across the street?" She shook her hair loose. "I can't see her, but she can see us. Anything that happens here tonight, Mr. Conner, she'll see."

She said it as a warning, and waited for a reaction from him. He was already at the easel, working more quickly than usual, anxious to get to the end. He didn't answer.

She should have known he wouldn't hear her. He never did.

In the morning, she thought, I wonder if the old lady will think she dreamed it—whatever it is she's going to see. Maybe she won't even tell anybody.

"Do you know, Mr. Conner," Jenny said, "that wouldn't surprise me in the least? And do you know why? Because it's not polite to go around telling other people your nightmares. It makes them nervous. Haven't you ever noticed that nobody wants to get mixed up in your nightmares? They just don't want to get involved."

She could say anything at all to him and he wouldn't pay any attention to her, but if she moved so much as a hair he noticed.

She couldn't stand the weight of her hair. She was suffocating under it. Funny, it had never bothered her. Tonight was different. Tonight she remembered why she had let it grow: to please Charlie.

She felt her chin drop forward. Most of the time, she thought, don't they shave heads first? I wish someone would come in and do mine now. —What a weird and wild idea! She shook herself violently and sat very straight.

From across the studio, she heard him say, "Getting tired?"

"Charlie says I do, because I let people take advantage of me. Don't you think it's funny that when he said *people,* he didn't include himself, Mr. Conner? And he was the worst—"

"What do you mean?"

She smiled sadly. "The one time I didn't want you to hear me, you did. Do me a favor? Forget it. It's nothing I'm very proud of."

"All right." Then he said, "I'm going to tell you something, Mrs. Frye. I could have finished without you. I haven't really needed you right along, but it kept you from the easel. I had a reason for not wanting you to see this until it's done."

There was no sound in the room, except for a big clock ticking. Strange she had never heard it before. Each beat was slow and heavy, and seemed to come from inside her. It took a moment to realize there was no big clock; only the beating of her own heart. If it beat any louder, she would split wide open.

"I would have gone on perfectly happy painting faces on dolls. You wouldn't let me."

"Oh, please, I didn't mean to make you do anything you didn't want to do. All I said was—"

"Hoodoo," he said softly. "You called me hoodoo. Admit you made me do it, Mrs. Frye."

"I'm sorry," Jenny said, "I'm sorry. I'm sorry."

"It's too late for that now."

"I suppose it is," she agreed tonelessly.

Then for no reason at all, or maybe for the best one, Jenny remembered a slaughterhouse she had been taken to once. Why she had gone and who had taken her was something she couldn't remember. What she couldn't ever forget was the crazed terror in the eyes of the animals: the flaring, pulsing nostrils that smelled death, and the big bodies that were herded unwillingly, but almost docilely.

She had silently pleaded with them to break loose and trample every human being in sight, even if it meant her, as well. They were stronger. They could have fought back. Or tried. They didn't because they were dumb animals. Maybe they deserved to have their flesh eaten. She didn't know.

What she did know now was that she would deserve anything that happened to her if she simply let herself be led to slaughter. With Charlie gone, maybe she didn't have much. Still, life was worth holding onto even if it meant just being alive.

Or, if I give up without a fight, she decided, shouldn't it be for something or somebody worth while? But for Charlie? That would make it cheap, the one thing Mr. Conner had said she wasn't. She would prove it to him, by holding on any way she could.

"Were you very much in love with that other model?" she asked.

Startled by the suddenness of the question, he said, "Why talk about her tonight?"

"Because tonight my portrait is finished, and I'm remembering what happened to that other model on the night you finished hers."

"That night has nothing to do with you." He was more than impatient with this unexpected turn of conversation. It seemed to Jenny that the scar on his cheek had grown more jagged, even lumpier.

She forced herself to look at it. "Do I remind you very much of her?"

"No!"

"She had long hair, too, didn't she?—Tied it back with a ribbon or just let it fall loose?"

"Did they tell you that?"

"My hair is blonde, Mr. Conner," she said soothingly. "Can't you see what a mistake you've made? Her hair was more on the auburn. You mixed all the wrong colors to do me. I pointed that out to you when you started, remember?"

He tried to interrupt. "Mrs. Frye."

But she continued feverishly. "If the only resemblance between me and that other girl is long hair, would you call that a resemblance? Be honest, Mr. Conner."

"You're nothing alike. If they told you that, they lied."

If she could only explain it to him, make him understand the way she did. It was so obvious—then there was still a chance to save herself. "You wanted to paint me, because I do resemble her—a little. Isn't that why, Mr. Conner? You wanted to do it all over again because you loved her."

He looked hard at the new portrait. "You don't know what you're talking about. I wished her dead. A hundred times over I wished her dead."

She whispered, "And did you wish it very hard?"

"Hard enough," he confessed. "Or so I thought for a very long time—to have dug death into the canvas and buried it there."

"I saw that painting. Alice showed it to me. I'm afraid I have to admit it didn't look like an accident." Hastily she added, "But I believe you. It could have happened."

He jammed the paintbrush into the jar with such violence that it turned over. Brushes spread over the table. A few of them rolled onto the floor along with some of the tools. He didn't bother to pick them up.

"There's a stench of hell about that woman!" he shouted. "What did she have to gain by showing it?"

"She had nothing to gain. Nothing at all. She was trying to help me."

He didn't move from the easel. "Come here," he said, "and look at this."

Explaining about the other model hadn't worked. He didn't understand. Or if he did, he didn't care. All he cared about now was to make this new portrait come out the way he had planned. Hadn't he told her once it was coming out exactly the way he planned?

"I just realized," she said lightly, "I'm wearing the wrong top, Mr. Conner. You'll have to do this last sitting over again. Only I won't be here. Isn't that too bad? You see, my agent—"

"It doesn't matter what you're wearing tonight—what you wore yesterday. Come here. Or I'll turn it so you can see it. Is that what you want?"

"No!" She was closer to the door than he was. If she reached it first—

She heard him yell, "Mrs. Frye!" And then he swooped down on her.

Jenny wondered what he had done with the black-hooded cloak he had been wearing. She could have sworn he had been wearing a black-hooded cloak.

His nails dug into her arm. With big hands and strong arms he swept her half across the studio.

She looked back dazedly in time to see the big mirror, which had been standing behind her, sway back and forth before it finally smashed into hundreds of pieces of glass.

"You could have been killed," he said, breathing heavily. "You knocked against it when you stood up."

"Such a big mirror," Jenny whimpered. "I bet it's about a million years of bad luck to break that."

"Never mind. Look at the painting."

"No!"

Only one mirror had broken. There was still the one over the sink, the little one that had taught her she didn't know the size of her own face. It was showing her something far more frightening now. It was showing her herself with eyes like those steers in Chicago—sprung wide with the same crazed terror. Her own nostrils were flared and pulsing. He had turned her into an animal.

She dropped down on all fours and began to move away from him.

"Mrs. Frye," he said, "if there's hoodoo here, get up on your feet and look into the face of it. The only way not to be afraid is to look into the face of it."

"No," she said, "I don't want to."

She lowered her head. The whole floor was alive with fragments of mirror.

"If I could find a way to thread these," she said, "I could make the prettiest costume—the most beautiful—"

"Stop it," he ordered. "Get up and look at this. Do as you're told."

Behind her, lying with the broken glass, was a brush that had fallen from the work table, and a knife—the very sharp one he had used to slash the first portrait.

"Will you get up, Mrs. Frye?"

Obediently she said, "Yes," at the same time fumbling for the knife handle.

And at the moment her fingers found it and curved around it, Jenny seemed to stand apart from herself again, as she had when they left her room. She saw the girl she never had difficulty recognizing as herself in any nightmare she had ever slept through. She saw the girl with the dancer's body rise effortlessly without using her hands for assistance or support. One hand behind her back held the knife.

"That's better," he said.

Jenny saw her smile. That's it, she thought, get it over with. You're a good girl. What you do for a living doesn't make you bad.

Or was that what Mrs. Keefer had said? Never mind. It wasn't important.

"Come here," he said.

"Don't be afraid, Jenny," she whispered. "Poor little dear, you've been so stubborn."

She waited only a moment more, knowing that if she stood perfectly still and gathered strength he was sure to come for her. When he did, she lunged forward. The knife went into him soundlessly. She kept her hand on the handle until she felt something sticky spread over it. Then she let go.

He didn't look anything except surprised and he sagged heavily on top of her before he fell, almost dragging her down with him. She thought she heard him say one word—"hoodoo"—but couldn't be sure. Then she went over and looked at the painting.

The two women found her there, sitting in front of the easel. She was holding his head in her lap and rocking him back and forth as if he were a child. They found her singing to him very softly and sweetly.

On the floor around Jenny, they found the broken pieces of a mirror, and on the easel was a self-portrait of Mr. Conner.

Much later, in Mrs. Keefer's apartment on the first floor, Alice Molland sucked chocolate icing from spongy fingertips and said, "I want that portrait, Mildred."

Mrs. Keefer didn't turn from the window. "Why?"

"Because I've got the other. It'll make a pair." She sucked

16

noisily. "I overpaid for that first one. Getting this for nothing will make up for it. You'll let me have it, won't you? It's yours to give —your house—your property—"

"I don't want it," the landlady said, and lifted the sheer curtain higher.

The street was almost deserted. Less than an hour before, the sidewalk in front of the brownstone had been jammed.

People had poured from neighboring brownstones or smelled excitement blocks away and came running. It had been close to eleven o'clock, but some of the women held infants who slept through the blast of sirens.

Police had the most trouble with children. They ducked under the bridges made by tall men's spread legs to watch white-jacketed men from the ambulance carry down a stretcher.

One of the women supported her baby with one hand and crossed herself with the other. A teen-ager, wearing a leather jacket, swore and said to his companion, "It was your idea to break up the game for this and we can't see a damn thing. They got the fink all covered up. Hey—here comes the blonde."

Jenny came out of the house, a policeman on either side of her. One of them held her by the arm. She stopped briefly halfway down the stone steps. When she saw two familiar faces at a first-floor window, she called to them.

"I knew he couldn't get my hair with colors like that. I told him they were wrong." She smiled. "Anyway, I want to thank you both for trying to help me. It was nice of you. I'll be sure to tell Charlie."

Mrs. Keefer let the curtain drop and turned back into the room.

"Good cake. Do you have any more cake?" Alice asked.

"Don't you ever stop feeding your face?"

At first her guest was too taken aback to answer; then she said quietly, "What did you say?"

"I said you eat too much."

"That's none of your business."

"It is if it's my food you're eating."

Alice seemed to be proceeding cautiously now. She reached into the deep pocket of her purple dress and took out a cigar. "What's the matter, Mildred?"

"You're not even upset about what happened, are you?"

"Admit you are, only because you have two rooms to rent again."

"Three," the landlady corrected. "I want yours."

"You wouldn't dare throw me out," Alice Molland said furiously. "You wouldn't dare."

"Six years back rent. That's reason enough. I've got a better one—what happened in my house tonight."

Alice bit off the end of the cigar and spat it out. "Are you even suggesting any of this is my fault?" The words she spoke next were out of place in a brownstone room on New York's West Side. They were out of tune with time—almost off-key. "Whatever image he took had to bring destruction to that subject. If evil angels sowed the seeds of death and she was assigned to reap those seeds, am I to blame?"

Mrs. Keefer stood very still and listened. She seemed to have stopped breathing.

"More than that—I warned her. I told her what was in the cards. You were there. You heard her defy the mysteries—heard her deny their existence. She laughed at them, and she was punished." She leaned forward in the kitchen chair that groaned under her weight. "Madness, Mildred, is a supernatural punishment." After making this pronouncement, she drew a match from the little box on the table and struck it crisply, as if to end further discussion of the matter.

Mrs. Keefer said, "Fire!" and deliberately blew it out.

"Have you lost your mind, too?" Alice demanded hoarsely. She saw her pick up the matchbox and light another match, watched her scratch one after another to life and toss away burned-out sticks—until the floor was littered. "You are insane."

"Fire!" Mrs. Keefer repeated. "You yelled it loud enough and long enough until that poor girl thought she was on fire. Then you set a match to her." She lit the last one. "Yes," she accused, "you are to blame."

Alice lashed out and grabbed the thin wrist. She smiled as she felt the other woman cry out with pain and fear. She held on even more tightly to steady the trembling hand, then leaned forward and lit her cigar. "You'll feel better after a good night's sleep. Make more coffee, and look for more cake." Deliberately she placed the cigar in the ashtray, brought out the tarot cards and began to shuffle. "I'm going to give you a reading tonight, Mildred. You'd like that, wouldn't you? Haven't the cards always advised you well in the past? Remember how well."

Mrs. Keefer let out a thin wail, and whacked the cards to the floor.

Alice was on her feet immediately, looking stunned. Her eyes blazed. "You'll regret this. Ignorant old fool. Pick them up. Pick them up this minute and give them to me."

"I'm going to clean her room," Mrs. Keefer told her calmly.

"I don't want you here when I come back. You turn my stomach. I told you once, I have a very delicate stomach." Just before she left the room she said, "I don't think I will feel much better in the morning. You're wrong about that, too. I don't expect to sleep very well. Tell me, Miss Molland," she asked, addressing her with the old formality, "what kind of dreams do *you* have? Will Jenny Frye be in them tonight? Will she be in them again tomorrow night, and the night after that . . ." She let her voice trail off. "I wouldn't be at all surprised," she said.

She closed the door after her and walked up the stairs where three months before a girl had huddled against a banister—afraid to pass a colored man with a beard.